CORKY'S BROTHER

Books by JAY NEUGEBOREN

Big Man

Listen Ruben Fontanez

Corky's Brother

Jay Neugeboren

Corky's Brother

FARRAR, STRAUS AND GIROUX

 *New York*

Copyright © 1964, 1965, 1966, 1967, 1969
by Jay Neugeboren
Library of Congress catalog card number: 78-87214
All rights reserved
Third printing, 1970
Published simultaneously in Canada by
Doubleday Canada Ltd., Toronto
Printed in the United States of America
Designed by Charles E. Skaggs

for ROBERT

Contents

NOTE

THESE STORIES, including the six "Brooklyn stories," were written between the years 1962 and 1969. My thanks to friends who have gone through these years, these stories with me. I would like to thank, in particular, those friends whose professional help during these years has been especially warm and kind. My deep gratitude, then, to Betsey Bendorf, Jerome Charyn, Joyce Hartman, Emilie Jacobson, William E. Wilson, Martha Winston, William Wiser, and the late Richard Chase.

Joe McCrindle and Heathcote Williams of *Transatlantic Review* have been very generous—my thanks to them, and also to the editors of the publications in which some of these stories, in different form, first appeared, as follows: "The Application," *Transatlantic Review 17*, 1964; "The Child," *Minnesota Review*, 1965; "Luther," *Commentary*, 1966; "The Zodiacs," *Transatlantic Review 20*, 1966; "Ebbets Field," *Transatlantic Review 24*, 1967; "Corky's Brother," *Transatlantic Review 25*, 1967; "Something Is Rotten in the Borough of Brooklyn," *Ararat*, 1967; "A Family Trip," *Transatlantic Review 33*, 1969; "The Pass," *Mademoiselle*, 1969; and "Elijah," *Works*, 1969.

JAY NEUGEBOREN

Spéracèdes
Alpes Maritimes
March, 1969

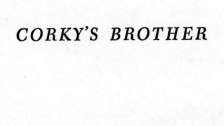

CORKY'S BROTHER

Luther

LUTHER ARRIVED at Booker T. Washington Junior High School (Columbus Avenue and 107th Street, Manhattan) in September of 1955, six months before I did. I met him at the end of February, the third week I taught there, when one of the assistant principals asked me to cover the cafeteria during fifth period for a teacher who had to be at a conference. "Good luck with the animals," I remember him saying.

I was on my guard when I entered the cafeteria; perhaps even a trifle scared. The stories I had been hearing in the teachers' lounge had prepared me to expect anything. During the winter months the students were not allowed to leave the lunchroom and the results of keeping them penned in—the fights, the food throwing, the high-pitched incessant chattering in Spanish, the way the Negro and Puerto Rican boys and girls chased each other around the tables—such things did, I had to admit, give the room a zoo-like quality.

The day I was assigned, however, was a Catholic holy day and many of the students were absent. Those who remained filled a little less than half of the large room and though they were noisy it was relatively easy to keep them in order. Luther sat at a table by himself, near the exit to the food line. Occasionally, I noticed, a few boys would come and sit next to him. The third time I patrolled his area, however, his table was empty and he stopped me.

"Hey, man," he said, poking me in the arm to get my attention, "you new here?"

He had a stack of about ten cookies in his other hand and he put one into his mouth as he waited for an answer. When I told him that I was not new, he nodded and looked at me. "You have any trouble yet?"

"No," I said, as sternly as possible. Despite my feelings of sympathy for the students, I knew that if I ever hoped to get anywhere with them I had to appear tough and confident. "No," I repeated, almost, I recall, as if I were challenging him. "I haven't."

Luther cocked his head to one side then and smiled slowly. "You will," he said, and went back to his cookies.

In the teachers' lounge, the first time I told the story, somebody asked if the boy who had stopped me was a little Negro kid, very black, with a slight hunchback. I said he was. The teachers laughed. "That's Luther," one of them said.

"He's batty," said another. "Just leave him be."

I repeated the story endlessly. It was the first anecdote of my teaching experience that excited admiration and some sort of reaction from those I told it to, and this was important to me then. I had no more direct encounters with Luther that term, though I did see him in the halls, between classes. I always smiled at him and he would smile back—or at least I thought he did. I could never be sure. This bothered me, especially the first time it happened. Through my retelling of the story, I realized, he had become so real to me, so much a part of my life that I think I took it for granted that our encounter had assumed equal significance in his life. The possibility that he had not even repeated the story to a single one of his friends disturbed me.

Once or twice during the term I spotted him wandering around the halls while classes were in session, slouching down a corridor, his body pressed against the tile walls. When I asked the other teachers if he was known for cutting classes, they told me again to just leave him be—that the guidance counselor had suggested the teachers let him do what he wanted to. He was harmless, they said, *if* you left him alone. Those teachers who had him in their classes agreed with the guidance counselor. Left alone, he didn't annoy them. When he wanted to, he worked feverishly—and did competent work; but when he didn't want to work he would either sit and stare or just get up, walk out of the room, and wander around the building. He was, they concluded, a mental case.

I returned to Booker T. Washington Junior High School the following September, and Luther turned up in one of my English classes. He had changed. He was no longer small, having grown a good five inches over the summer, and he was no longer quiet. When classwork bored him now, he would stand up and, instead of leaving the room, would begin telling stories. Just like that. He had his favorite topics, too—his cousin Henry who had epilepsy, Willie Mays, what was on sale at the supermarket, the football team he played on, the stories in the latest *Blackhawk* comic book. When he ran out of stories, he would pull *The National Enquirer* out of his back pocket and begin reading from it, always starting with an item in the "Personals" columns that had caught his eye. I never knew what to do. When I would yell at him to sit down and be quiet, he would wave his hand at me impatiently and continue. Moreover, no expression on his face, nothing he ever said, indicated that he thought he was doing anything wrong. An hour after disrupting a class, if I would see him in the corridor, he would give me a big smile and a hello. After a while, of course, I gave up even trying to interrupt him. I listened with the other students—laughing, fascinated, amazed.

I tried to remember some of his stories, but when I retold them they never seemed interesting, and so I purposely gave Luther's class a lot of composition work, trying to make the topics as imaginative as possible—with the hope, of course, that he would use one of them to let loose. But all the topics, he declared, were "stupid" and he refused to write on any of them. Then, when I least expected it, when I assigned the class a "How to—" composition, he handed one in. It was typewritten on a piece of lined notebook paper, single-spaced, beginning at the very top of the page and ending just at the first ruled line. It was titled "How To Steal Some Fruits."

```
    How To Steal Some Fruits, by Luther
Go to a fruit store and when the fruitman isn't
looking take some fruits. Then run. When the
fruitman yells "Hey you stop taking those
fruits" run harder. That is how to steal some
fruits.
```

The next day he sat quietly in class. When I looked at him, he looked down at his desk. When I called on him to answer a question, he shrugged and looked away. At three o'clock, however, no more than five seconds after I had returned from escorting my official class downstairs, he bounded into my room, full of life, and propped himself up on the edge of my desk.

"Hey, man," he said. "How'd you like my composition? It was deep, wasn't it?"

"Deep?"

"Deep, swift, *cool*—you know."

"I liked it fine," I said, laughing.

"Ah, don't put me on, man—how *was* it?"

"I liked it," I repeated, my hands clasped in front of me on the desk. "I mean it."

His face lit up. "You mean it? I worked hard on it, Mr. Carter. I swear to God I did." It was the first time, I remember, that he had ever addressed me by my name. He stopped and wiped his mouth. "How'd you like the typing? Pretty good, huh?"

"It was fine."

"Christ, man," he said, stepping down from my desk and moving to the blackboard. He picked up a piece of chalk and wrote his name, printing it in capital letters. "How come you so tight? Why don't you loosen up? I ain't gonna do nothing. I just want to know about my composition. That's all."

I felt I could reach him, talk to him. I wanted to—had wanted to for some time, I realized—but he was right. I was tight, uncomfortable, embarrassed. "Where'd you get a typewriter?" I offered.

He smiled. "Where I get fruits," he replied, then laughed and clapped his hands. I must have appeared shocked, for before I could say anything he was shaking his head back and forth. "Oh man," he said. "You are really deep. I swear. You really are." He climbed onto my desk again. "You mind talking?"

"No," I said.

"Good. Let me ask you something—you married?"

"No," I said. "Do you think I should be married?"

"It beats stealing fruits," he said, and laughed again. His laugh was loud and harsh and at first it annoyed me, but then his body began rocking back and forth as if his comment had

set off a chain of jokes that he was telling himself silently, and
before I knew it I was laughing with him.

"I really liked the composition," I said. "In fact, I hope
you don't mind, but I've already read it to some of the other
teachers."

"No shit."

"They thought it was superb."

"It's superb," he said, shaking his head in agreement.
"Oh, it's superb, man," he said, getting up again and walking
away. His arms and legs moved in different directions and he
seemed so loose that when he turned his back to me and I
noticed the way his dirty flannel shirt was stretched tightly over
his misshapen back, I was surprised—as if I'd noticed it for the
first time. He walked around the room, muttering to himself,
tapping on desks with his fingertips, and then he headed for
the door. "I'm superb," he said. "So I be rolling on my superb
way home—"

"Stay," I said.

He threw his arms apart. "You win!" he declared. "I'll
stay." He came back to my desk, looked at me directly, then
rolled his eyes and smiled. "People been telling stories to you
about me?"

"No."

"None?" he questioned, coming closer.

"All right," I said. "Some—"

"That's all right," he said, shrugging it off. He played with
the binding of a book that was on my desk. Then he reached
across and took my grade book. I snatched it away from him
and he laughed again. "Oh, man," he exclaimed. "I am just so
restless! —You know what I mean?"

He didn't wait for an answer but started around the room
again. The pockets of his pants were stuffed and bulging, the
cuffs frayed. The corner of a red and white workman's hand-
kerchief hung out of a back pocket. He stopped in the back of

the room, gazed into the glass bookcase, and then turned to me and leaned back. "You said to stay—what you got to say?"

The question was in my mind, and impulsively I asked it: "Just curious—do you remember me from last year?"

"Sure," he said, and turned his back to me again. He looked in the bookcase, whirled around, and walked to the side of the room, opening a window. He leaned out and just as I was about to say something to him about it, he closed it and came back to the front of the room. "Man," he exclaimed, sitting on my desk again. "Were you ever scared that day! If I'd set off a cherry bomb, you'd have gone through the fan." He put his face closer to mine. "Man, you were scared green!"

"Was I scared of you, Luther?" I asked, looking straight into his eyes.

"Me? Nah. Nothing to be scared of." He hopped off the desk and wiped his name off the blackboard with the palm of his hand; then he started laughing to himself. He looked at me, over his shoulder. "Bet I know what you're thinking now," he said.

"Go ahead—"

"You're thinking you'd like to *help* a boy like me. Right? You're getting this big speech ready in your head about—"

"No," I interrupted. "I wasn't."

He eyed me suspiciously. "You sure?"

"I'm sure."

"Not even with compositions? Oh, man, if you'd help me with compositions, before we'd be through with me, I'd be typing like a whiz." He banged on a desk with his palms, and then his fingers danced furiously on the wood as he made clicking noises inside his mouth. "Ding!" he said, swinging the carriage across. "Ain't it fun to type!"

"Okay," I said. "Okay. Maybe I was thinking that I would like to help you."

"I knew it, man," he said to himself. "I just knew it."

"You have a good mind, Luther—much better than you let on."

"I do, I do," he muttered, chuckling. I stood up and went to the closet to get my coat. "Okay. What do I get if I work for you?" he asked.

I shrugged. "Nothing, maybe. I can't promise anything."

"I *like* that, man," he said.

"Could you call me Mr. Carter?" I asked somewhat irritably. "I don't call you, 'Hey, you'—"

"Okay, Mr. Carter," he said. He took my coat sleeve. "Let me help you on with your coat, Mr. Carter."

We walked out of the room and I locked the door. "You ain't a *real* social worker like the others," he commented as we started down the stairs. He held the door open for me. "I do like that."

I nodded.

"Playing it close to the vest again, huh? Tight-mouthed."

"Just thinking," I said.

When we were outside, he asked me what he had to do.

"For what?" I asked.

"To get you to help me to be somebody, to educate myself—all that stuff."

"Do what you want to do," I said. "Though you might start by doing your homework. Then we'll see—"

"I know," he said, cocking his head to one side again. "If I play ball with you, you'll play ball with me. Right? Okay, okay. I know."

Then he was gone, running down the street, his arms spread wide as if he were an airplane, a loud siren-like noise rising and falling from him as he disappeared from view.

The next few months were without doubt the most satisfying to me of any during the eight years I've been a teacher.

Luther worked like a fiend. He was bright, learned quickly, and was not really that far behind. He did his homework, he paid attention in class, he studied for tests, and he read books. That was most important. On every book he read I asked him to write a book report: setting, plot, theme, characters, his opinion of the book—and once a week, on Thursday afternoons, we would get together in my room for a discussion. During the remainder of the term he must have gone through at least forty to fifty books. Most of them had to do with sports, airplanes, and insects. For some reason he loved books about insects. All the reports came to me typed, and on some he drew pictures—"illustrations" he called them, which, he claimed, would be a help to me in case I had not read the book.

When we would finish talking about books, I would help him with his other subjects, and his improvement was spectacular. I looked forward to my sessions with him, to his reports, to just seeing him—yet from day to day, from moment to moment, I always expected him to bolt from me, and this pleased me. Every time he came to me for a talk I was truly surprised.

When the term ended, he asked if I would continue to help him. I said I would. He was not programmed for any of my English classes during the spring term, but we kept up with our weekly discussions. As the weather improved, however, he read less and less; I didn't want him to feel that he *had* to come see me every Thursday, and so, about a week before the opening of the baseball season, I told him I thought he had reached the point where he could go it alone. "When you feel like talking, just come knocking," I said. "We don't need a schedule." He seemed relieved, I thought, and I was proud that I had had the sense to release him from any obligation he might have felt.

Then, suddenly, I didn't see him anywhere for three weeks. I asked his homeroom teacher about him and she said she hadn't seen him either; she had sent him a few postcards but had received no reply. That very night—it was almost as if he had been there listening, I thought—he telephoned me at home.

"Is this Mr. Carter? This is Luther here."

"Hi, Luther," I said.

"I looked you up in the telephone book. You mind me calling you at home?"

"No, no. I don't mind."

"Okay," he said, breathing hard. "I just wanted to let you know not to worry about me because I'm not in school. Okay?"

"Sure," I said. "Sure."

"I had some things to take care of—you know?"

"Sure," I said.

"Man, you *know* you're itching to ask me *what?*" He laughed. "You are deep. I'll be back Monday."

That was all. On Monday, as he'd promised, he returned to school and came to visit me in my room at three o'clock. We talked for a while about the way the pennant race was going, and then he said, "Okay, let's cut the jazz, man. I got something to say to you." He seemed very intense about it and I told him that I was listening carefully. He pointed a finger at me. "Now, we stopped our sessions, right?"

"Right," I said.

"And the day after we stopped, I began to play the hook for three straight weeks, right?"

"Right."

"Okay. Now you can tell me it ain't so, but I'll bet you'll be thinking it was your fault. It ain't. If you want the truth, I ain't done a stick of work all term for *any* teacher—so don't go thinking that I stopped being a good student cause we stopped our meetings." He let out a long breath.

"I'm glad you told me," I said.

"Shit, man," he said, getting up and going to the door. "Don't *say* anything, huh? Why you got to *say* something all the time?" He came toward me. "*Why?*" He was almost screaming and I slid my chair back from the desk. He shook his head frantically. "Why, man?" he said. He reached into his side pocket and I started to stand up. Abruptly, he broke into laughter. "Oh man, you are deep! You are just so deep!" He clapped his hands and laughed at me some more. "Ra-ta-tat-tat!" he said as he banged on a desk. "You're real sweet, man! Just so sweet! Ra-ta-tat-tat! Comin' down the street!" He sat down in one of the seats. "But don't you worry none. I got seven liberry cards now and books growing out the ceiling. I got a liberry card for Luther King and one for Luther Queen and one for Luther Prince and one for Luther Jones and one for Luther Smith and one for Luther Mays and one for Luther B. Carter." He banged on the top of the desk with his fist, then drummed with his fingers again. "But don't you worry none—ra-ta-tat-tat—just don't you worry—"

"I'm not," I said.

"That's all," he said, and dashed out of the room.

He attended classes regularly for about two weeks and then disappeared again for a week. He returned for a few days, stayed away, returned. The pattern continued. In the halls when we saw each other he would always smile and ask if I was worrying and I would tell him I wasn't. Once or twice, when he was absent, he telephoned me at home and asked me what was new at school. He got a big charge out of this. Then another time, I remember, he came riding through the schoolyard on a bicycle during sixth period, when I was on patrol. "Don't report me, man!" he yelled, and rode right back out, waving and shouting something in Spanish that made everybody laugh.

Near the end of May, the assistant principal in charge of the eighth grade called me into his office. He knew I was friendly with Luther, he said, and he thought that I might talk to the boy. For the past six or seven months, he told me, Luther had been in and out of juvenile court. "Petty thefts," the assistant principal explained. I wasn't surprised; Luther had hinted at this many times. I'd never pressed him about it, however, not wanting to destroy our relationship by lecturing him. The assistant principal said he didn't care whether I said anything to Luther or not. In fact, he added, he would have been just as happy to get rid of him—but before he was shipped off to a 600 school or put away somewhere else, he wanted to give me an opportunity to do what I could. More for me, he said, than for Luther.

About a week after this, on a Friday, Luther telephoned me.

"How've you been?" I asked.

"Superb, man," he said. "Hey, listen—we ain't been seeing much of each other lately, have we?"

"No—"

"No. Okay. Listen—I got two tickets to see the Giants play tomorrow. You want to come?" I didn't answer immediately. "Come on—yes or no—tickets are going fast—"

"I'd like to," I said. "Yes. Only—only I was wondering where you got the money for the tickets." I breathed out, glad I had said it.

Luther just laughed. "Oh man, you're not gonna be like that, are you? You been listening to too many stories again. That judge from the court must of been gassing with you. Tell you what—you come to the game and I'll tell you where I got the tickets. A deal?"

"A deal."

"Meet you in front of the school at eleven o'clock—I like

to get there early to see Willie go through batting practice. Batting practice—that's more fun than the game sometimes. You know?"

He was waiting for me when I got there a few minutes before eleven the following day. "Let's go," he said, flourishing the tickets. "But don't ask me now, man—let's enjoy the game first. Okay?"

I did enjoy the game. The Giants were playing the Cardinals and to Luther's delight Willie Mays had one of his better days, going three-for-four at bat, and making several brilliant plays in the field. For most of the game I was truly relaxed. Along about the eighth inning, however, I began to think about the question again—to wonder when would be the best time to ask it. Luther, it seemed, had forgotten all about it. The Giants were winning 5–2.

"Oh man," he said. "If only that Musial don't do something, we're home free. Look at Willie!" he exclaimed. "Ain't he the greatest that ever lived. He is just so graceful! You know? How you like to see a team of Willie Mayses out there? Wow!" Wes Westrum, the Giant catcher, grounded out, short to first, and the eighth inning was over. "One to go, one to go," Luther said. Then he jabbed me in the arm with his finger. "Hey, listen —I been thinking. Instead of an All-Star game every year between the leagues, what they ought to do one year is have the white guys against our guys. What you think?"

I shrugged. "I don't know," I said.

"Sure," he said. "Listen—we got Willie in center. Then we put Aaron in right and Doby in left. He's got the raw power. Some outfield, huh? Then we got Campy catching and Newcombe pitching. You can't beat that. That Newcombe— he's a mean son-of-a-bitch, but he throws. Okay. I been thinking about this a long time—" He used his fingers to enumerate. He was excited, happy. "At first base we put Luke Easter, at second Junior Gilliam, at short Ernie Banks, and at third base we bring in old Jackie Robinson, just to give the team a little class—you know what I mean? Man, what a line-up! Who could you match it with?"

When I said I didn't know, Luther eyed me suspiciously. "C'mon—Musial, Mantle, Williams, Spahn—you name 'em and I'll match 'em, man for man, your guys against ours." He stopped and cheered as a Cardinal popped out to Whitey Lockman at first. "What's the matter—don't you like the idea? Ha! Face it, man, we'd wipe up the field with you. Swish! Swish!" He laughed and slapped me on the knee. "Hey, I know what's bugging you, I bet—" He leaned toward me, cupping his hand over his mouth, and whispered in my ear. "Tell the truth now, would you have ever offered to help me if I wasn't colored?"

"Would I—?" I stopped. "Sure," I said. "Of course I would. Of course—"

Luther smiled, triumphantly, dubiously.

"Look," I said. "As long as we're asking questions, let me ask you something."

"About the tickets, right?"

"No," I said. "Forget the tickets. No long lectures, either. Just a question. Just one: how come you steal?"

"Oh man," he said, laughing. "That's an easy one! Because I'm not getting what I want and when you don't get what you want, man, you got to take. Don't you know that?"

I stared at him, not sure I had heard right. He winked at me. "Enjoy the ball game, man! Say hey, Willie!" he shouted as Mays caught a fly ball, bread-basket style, for the second out. "Ain't he the sweetest!"

A minute later the game was over and the players were racing across the field toward the clubhouse in center field, trying to escape the fans who scrambled after them. "They won't get Willie," Luther said. "He's too swift, too swift."

When we were outside, I thanked Luther and told him how much I'd enjoyed the game. "How about a Coke or something?" I offered.

"Nah," he said. "I got things to do." He extended his hand quickly and I shook it, the first time we had ever done that. "Okay. You go get spiffed up and get a wife. Time you were married." He tossed his head back and laughed. "Ain't you married yet? No, no. *Smile,* man—how you gonna get a wife, never smiling." He started away, through the crowd. "Stay loose," he called back. "Don't steal no fruits."

I never questioned him again about stealing, but even if I'd wanted to, I wouldn't have had much opportunity. He didn't come to see me very often the rest of that year. When he returned to school in September of 1958 for his last year of junior high school, he had grown again. But not up. He never did go higher than the five-five or five-six he had reached by that time. He had taken up weightlifting over the summer, however, and his chest, his neck, his arms—they had all broadened incredibly. Instead of the dirty cotton and flannel shirts he had worn the two previous years, he now walked through the halls in laundry-white T-shirts, the sleeves rolled up to the shoulder, his powerful muscles exposed. There were always a half-dozen Negro boys following him around and they all dressed the way he did—white T-shirts, black chino pants, leather wrist straps, and—hanging from their necks on pieces of string—miniature black skulls.

The guidance counselor for the ninth grade came to me one day early in the term and asked me if I could give him any evidence against Luther. He claimed that Luther and his gang were going around the school, beating and torturing those students who refused to "loan" them money. All of the students, he said, were afraid to name Luther. "The kid's a born sadist," he added. I told him I didn't know anything.

The term progressed and the stories and rumors increased. I was told that the police in Luther's neighborhood were convinced that he and his gang were responsible for a series of muggings. I tried not to believe it, but Luther all but gave me conclusive proof one afternoon right before Christmas. He came into my room at three o'clock, alone, and said he had something for me. He said he trusted me not to tell anybody about it or show it to anyone. I said I wouldn't.

"Okay, man—here it is—" His eyes leapt around the room, frenzied, delirious. He took a little card from his wallet. "You might need this sometime—but don't ask me no questions. Ha! And don't you worry none. I'm doing okay. Expanding all the time. Don't you worry." I took the card from him. "See you now, Mr. Carter. See you, see you."

He left and I looked at the card. Across the top was printed THE BLACK AVENGERS, and below it was written: "Don't touch this white man. He's okay." It was signed by Luther and under his name he had drawn a skull and crossbones. I put the card in my wallet.

In January, to no one's great surprise, Luther was sent away to reform school in upstate New York. I was never exactly clear about the precise event that had led to it—the policeman assigned to our school said it had to do with brutally beating an old man; Luther's friends said it had to do with getting caught in a gang war. They claimed the fight was clean but that the cops had framed Luther. There was nothing in the papers, Luther had not contacted me, and I did not find out about it all until he'd already been shipped off.

I received a postcard from him that summer. It was brief.

I hate it here. I can't say anymore or they'll beat shit out of me. I hate it. I'm reading some. I'll visit you when I get out and we'll have a session.

I answered the card with a letter. I told him I was sorry about where he was and that I'd be glad to talk to him whenever he wanted. I gave him some news of the school and included some current baseball clippings. I asked him if there was anything he needed and if there was anybody in his family he wanted me to get in touch with. I told him that in return for the time he'd taken me to the baseball game I had ordered a subscription to *Sport* magazine for him.

He replied with another postcard.

Visiting day this summer is August 21. I'd like for you to come.

When I arrived, he seemed glad to see me, but I remember that he was more polite than he had ever been before—and more subdued. I wondered, at the time, if they were giving him tranquillizers. I was only allowed an hour with him and we spent most of that time just walking around the grounds—the school was a work-farm reformatory—not saying anything.

The visit, I could tell, was a disappointment to him. I don't know what he expected of me, but whatever it was, I didn't provide it. I wrote him a letter when I got home, telling him I had enjoyed seeing him and that I'd be glad to come again if he wanted me to. He didn't answer it, and I heard no more from him for a year and a half.

Then one day in the spring of 1961—just about the time of the Bay of Pigs invasion of Cuba, I remember—he popped into my room at school. He looked horrible. His face was unshaven, his clothes were filthy and ragged, his eyes were glazed. Underneath his clothes, his body had become flabby and he bent over noticeably when he walked. At first I didn't recognize him.

When I did, I was so glad to see him I didn't know what

to do. "Luther—for crying out loud!" I said, standing up and shaking his hand. "How the hell are you?"

He smiled at me. "I'm superb, man—can't you tell from looking at me?" He laughed then, and I laughed with him.

"You've gotten older," I said.

"Past sixteen," he said. "That means I don't got to go to school no more—"

He waited, but I didn't offer an opinion. "How about going down with me and having a cup of coffee? I'm finished here for the day—just getting through with midterms."

"Nah," he said, looking down and playing with his hands. "I gotta meet somebody. I'm late already. But I was in the neighborhood, so I thought I'd come let you know I was still alive." He came to my desk and looked down. He shook his head as if something were wrong.

"What's the matter?" I asked.

"Don't see no wedding ring on your finger yet." He looked straight into my face. "Hey, man—you ain't a fag, are you?"

"No," I said, laughing. "Not that I know of—"

He laughed, his mouth opening wide. "Okay. That's all the gas for today. I'll see you, man."

During the next few months he visited me several times. Sometimes he looked good, sometimes bad—but I never could find out what he was doing with his days. He never gave a straight answer to my questions. More and more, I felt that he was asking me for some kind of help, but when I would touch on anything personal or even hint that I wanted to do something for him, with him, he would become defensive.

I didn't see him over the summer, but the following fall he came by periodically. He seemed to be getting a hold on himself and sometimes he would talk about going to night school. Nothing came of the talk, though. In November he was arrested and sent to Riker's Island—to P.S. 616, the combination prison-school for boys between the ages of sixteen and twenty. His sentence was for eighteen months and during the first three months I visited him twice. Both times all he wanted to do was talk about the English class we had had and the stories and compositions he had made up. He said he was trying to remember some of them for the English teacher he had there, but couldn't do it all the time. He seemed to be in terrible shape, and I didn't have much hope for him.

So I was surprised when I began getting postcards from him again. "I am studying hard," the first one said. "There is a Negro who comes here to help me. I like him. I will be a new man when I come out. Yours sincerely, Luther." It was neatly and carefully written. The ones that followed were the same and they came at regular intervals of about five weeks. He told me about books he was reading, most of them having to do with Negro history, and about how he was changing. "Improving" was the word he used most.

I answered his cards as best I could and offered to come see him again, but he never took up any of my offers. When his eighteen months were up, I expected a visit from him. He never came. Sometimes I wondered what had become of him, but after the first few months passed and I didn't hear from him, I thought about him less and less. A year passed—two since we had last seen each other at Riker's Island—and then we met again.

I spotted him first. It was a beautiful summer night and I had gone up to Lewisohn Stadium for a concert. It had been good, I was relaxed and happy as I walked out of the stadium. Luther was standing at the corner of Amsterdam Avenue and 138th Street. He was wearing a dark blue suit, a white shirt, and a tie. He was clean-shaven, his hair was cut short, and he looked healthy and bright. He was stopping people and trying to sell them newspapers.

"How are you, Mr. Carter?" he asked when I walked up

to him. His eyes were clear and he seemed very happy to see me. "Interested in buying a newspaper to help the colored people? Only a dime—"

"No, thanks," I said. The paper he was selling, as I'd expected, was *Muhammad Speaks,* the newspaper of the Black Muslims. "You look fine," I added.

"Thanks. Excuse me a second." He turned and sold a copy to somebody. People snubbed him but this didn't stop him from smiling or trying. I waited. When the crowd had gone, he asked me where I was going. "Home," I said. "Cup of coffee first?"

"No, thanks," he said. "Thanks, but no thanks."

"When did all this start?" I asked, motioning to the newspapers.

"At Riker's Island," he said. He put up a hand, as if to stop my thoughts from becoming words. "I know what you're thinking, what you hear on TV and read in the newspapers about us—but don't believe everything. We're essentially a religious organization, as you may or may not know."

"I know," I said.

"And it's meant a lot to me—I couldn't have made it without their help. They—they taught me to *believe* in myself." His eyes glowed as he twisted his body toward me. "Can you understand that?" It seemed very important to him that I believe him. "*Can* you?" He relaxed momentarily and shrugged. "I don't believe everything they teach, of course, but I follow their precepts: I don't smoke, I don't drink, I don't curse, I don't go out with women who aren't Muslims—I feel good *inside,* Mr. Carter. Things are straightening themselves out." He paused. "It hasn't been easy."

"I know," I said, and smiled.

He nodded, embarrassed, I thought. "I'm going back to school also—"

"I'm glad."

"Even my body feels good! I'm lifting weights again," he said. Then he laughed and the sound tore through the warm night. His eyes were flashing with delight. "Oh man—some day I'll be the head of a whole damned army! Me and my old hunchback." He laughed again, pleased with himself. His laughter subsided and he patted me on the shoulder. "Oh man, you are still so deep, so deep. Don't worry none, Mr. Carter. I don't go around advocating no violence." He chuckled. "I've got to go," he said, extending a hand. "It's been good seeing you again. Sure you don't want to buy a copy?"

"I'm sure," I said, shaking his hand. "Good luck to you, Luther. I'm glad to see you the way you are now—"

"Thanks." We looked at each other for a minute and he smiled warmly at me. Then I started toward the subway station. When I'd crossed the street, he called to me.

"Hey—Mr. Carter—"

I turned.

"Let me ask you something—do you still have that card I gave you?" He howled at this remark. "Oh man, I'd save that card if I were you! I'd do that. You never know when you might need it. You never know—"

I started back across the street, toward him. He tossed his head back and roared with laughter. "You never know, you never know," he repeated, and hurried away from me, laughing wildly. I stared at him until he disappeared in the darkness. Then I just stood there, dazed, unable to move—I don't know for how long. Finally I made myself turn around, and as I walked slowly toward the lights of Broadway all I could feel was the presence of his muscular body, powerful, gleaming, waiting under his white shirt, his clean suit.

Joe

IN SEPTEMBER OF 1955, when President Eisenhower had his heart attack, Joe draped his delivery cart with black streamers and pedaled around our neighborhood in Brooklyn telling everybody that the Nazis were going to take over as soon as Ike died. Every time he delivered a carton of groceries to our house, he would give my mother details of how the takeover would be carried out. My mother never tried to interrupt him. She would listen quietly and patiently until he finished. Then she would give him a tip and he would take off his baseball cap and thank her. "But don't you worry," he'd say then, slipping the coins into his apron pocket. "I'll protect Howie and all the other little kids. The Nazis won't get them if I can help it."

When he'd gone, my mother would always praise me for not having laughed at him. Joe must have been in his forties or fifties then, and for as long as I could remember he'd been the delivery boy for Mr. Fontani's fruit and grocery store on Rogers Avenue. One of the big treats of my life, I remember, was being allowed to go with Joe on a round of deliveries. While my

25

mother was doing her shopping, I'd sit on top of Joe's cart—it was made of wood, not aluminum—and we'd zoom through the streets, in and out of traffic—up Linden Boulevard, down Nostrand Avenue, through Martense Street, Church Avenue, Lenox Road, into courtyards, backyards, through alleys, down cellars. "Fast enough for you, Howie?" he'd always shout, and he'd speed up until I felt I was going to be blown off the top of his cart. Then I'd scream for him to slow down and he'd laugh a lot. At one time or another all my friends had been taken for rides by Joe, and when we were together we'd swap tales of our trips, each of us claiming to have come closest to getting killed.

Joe was tremendous in size. He was over six feet tall and must have weighed at least two hundred and fifty pounds. His eyes were small and pale blue, his nose was large and red, his ears stuck out, his face was usually unshaven, and his long hair, which was silver-gray, stuck out in wild curls from under his baseball cap. It was inevitable, I guess, that we called him Mighty Joe Young. If any of us had ever been caught under the wheels of a car or truck, we were sure that Joe would have appeared, lifted the truck, and saved our lives. Watching him carry crates of vegetables into Mr. Fontani's store, or sides of beef into Mr. Klein's kosher butcher shop, we used to make bets about how many pounds he could lift. The figures usually started at five hundred.

In March of 1956, when President Eisenhower announced that he would seek re-election, Joe removed the black streamers from his cart and in their place he put a smiling picture of the President, framed in red, white, and blue. By that time, though, it wasn't the outside of his cart that interested us. We were all about twelve or thirteen then, most of us in the sixth or seventh grade at P.S. 92, and for almost a year—starting the previous spring—the inside of Joe's delivery cart had been the center of our lives, a treasure chest of pornography.

It contained everything—photography magazines, decks of playing cards, glossy eight-by-ten's of naked women, calendars, rubber dolls, comic books, stories, books on exotic methods of love-making, and these dull brown photos of live men and women making love and doing things in positions that drove us wild. Joe kept his collection carefully stored behind wooden slats that he'd removed from orange crates and had nailed to the insides of his cart. He'd show us the same books and pictures again and again, always telling us how much he'd paid for an item, always pointing and asking, "Do you like that, huh?" We must have looked through some of those books a thousand times during that year, but every time we'd get together with him it was as if each of us was seeing it all for the first time. "I got some collection, huh?" he'd say proudly, and we'd always tell him that he did, and then we'd ask to see the three or four photos he kept in his wallet, the ones we knew were his favorites.

We usually met in a cellar of one of the big apartment houses on Linden Boulevard or Lenox Road—no more than six or seven of us at a time. We always entered and left in groups of two's, so that it wouldn't look suspicious. Sometimes, though, when we were sure it was safe and Joe was scheduled for a delivery, we'd get together in one of our own homes and Joe would carry his collection upstairs in a grocery carton. And sometimes—right in my own house—Izzie and Corky would get on my parents' bed and try to see if the positions in the pictures were possible for human beings. They'd say all kinds of crazy things to each other—the way people in the comic books did while they were doing things—and we'd go out of our minds laughing at them. Joe liked to watch them fool around and he'd laugh and try to help them get their legs and arms going the right way.

The biggest thrill that year came when Joe invited us up

to his apartment. He lived on the top floor of an apartment house on Linden Boulevard, right around the corner from Mr. Fontani's store. We came on a Sunday morning in June, about two weeks before school was out. There were fifteen or twenty of us: Izzie, Corky, Louie, Marty—most of the guys from our baseball team, and a few others we'd invited. We came in small groups, with our bats and balls and gloves—we all told our parents we had a game at the Parade Grounds—and we made up that if anyone asked us questions we would say we were looking for Kenny Murphy, who lived on the third floor of Joe's building. I got there with Izzie and Louie at about eleven o'clock, and there were already a half dozen guys sitting around eating cookies and fruit and drinking sodas.

Joe was dressed in a white shirt and tie and almost before he'd closed the door behind us he was asking what we wanted to eat. In the middle of the living room he'd set up a table and piled it high with all kinds of food—apples, oranges, peaches, pears, cookies, candy bars, potato chips, soda, milk, even lettuce and tomatoes and mushrooms, I remember—and all the while we were there he kept bringing new supplies out of his kitchen to refill the plates we were emptying.

He served ice cream, too—Mel-o-rolls and Dixie cups—and he was as happy as I'd ever seen him, just going around and asking us again and again if we were having a good time, if we had enough to eat. We were all surprised, I think, at what his place looked like. It was neat and clean, and the furniture seemed to be almost brand-new. When Louie went up to him and told him how much we all liked his place, his face lit up and he began telling us how much each thing had cost him. At the time, I remember, his place reminded me of a motel I'd been in once on a trip to Connecticut with my parents—mainly because of the bright-colored slipcovers and rugs, and the wrought-iron supports on the couches and chairs and tables. On the walls, though, instead of a few neatly framed pictures,

Joe had taped up his own drawings of naked men and women, some traced on tissue-thin paper with pencil, others copied free-hand with crayons. At about noon, when all the guys were there, Joe got out his collection from under his bed and began passing around books and pictures and dolls for us to look at, but I wasn't too interested. I just kept looking at his own drawings. There seemed to be thousands of them in all different sizes, drawn on all kinds of paper—flattened-out paper bags, strips of wallpaper, colored poster paper, envelopes, shirt cardboards—and they covered the walls of his three rooms.

We stayed until about four o'clock that day. When we were about to leave, Joe made us swear not to tell our parents, the way he always did when we'd finished a session. He never threatened to do anything to us if we did tell—he just asked us not to, because he said it would get him into trouble with Mr. Fontani if any customers found out. Then he told us that he was saving his money and he promised that the next time we came over, after the summer, he'd have a movie projector and a bunch of French films he was planning to buy. He had a lot of money saved, he said, but the films were very expensive. We thanked him, and those of us who were going to the country or to camp for July and August promised we'd send him postcards.

We never got to see the French films at Joe's apartment. The next fall, one day about a month or so after I'd gotten back from camp, Izzie gave me the news. We were in the schoolyard, shooting around, waiting to get enough guys to start a game. "You won't believe it," he said, "but Joe is getting married."

"*What*—?"

He shook his head. "Yeah. I didn't believe it either—but Mr. Fontani told my mother that it's the truth."

After supper that night I ran out of the house and met the

guys at the corner of Linden and Rogers, where we always hung out. They'd all heard the news by then and they all seemed very sad about it. We kept shaking our heads in disbelief and asking each other if it was really true. Before we went home that night we made up that Kenny and I would go by Mr. Fontani's store the next morning and ask Joe ourselves. He couldn't get married, we told each other. He just couldn't.

But the next morning Joe told us that it was so. "Wait till you see her," he said, with this big smile on his face. "My aunt got her for me—but that don't matter. Wait till you see her." We talked for a while, he thanked me for the postcard I'd sent him, and then—we were standing by the curb, I remember— he put down a big sack of potatoes he'd been carrying, wiped his hands on his apron, and after looking around to make sure nobody could hear him, he rolled his eyes and whispered to us: "Who needs pictures when you can have the real thing, huh?"

When we reported to the other guys later that day, they all seemed to feel betrayed in the way we did—and about the only thing that cheered us up was Louie's suggestion that we chip in and offer to buy Joe's collection from him. But even if he would sell, we realized, none of us was brave enough to keep the stuff in his house.

Joe was married sometime around Thanksgiving—I was never exactly sure where and how—and the first time any of us ever saw his wife was the week after Thanksgiving. We were standing on the corner when Corky spotted them. They walked toward us slowly, arm in arm. Joe was wearing a blue suit, a shirt and tie, and instead of his baseball cap, a new straw hat. He was smoking a cigar and nodding proudly to everyone he passed. His wife seemed to be just as proud as he was—and when they reached us and Joe introduced her to each one of us, she smiled and repeated our names. She was very short— maybe a little over five feet—plump, but not fat. She seemed to be much younger than Joe—thirty-three or thirty-four at the most—and she had very pretty, reddish-colored hair which was cut short and straight. Her face was oval, pushed-in, fleshy—to be truthful, it was pretty obvious to all of us that if she wasn't a true Mongolian idiot, she was pretty close to it. You could tell just from the way she walked, kind of duck-footed.

"Why'd he do it?" Corky kept asking after they'd gone. "Why'd he do it?"

The following night Joe and his wife came by at about the same time, arm in arm, and we went through the introductions all over again. At about the end of a week Joe stopped introducing us and would just walk by and say something like "Nice evening for a walk with your wife, huh?" and keep going. That fall he took her for a walk every night, and on Saturday and Sunday afternoons we sometimes saw them in Prospect Park, sitting by the lake. After a while we took them pretty much for granted and hardly gave them much thought when we'd see them together.

After the first snow they came by only about once a week. When they did appear, she would always be dressed warmly in a heavy Persian lamb coat that was too big for her. During Christmas vacation they didn't go walking at all. One night, though, Joe came down by himself and stopped to talk to us.

"I'm going to the store to get something to eat for me and my wife," he said, smiling.

"Is she feeling okay?" Louie asked. "We haven't seen her for a while."

"Oh, she's fine," Joe said. "She's just fine."

Then Izzie, trying to be a wise guy, I guess, looked up at Joe and as seriously as he could, in a man-to-man voice, asked: "Tell us something, Joe—how do you like married life?"

Joe burst into a big smile then. "I like it fine," he said. He shook his head up and down a few times before he spoke again.

"It's really good for a man to have a wife. I mean it. Everybody should get married." Then he stopped and lowered his huge head toward us. "I'll tell you something, though. C'mere—" We gathered closer to him and he spoke to us softly, confidentially. "I'll tell you something—it's true what they say about that sex stuff." Nobody said anything. Joe shook his head vigorously, as if agreeing with himself, then he shrugged. "It's good, but after a while the thrill wears off. You'll all see some day—"

During the winter we didn't think very much about Joe and his wife, and we hardly ever saw them. It snowed a lot and because it got dark so early most of our parents didn't let us stay outside too late anyway. When it started to get warmer, though, and we began to get together again every night after supper, we expected to begin seeing Joe and his wife take their walks again. In a way, I think, we were looking forward to it. At the end of February Joe came down alone a few times and we asked him how his wife was. He said she was fine, but he didn't stop to talk to us. During the month of March he kept going for his walks—almost every night now—but he still took them by himself.

When the warm weather came in the middle of April, Joe was still going for his walks alone. May came and we realized that nobody had seen his wife for over four months. More important, when Joe passed us at night and we asked him about her, he never answered any more. He just kept walking—almost as if he were angry with us. We began to speculate. Izzie started to make up wild stories about what he was probably doing to her, and Corky kept insisting that she'd been dead since New Year's but that Joe didn't know what to do with the body. A few of the guys even began talking about calling the police—that maybe he'd murdered her or chopped her up— you don't know the things you can dream up standing on a corner at night with a bunch of guys.

The second or third week in May we decided to do something. One night when Joe came down we stood around so as to block him from getting by. We did it casually—then, when he'd stopped, Izzie took out a cigarette and asked him if he had a match. While Joe was reaching into his pocket, we shot our questions at him. He lit Izzie's cigarette for him and looked at us. "Okay," he said. "I'll tell you guys. C'mere—" We moved back from the curb, toward the fence that surrounded the garden of the corner apartment house. "Do you guys listen to the radio?" he asked. "All you hear about is women getting raped and beat up. I'm not kidding." He took out a page from a newspaper he had in his pocket and unfolded it for us. There were pictures of four different women on the page, all of them in bad shape—bloody, bruised, their dresses torn, their legs or breasts cut and mangled. "Look at what happens nowadays, huh? I gotta protect my wife. The streets aren't safe for women. I could handle one or two guys, but if a whole *bunch* attacked her, I just don't know . . . you see what I mean?"

We nodded and mumbled that we did, but for some reason none of us could accept what he'd told us as the whole truth. Nobody said so right away. The next night, though, Izzie and Corky started in again with their descriptions of what he was probably doing to her. Even I joined in now—not making up stories the way they did, but just pointing out things, such as the fact that it didn't get dark until late and that our neighborhood was pretty well-lit and safe. I could see why he might not want to take her walking late at night—but what was unsafe about going down Linden Boulevard or into Prospect Park on a Saturday or Sunday afternoon?

The first two weeks in June came and went and we realized that Joe's wife hadn't been seen for six full months. We held a meeting in Marty's house and talked about going to the police, but we were afraid to. Not only for what they would do to us if we were sending them on a wild-goose chase, but because they might tell Joe about us. We didn't want to cross him. Kenny suggested going upstairs to Joe's apartment and saying his mother needed to borrow something—but after he'd suggested the idea, he chickened out. What if Joe came to the door—

"There's only one thing to do, then," I said after a while. "We've got to climb the fire escape and get a look around."

Everybody admitted that I was right, and since it was my suggestion, I was elected to do the climbing. The next afternoon, after school, I changed into my sneakers and met the other guys in the courtyard behind Joe's building. Kenny pointed out which window was Joe's. We stationed guys at the entrance and exit to the cellar, inside the cellar, and on the street in front of Joe's building, forming a relay team to send a message in case there was any trouble. We didn't see Joe's delivery cart around anywhere, and it wasn't six o'clock yet, when he'd be finished with his deliveries, so we figured it was a safe time.

The guys who weren't on the relay squad waited below the fire escape. A few of them sat on the ground reading comic books and sports magazines. Izzie and Kenny played catch with a rubber Spalding and the other guys stood in a line, making believe they were playing Chinese handball against the side of the building, but keeping their eyes on the windows and doors that led to the other buildings.

"If anybody sees us," I said, "start making a lot of noise or fighting or something so they don't look up at me."

Then I started up the fire escape. My heart was pounding. "Are you okay?" Izzie asked when I got to the second story. I nodded. At the next level I almost knocked over somebody's potted plant. When I got to the fourth story, I looked down and had to stop for a few seconds, I was so scared. The guys looked small and funny from where I was. "Go on, go on," they called, whispering. "Go on—"

My fingertips were cold and I almost lost my grip as I started up toward Joe's floor. *I was doing it.* That was the sentence in my head, and it kept me going. I think even then I knew that for months—maybe years afterwards—the guys would always talk about the time I'd climbed the fire escape to spy on Joe. I looked down, then walked carefully up the ladder to the fifth-floor fire escape. I shot my head up quickly, then lowered it. The shade was up and I could see straight into the window. Keeping my head down and moving on my hands and knees, I managed to get to the side of the window. I rested for a few seconds in a deep knee-bend position. There were a few old bricks and flowerpots on either side of the window and on the ledge, and there was a stack of old magazines. I looked down through the spaces between the iron rails and I saw that the guys were all standing there, watching me. I waved frantically at them, and they got the hint and started playing again. I took a deep breath and crawled in front of the window, slowly raising my head.

To my relief, Joe's wife was sitting there, her back to me, watching television. She was eating a banana. She looked very peaceful, I remember, just sitting and eating, not knowing I was spying on her. She seemed to have gotten much fatter, but somehow I felt she was happy, I don't know why. I watched her for a while, then looked around the room. The furniture was the same as it had been, except for the walls. All of Joe's drawings were gone and in their place were neatly framed pictures of flowers and landscapes.

The room looked nice. On the orange couch at the side there was a pile of clothes, and next to it an ironing board had been set up. I don't know how long I watched Joe's wife sitting there—though I do remember that after she'd finished the banana she immediately picked up an apple and started eating it. All I know is I was suddenly aware that the guys were trying to get my attention. I looked down, but the crisscross of the rails blocked my view and I couldn't hear what they were whispering. I motioned to them to wait a minute. Then I got onto my hands and knees and started to crawl toward the staircase. Just before I passed the window, though, I wanted to get one last look—to assure myself again that nothing was wrong. I turned my neck around to look in through the corner of the window —and Joe's huge head was glaring at me through the glass. I screamed like a madman and grabbed onto the side of the fire escape. I could see myself falling the five flights. The guys in the yard were yelling. Joe's face got redder and redder, his chest bigger. I heard my heart going, loud, and I didn't know what to do.

"Hey, what are you doing up there?" some woman called, I didn't know from where. "Get down offa that fire escape." Other windows opened. I looked at Joe. Neither of us could move. We just stared at each other. His eyes looked as if they were going to pop out of his head. His mouth turned but I didn't hear anything. There was more silver in his hair. Finally I let go of the side of the fire escape and scrambled across it, skinning my knees, but making it to the ladder before Joe got the window open.

I don't know how I did it—I don't remember going down at all—but the next thing I knew, I was at the first landing. "Jump!" somebody yelled, and I jumped the last eight or ten feet, not bothering with the hanging ladder. The guys were all standing in the archway that led to the cellar and the street. Something crashed near me. Some of the guys ran. I looked up and saw that Joe was out on the fire escape now.

I stood up and walked into the middle of the courtyard to get a full view of him.

"Are you crazy!?" one of the guys yelled. "Get under cover! He's out of his mind—!"

Joe stood at the rail now, hanging over, bellowing out

words that I couldn't understand and hurling down bricks and
flowerpots and fruit—whatever he could get his hands on. None
of them came close to hitting me. Windows were open all
over—the women were yelling across the courtyard that Joe
was going crazy, the guys were yelling at me to make a run
for it, but I just stood there, transfixed. Finally I cupped my
hands over my mouth and yelled, "I'm sorry, Joe—I'm *sorry!*"
as loud as I could. I don't think he understood me. He just kept
shouting and throwing things. He never even tried to follow
me down the fire escape. The things he shouted were blurred
and thick, and I couldn't make them out. It even seemed to me
that he was crying. I felt so bad and wanted so much to be able
to do something, but I knew there was nothing to do, and after
a few minutes I shouted again that I was sorry and then I ran
through the cellar and out into the street, looking for my
friends.

The
Application

IT HAD STARTED RAINING again, a thin mist-like drizzle through which the workers passed as they filed slowly into the Indiana Auto Works, droning conversation to each other. In the few minutes when most of the men on the first shift were washing up and the second shift had not yet started, the usual fierce noises had subsided to a dull rumble.

Josh walked to his locker and changed from his neatly pressed black double-breasted suit to his factory clothes. When he arrived at his three-cornered stool, next to his welding press, the paper was already there:

APPLICATION FOR THE NAACP

Name (to best of your knowledge): ....

Mother's name: ....

Father's name (list first three possibilities): 1. ....

2. .... 3. ....

Place of birth (check one):

1. County Hospital .... 4. Cotton patch ....
2. Belgian Congo .... 5. Bathroom ....
3. Swamp .... 6. Brothel ....

Number of children (approximate): ......
Number of gold teeth: ......
Number of wives (including those legally married): ......
Age (to nearest 5-year figure): ....
Species (check one): Big Black Buck ....
Boogie Brown .... Sambo Tan ....
How often do you have your hair straightened? ....
List three most prominent identifying scars: 1. ....
2. .... 3. ....
Make of car (check one): Buick .... Cadillac ....
Number of Payments made: One.... Two .... Three....
Cost of accessories (don't count first $200): ....
Number of suits owned: .... *Number of lucky charms:* ....
Number of TV sets: .... *Color of favorite hat:* ....
Do you prefer a razor or switchblade? ....
Length of blade: ....
Court convictions (list number of times): 1. Burglary .....
2. Rape .... 3. Car theft .... 4. Other ....
How many hours a day are you usually sober? None ......
One or two ...... More than two ......
How many loan and finance companies are you indebted to?
(roughly): ....
What was the last job you held for more than six months?
(pimping doesn't count) ....
*If you were given passage and $5 would you go back to
Africa?* ....
How do you prefer to be addressed? (check one):
Daddy-o ..... Like man ..... Blackie ..... Shine .....
Nigger-boy ..... Coon ..... Hey Jig .....

So that the fight between Emmett and Josh that everybody had been anticipating for three years finally came. It had
been brewing slowly, simmering, aging, until the moment came
when both were ready to make their immense stores of inner
hatred visible, tangible, explosive to themselves and to each
other. It was only waiting for an excuse befitting the amount of

hatred in each. Just any excuse wouldn't do. Over the years the workers had often speculated about the fight—how it would come, when it would come, who would win, what implements of battle would be used. Around the toilets, in the cafeteria, the Union Hall, in local taverns, at the Coke and coffee machines, and even in the foremen's offices and toilets and dining room, the speculation went on, coming up every now and then as a topic of conversation, a natural remark passed as a part of the day's work—another item to relieve the monotony of the work, to vary tried, tested, and tired conversation pieces as the half-assembled trucks moved down the lines.

Emmett had been open about his hatred. "He makes my blood boil," he would say. "Some day I'm gonna break his ass. The way he never says nothin' but looks at ya like he'd spit on ya and now wanted ya to beg his pardon fer bein' in the way o' his spit—black bastard. I'd give a month's pay for a chance to bloody that skin o' his . . ."

Josh never said anything. But in his mind, behind his blood-veined eyes, simmering beneath his haughty, dignified, proud demeanor, he hated Emmett every bit as much as Emmett hated him.

Not even the few friends he had knew the depths of his hatred. But day after day, sitting on his three-cornered stool, pressing the buttons that made the top half of the press meet the bottom and weld the two door sections together, he had his eye on Emmett. And he vowed to himself that if he ever killed a white man it would be Emmett Rumple. Because in Emmett's eyes he saw that look of savage disgust he remembered from his childhood, from the white men of Bullett and Troy (Alabama) when a nigger "forgot his place," that supercilious hateful glare, mixed with, arising from, fear of niggers like Josh who wouldn't stay in their place but assumed the walk and talk and attitude of any man.

He wondered now. Exactly when was it that he had

made his vow? When he was already on the bus heading north? When he was working in the garage? When he'd left school? When he was twelve years old and his father had strapped him for talking back to a white man? He didn't remember and it didn't matter. It might have been at fourteen and it might have been at forty. Or it might have been none of those times. That was more likely. It was more likely that the vow had never been made but had simply been there; the vow that some day he would pick out a single white man, would *select* him. Many nights, walking the streets of the Indiana city, he'd seen men who almost qualified. He'd hated them all, and had almost hated those who'd smiled at him or nodded to him more than those who ignored him.

Long nights alone in his apartment, the thought had kept him alive. In fact, he knew that if the thought hadn't been there during those nights, hadn't sustained itself through wonderful dreams of revenge and blood, he'd have been in many fights long before this. Fortunately, though, he'd noticed the way Emmett had looked at him one day. Not indifference in that look. It was the look, the face, that could fill the dreams; and daytime, thinking of Emmett, of spreading his white man's blood on the coal-black floor of the factory, Josh had developed the twitching habit of touching his side pocket to feel the knife, of laughing. Aloud. He knew many of the men mocked the habit and the laugh, but he didn't care. He'd have the last laugh.

Now, as he began reading the piece of paper, he laughed again. When he looked up, most of the men on his assembly line were already in their places.

"Get me my relief man," Josh said to his foreman, not waiting to get an O.K. from the foreman but already walking in Emmett's direction, the paper now folded in one hand, the other hand loose at his side, itching for the pocket.

"Whaddaya mean? Hey, Russell! Where you going? Come back here. We gotta get the line started up. Goddamn you—I said come back or I'll slap a reprimand on you. . . ."

Emmett heard him approaching (he was leaning over his toolbox, getting out his electrician's holster), but he didn't look up.

"I'm thinking you left somethin' over by my chair, mister," Josh said, his voice low, cracking just a bit with nervousness.

"What?" Emmett said, looking up and seeing Josh's eyes gleaming at him as if there were little flashlight bulbs behind the lenses. For the first time he seemed to notice Josh's size, his hulking broad body. But he'll be slow, Emmett thought, and if I have a little room I'll be too quick for him. And too smart. This nigger can't be as smart as he tries to put on. "You addressin' me?"

"You heard me."

"Well, as far as I can figger, I ain't fergot nothin'. You better be gettin' to work."

Emmett strapped on his holster and turned, walking out into the aisle toward the intersection, where there would be more room. He passed Jim Bryant, his buddy, and winked. Already the men in the vicinity had stopped whatever they were doing and were waiting, their eyes eager for the violence they anticipated. Within a minute, by the time Emmett had reached the intersection of the aisles, men were closing around, and groups of Negroes sauntered slowly over, already hearing the whispers that the fight between Em and Josh had come.

Josh followed Emmett, not hurrying, knowing that Emmett wanted to fight, to get it over with also.

"Hold it there, mister," Josh said. "I was talkin' to you. I haven't finished."

"What else ya got to say?" Emmett said, turning on Josh,

a slight smile at the corner of his mouth, his hand resting on the hammer that hung in his holster.

"You recognize this?" Josh said, showing him the application.

"Oh, this—?" Emmett said, and laughed for the benefit of the men circled round them. A mule driver honked to get through but stopped as soon as he saw the two men facing each other. "I didn't forget it. I figgered I was doin' ya a favor. Figgered ya might be interested in fillin' it out."

One of the men started to laugh but stopped quickly, noticing a group of Negro workers to his right.

"Ya mean ya got it filled out already? You're pretty smart fer a—fer a—"

"Nobody treats me like dirt, mister," Josh said, moving slowly forward. The circle around them was wide now, fifteen feet in diameter.

"I put five bucks on ole Josh," one man whispered.

"I'll cover that."

"Any o' you boys wanna bet?" Jim Bryant said to a group of Negro workers. "I got fifteen bucks I'd like to double."

"We'll cover it, man. Be like pickin' cherries."

"Nobody pushes me around, mister," Josh said. He thrust his arm forward, the application clenched in his fist. Emmett started back, whipping the hammer out of his holster. Betting stopped. "You better say you're sorry and bend down and pick up this thing and tear it up or I'll cut you from your belly button to the tip of your ugly head."

Josh tossed the piece of paper in front of him. Emmett rubbed his palms with his fingertips. Wet. But nobody'd make him cower before a nigger. Not in front of all the men.

"Sure," Emmett said, moving a step forward. "I'll pick it up."

He held the hammer in his hand as he began to bend

over in front of Josh. But then, his body bent over, his hand darted up suddenly in whiplash and the hammer glanced off Josh's cheek, red blood showing immediately on the black perforated face. With his other arm he grabbed Josh's leg behind the knee and tripped him, falling upon him and raising the hammer to his full arm's length and starting it in its downward arc, but never landing another blow because even while Josh was falling backward he had slipped it out of his pocket and as Emmett fell on top of him you could hear the intake of breath as every last man saw the light flash, glint from the switchblade.

Emmett rolled off Josh, clutching at his stomach, and Josh stood up and bent his shoulders down, the knife now visible to all, its silver blade tipped with a dripping of blood, crimson and liquid. Emmett backed away, breathing in deeply, cursing under his breath, gasping.

"Gimme yer bottle o' whiskey, Jim. Damn it. Where are ya? Gimme yer bottle."

Bryant reached into his side pocket. He took the bottle out of its paper bag and handed it to Emmett. Emmett took a quick swallow and moved backwards along the rim of the circle, watching, waiting, while Josh just glared and followed him with his eyes, not saying a word; but even Emmett could read the expression in his eyes now. Emmett looked to the side and lifted the bottle, bringing it down with a gurgling crash against a post.

"We're even now, big man," he said, dropping the hammer to the floor and holding the jagged edges of the bottle forward. "Yer yeller'll show now."

Josh continued stalking.

"Man, he looks like the old Brown Bomber now, don't he?"

"Don't look like no Brown Bomber to me."

"Five bucks says he mops the floor with your boy."

"Make it ten."

"You're on, man."

Emmett smiled now, despite the pain that seemed to be somewhere in his back, pulling down and ripping, but he smiled because he felt the worst was over. He wouldn't be stupid enough to get that close again. Because Josh might be fast with that knife, but he'd be slow otherwise, like all niggers, slow at everything except running. Them nigger boys could run. That was one thing. Like when they used to hell up down in Louisville when he was a kid and get one of them alone and paint on him in white: *Keep this nigger running. Keep this nigger running.*

Emmett lunged forward, but Josh parried with his forearm and they backed away from each other. Good, Emmett thought. I'll set him up. He lunged again, and again Josh parried with a sweep of his arm, cutting Emmett's sleeve with the knife. Emmett backed away and then came forward a third time and lunged. Josh went to parry, but before he could, Emmett had ducked his head and his hand wasn't there when Josh's arm went flailing out to meet it. Instead, Emmett's fake had worked and he had ducked his head and had come plowing into Josh's midsection, the glass edges aimed for Josh's groin. In missing Emmett, though, Josh stumbled and avoided the brunt of Emmett's charge, so that the broken bottle ripped into his thigh and with his left hand Josh clubbed the top of Emmett's head as he went by. Emmett fell to the floor.

The broken bottle slid across the floor and shattered. Josh moved in for the kill now, hulking above Emmett.

"Lift his liver, man," someone shouted to Josh.

"I got another ten on Josh if anyone'll see me."

"Who's got a knife?" Jim Bryant asked. He turned toward two Negroes. "One of you got a knife or a razor?"

"You talkin' to us, Jim?"

"Keep it fair. Throw Em a knife."

The boys looked at each other, then one of them shrugged, reached into his pocket, and flipped a knife into the open circle. Josh kicked it at Emmett, who picked it up and rose to one knee. Josh moved forward slowly, wary now. Emmett watched him, seeing two Joshes as his head refused to clear. He flicked the knife open and waited. The two black faces merged into one and then separated, then merged again. There was a dull ache at the back of his head and his legs felt cold and damp. Above him he saw the black figure coming and he began to lift up from his knee but then everything went blank and the only thing he remembered was being thrown back down and then the sound of something dull, like punching against a sponge, and a warm, liquid feeling all over him, a quiet, almost peaceful feeling, doubled up, his knees trying to reach his chest, his arms rigid, straining.

Josh saw his chance and was on Emmett before he could rise, knocking away the knife and crashing his body against him, driving the knife up to its hilt into the flesh of Emmett Rumple. Satisfaction came with the plunge and he licked his lips and there was no world for him in that instant but only a pale white face before him, under him, and the knife red, withdrawn from the soft bodyflesh, and now a speck of blood on that white face and now another and the eyes that had hated him all these years started to close. Then he hesitated. The factory was still: a hush, funeral quiet in which the workers paid their respects to the act they were waiting for him to conclude.

The silence startled him; he wouldn't be satisfied! It seemed impossible. It hardly seemed fair. The thought terrified him and his body hurried to carry out the execution; but in the backlash his mind had already reverted, and he was utterly disappointed, petulant, child-like—and he knew it was all over for him. The knife hung in the air, and seeing it there, seeing the doubt on his face, Jim Bryant took advantage and rushed into the circle, knocking him away. Nobody said anything, or even began to collect on the bets. They just stood there, staring, quiet.

The Zodiacs

WHEN I WAS in the seventh grade at P.S. 92 in Brooklyn, Louie Hirshfield was the only one of my friends who wasn't a good ballplayer. Which is putting it mildly. Louie was probably the worst athlete in the history of our school. He was also the smartest kid in our class and you'd think this combination would have made him the most unpopular guy there, but it didn't. He wasn't especially well liked, but nobody resented him. Maybe it was because he let you copy from his homework—or maybe it was just because he didn't put on any airs about being smart. In fact, Louie didn't put on airs about anything. He was one of the quietest kids I'd ever met.

The only time I ever saw him excited—outside of what happened with him and our baseball team—was when our fathers would take the two of us to baseball games at Ebbets Field. Louie lived one floor under me, in my apartment building on Lenox Road, and we'd grown up together, so I knew lots about Louie that nobody at school knew. He was an interesting guy, with lots of hobbies—tropical fish, rocks, stamps, Chinese puzzles, magic tricks, autographs.

That was the one thing the guys did know about. I don't know how many days he'd waited outside Ebbets Field to get them—all I know is he had the best collection of baseball players' signatures of any guy in school. Lots of them were addressed personally, too—like "To Louie, with best wishes from Jackie Robinson." What amazed me most about Louie, though, was that he could figure out a player's batting average in his head. If a guy got a hit his first time up in a game, Louie would say, "That raises his average to .326"—or whatever it was—and sure enough, the next time the guy came up, when the announcer would give the average, Louie would be right.

Louie had no illusions about his athletic ability—he was never one of those guys who hangs around when you're choosing up sides for a punchball or stickball game so that you *have* to pick him. Whenever he did play—like in gym class at school —he did what you told him and tried to stay out of the way. That was why I was so surprised when he came up to my house one night after supper and asked if he could be on our baseball team.

"Gee, Louie," I said, "we got more than nine guys already —anyway, we're not even an official team or anything. We'll be lucky if we get to play more than five or six games all year."

"I don't really want to play," Louie said. "I—I just want to be on your team."

"Well, I suppose you can come to practices and games," I said. "But I can't promise you'll ever get in a game."

"Honest, Howie—I know all the guys on your team are better than me. I wasn't even thinking of playing.—What I'd like to do is be your general manager." His eyes lit up when he said that. I looked at him, puzzled.

"Look," he said. "What do you think makes the Dodgers draw almost as many fans as the Yankees? What was it that made people stick with the Dodgers when they were hardly in the league?"

"I don't know," I said. "They were just Dodger fans, I guess."

"Sure—that's it. Don't you see? Being a Dodger fan means something because being a Dodger means something colorful to the fans. And you know why? Because the Dodgers have what my dad calls 'a good press'—they know how to get headlines in the papers whether they're winning or losing."

I nodded. "But what's that got to do with us?"

"What's your team like now? I'll tell you. It's the same as ten thousand other teams of guys our age all over Brooklyn. Nobody cares if you win or lose—except maybe you guys. If I'm general manager, Howie, I'll promise you this—your team will be noticed. Guys won't say, 'We got a game with Howie's team.' They won't come to the Parade Grounds to see all the older guys play. They'll come to see *The Zodiacs!*"

"The who—?"

Louie stopped for a second and I realized that I'd never heard him speak so fast before. "That's—that's the first thing you have to do, it seems to me." He spoke more hesitantly now, the way he usually did, not looking right at you. "You have to have a name that's different."

"What's wrong with calling ourselves the Sharks?"

"Nothing's wrong with it—but don't you see, nothing's right with it, either. I'll bet there's a hundred teams in Brooklyn alone called the Sharks. Sharks, Tigers, Lions, Phantoms— every team has a name like that. But calling ourselves—I mean, your team—*The Zodiacs*, will make them different—"

"Sure—but giving us a crazy name isn't going to win us any games."

"Right. What will win you games? I'll tell you. A good pitcher. I've been going down to the Parade Grounds to watch games, making a study of the teams there, and I've found that pitching is about ninety percent of winning. Especially at our age, when we're not fully built up yet. Did you know, for example, that on high school teams pitchers average about eleven strike-outs a game? It's like with baseball teams in spring training—the pitchers are way ahead of the hitters, because the hitters' reflexes aren't developed yet."

"Izzie's a pretty good pitcher," I said. Izzie was my best friend, and the pitcher for our team.

"Sure, but let's face it, he's not a real top-drawer pitcher. He's just not big enough to be. He's got good control, I'll admit that—but his fast ball is almost a change-up. If you let me be general manager, Howie, I'll get the best pitcher in our school to play for us."

"Who's that?"

"George Santini."

I gulped. *"Him?"*

"That's right."

George Santini was a year ahead of us at P.S. 92 and he was always getting in trouble with the teachers and the cops. He was about six feet tall, had black greasy hair which was long and cut square in back, and the biggest pair of shoulders I'd ever seen on a guy. He was also the best athlete in our school. The coaches and teachers were always talking to him about going straight and being a star in high school and college, but George never seemed to care much. He was the leader of this gang, which, as far as everybody in our section of Brooklyn was concerned, was the most dangerous gang the world had ever known.

What made George's reputation even worse was his older brother, Vinnie. Vinnie was about nineteen years old and he'd already spent two years in jail. He was a skinny guy—not at all like George—and the word on him was that he was really chicken. To listen to George, though, you would have thought that Vinnie was the toughest guy ever to hit Brooklyn. Whenever he wanted an audience, George would sit down on the steps of the school—on Rogers Avenue—and start telling tales of all the jobs he and Vinnie had pulled off. Sometimes, if we'd bother him enough, he'd tell us about the gang wars he had fought in with Vinnie—in Prospect Park, in Red Hook, in Bay Ridge. If he was sure no teachers or cops were around he'd show us his zip gun, the gun that Johnny Angelo—one of George's lackeys—claimed George had once used to kill a guy with.

"I don't know," I said. "If my mother ever caught me hanging around with him, I'd really get it—and, anyway, how would you get him to play for us?"

Louie smiled. "You leave that to me."

A few days later I got all the guys together at my house and I let Louie speak to them. He told them what he'd told me about how he would make our team special, maybe famous— and he also told them that George Santini had agreed to pitch for us. A few of the guys reacted the way I did to this news— they were scared. But when Louie insisted he'd be able to handle George, Izzie and I backed him up.

"I say it's worth a try," Izzie said. "Even though I'm pitcher and he'll take my place. I'll bet we could beat lots of high school teams with him pitching for us."

"Sure," I said. "You ever see the way he can blaze a ball in?"

A few more guys followed our lead, and after a while we all agreed that we'd probably be invincible with George Santini pitching for us.

"One thing, though," asked Kenny Murphy, our second baseman. "How'd you get him to play for us?"

"Simple," said Louie. "I offered him the one thing he

couldn't refuse—fame. I told him I'd get his name in the newspapers. It's not hard. All you have to do is telephone in the box score to the *Brooklyn Eagle* and they'll print it. My father knows a guy who works there."

For the next few weeks Louie was the busiest guy in the world—calling up guys at other schools, arranging games, getting permits from the Park Department, coming to our practices . . . When he started giving us suggestions on things, nobody objected either. He may have been a lousy ballplayer, but he knew more about the game than any of us. Izzie and I gave up playing basketball in the schoolyard afternoons and weekends and spent all our time practicing with *The Zodiacs*.

Our first game was scheduled for a Saturday morning the second week in April. Louie had gotten us a permit to use one of the diamonds at the Parade Grounds, next to Prospect Park, from nine to twelve in the morning, and we were supposed to play a team of eighth-graders from P.S. 246. I was at the field with Izzie by 8:30, but the other team didn't get there until after nine. We ran through infield practice and then let them have the field for a while. Kenny Murphy's father, who'd played for the Bushwicks when they were a semi-pro team, had agreed to umpire the game. By a quarter to ten neither Louie nor George had shown up and the other team was hollering that we were afraid to play them.

Since George had never come to any practices, some of us were a little worried, but at about five to ten he showed up. He was wearing a baseball hat like the rest of us, with a Z sewn on the front, and he looked a little embarrassed. He was smoking and he didn't say much to anybody. He just asked who the catcher was and started warming up. He wore a T-shirt, with the sleeves cut off. Looking at him, you would have thought he was too muscle-bound to be a pitcher, but when he reared back and kicked his left foot high in the air, then whipped his arm around, he was as smooth as Warren Spahn, only righty, with the natural straight overhand motion that every coach spends his nights dreaming about. Stan Reiss, our catcher, had to put an extra sponge in his mitt, but he was so proud, catching George with all the guys looking at the two of them, that I think he would have let the ball burn a hole in his hand before he would have given up his position.

"C'mon," George said after a dozen or so warm-ups. "Let's get the game going."

"We were waiting for Louie," I said. "He should be here any minute."

"Okay," George said. "But he better hurry. I got better things to do than spend all day strikin' out a bunch of fags."

He said the last thing loudly, for the benefit of the other team. Then he turned and spit in their direction, daring one of them to contradict him. No one did.

A minute later I saw Louie. He was getting out of his mother's car, on Caton Avenue, and he was carrying this tremendous thing. From my position at shortstop I couldn't make it out, but as he came nearer, running awkwardly and holding it in front of him like a package of groceries, I realized what it was: his old victrola.

"Hey, George!" Louie called. "You ready to break Feller's strike-out record?"

George laughed. "Anytime they get in the batter's box—"

"Wait a second," Louie said. He put the victrola down next to the backstop. He started fiddling with it, cranking it up the way you had to to get it to work, and then he started playing a record. At first it wasn't cranked up enough and you couldn't tell what kind of music it was. But then Louie cranked some more—and I whipped off my hat and stood at attention as the strains of "The Star-Spangled Banner" came blasting across the infield. I looked at George and he was smiling as broadly as he could, holding his cap across his heart, standing rigid, at attention. The team from P.S. 246 must have been as shocked as we were, but by the time the music got to "and the rockets' red glare" both teams were standing at attention, saluting, listening, while Louie kept cranking away so that the music wouldn't slow down. People sitting on benches, guys playing on other diamonds, men and women walking along Caton Avenue, a few park cops—they all stopped and started drifting toward our diamond. When the record was over, Louie —in the loudest voice I'd ever heard—shouted "Play ball!" and we started the game. We must have had a crowd of over fifty people watching us play our first game, and I told myself that if George had been pitching for a Major League team that day he would have pitched at least a shut-out.

He struck out all but two of their men—one guy hit a grounder to me at shortstop, and another fouled out to Corky Williams at first base. He also hit four home runs. I got a double and two singles, I remember. We won, 19–0, and the next day, as Louie'd promised, our box score was in the *Brooklyn Eagle*.

Louie got us six more games during the next two weeks, and we won all of them. George gave up a total of seven hits in the six games, and he was a pretty happy guy during that time. He had clippings of the box scores of all the games in his wallet, the way we all did. Clippings of the box scores—and then, the first week in May, the best clipping of all: an item in Jimmy O'Brien's column in the *Brooklyn Eagle* about our team, mentioning George, and Louie's victrola. I think I carried that clipping around with me until my third year in high school.

After that we began getting even more attention and teams from all over Brooklyn were challenging us to games. We played as many of them as we could—and George kept shutting out every team we played.

In the meantime Louie devised another plan. He called

a meeting of the team the second week in May to discuss it. He told us that a team with our ability and prestige had to live up to its name. We said we were—we were winning games, weren't we?

"Sure," Louie said. "But what do you look like out on the field? People are starting to come in pretty large numbers to see us play—they hear about us, we got a reputation—and then when they see us, we look like a bunch of pick-ups." He lowered his voice and went on. "What we have to do," he said, "is develop some class. And I've got the plan worked out. It's not new, I'll admit—lots of the high school guys use it. I say we run a raffle and use the money to buy ourselves jackets and uniforms."

We all liked the idea of jackets and uniforms, naturally, but they cost a lot of money—especially the kind of uniforms and jackets we wanted to have.

"I got it all figured out," Louie said, pulling out some pieces of paper. Then he started talking about numbers, and once he did that, I knew we'd get those uniforms and jackets. It turned out that Louie could get a clock radio at a discount from an uncle of his. Then he said he could get Levy's Sporting Goods Store, on Flatbush Avenue, to donate a glove and ball for the raffle. He also said they'd sell us the uniforms and jackets at cost if Jimmy O'Brien would mention them in his column sometime. Louie said his father could take care of that. We'd make the radio first prize and the glove and ball second prize, but we'd tell the kids at school that if they won first prize we'd give them the glove and ball anyway. There were fifteen of us and if we each sold five books of ten chances at a quarter apiece, that'd be almost two hundred dollars. Louie said that he himself would sell at least fifteen books, and he expected most of us to sell more than five. If we took in three hundred dollars in the raffle, we could have the uniforms and jackets.

George was at the meeting this time—in Louie's house—

and he volunteered to get his gang to sell chances. All of us were pretty glad then that we'd be on the selling end of the raffle during the next few weeks. Louie smiled and said he'd already had the raffle books printed and that the drawing would take place on Friday afternoon, June 1. On June 2, we all knew, we had a big game with the Flatbush Raiders, a team from P.S. 139 that had lost only one game. Louie said that if we could give Levy's a down payment of one hundred dollars they'd go ahead and get the uniforms and jackets made in time for the game against the Raiders.

We only had two games during the next week, and the rest of the time all of us were running around getting everybody we knew—friends, relatives, neighbors, teachers, store owners—to buy chances. By the following Friday, Louie reported that we had more than a hundred dollars and that Levy's had already started making the uniforms and jackets. The uniforms would be gray with orange lettering and the jackets were going to be made of an orange and black material that felt like satin, with *The Zodiacs* written across the back in bright yellow.

By the middle of the following week Louie reported to us that if we went over three hundred dollars—and it looked like we would, the extra money would be used to get Louisville Sluggers and official National League baseballs for the team. Louie also told us that his father could probably get Jimmy O'Brien to come down to see our game against the Raiders.

On Wednesday afternoon, two days before the raffle drawing, Louie rode out on his bicycle to Marine Park, where the Raiders were playing a game, and when he showed up at our big meeting on Friday, June 1, he had a stack of scouting notes.

"Before we get to our skull session on the Raiders," he said, "we have to get this raffle business over with. First, some of you haven't given me all the money—or the leftover raffles."

While Louie took care of the final accounts on the raffle, George stayed by himself in a corner, looking through Louie's sports magazines. Although he spoke to a few of us a little more, you couldn't really say that any of us had become pals with him. At school he stayed pretty much with his gang, and after school—on the days when we didn't have games—we knew that he still hung around with his brother.

"Okay," said Louie. "I got it all figured out. Just a few things don't check. You, Marty, you took out seven books and only gave me fifteen dollars."

"I forgot," Marty said. He handed Louie a book of tickets. "I didn't sell these."

Louie crossed his name off. He seemed to be stalling, because he kept adding and subtracting figures and I knew that he never had that much trouble figuring things out.

"George?"

"Yeah?"

"According to my records you gave me raffle stubs from sixteen books, which means you owe forty dollars."

"So?"

"You only gave me twenty-eight so far."

We were all quiet. George wasn't looking straight at Louie. He had a magazine out, with a picture of Sal Maglie on the cover, and he made believe he was thumbing through it.

"Maybe you didn't give me sixteen books," George said.

"I did. It's right here in writing."

"Hell, anybody can phony up figures."

"I didn't phony them up." Louie's voice was loud. "You still owe twelve dollars."

"Prove it."

"Prove it? It's down here in black and white."

"Oh yeah? My word's as good as yours."

"It's not!"

"Are you callin' me a liar?" George stood up now and walked toward Louie.

"I'm just saying you owe twelve dollars. You better pay up, or—"

"Or what, smarty?"

"Or—" Louie stopped. "—Or you can't play tomorrow."

George laughed. But his laugh was forced. "Who needs to play with you guys, anyway? You can't win without me and you know it."

"You pay up or you don't play. I mean it, George. You won't get your uniform and you won't get to play in front of Jimmy O'Brien either . . ."

"I don't give a damn," George said. He walked up to Louie and pushed his fist at Louie's face. Louie didn't move. This surprised George. "I never should of given you the twenty-eight dollars either. And you know what you can do with your raffle—"

George didn't finish his sentence. Instead, he picked up the clock radio, raised it over his head, and then flung it to the floor, splattering its parts all over the room. Louie leapt at George, screaming curse words, but with an easy push George shoved him to the floor. Then he kicked him a few times and Louie started crying. He got up and went for George again, and this time I was ready. I grabbed George's right arm.

"C'mon, you guys, help me hold him." Izzie jumped on George's back and got him in a stranglehold. George tried to throw him off, but by this time Kenny and Corky and Stan and the other guys were all holding George. He fought and it took all our strength to hold him, but it was fifteen to one and these odds were too much, even for him.

"C'mon, Louie," I said. "Give it to him now."

"Yeah, c'mon," the guys yelled. "Let him have it . . .

right in the gut . . . he deserves it . . . give it to him good . . ."

Louie was still crying, but he came at George. "You're—you're nothing but a *bum!*" he screamed.

George spit at him.

"C'mon," Kenny said. "We can't hold him all day. Just give it to him—"

"Yeah, c'mon, ya little sawed-off runt—I hear they're gettin' up a girls' team at school for you to play on."

"You're just a big bum," Louie said, whimpering. He was breathing heavily. "I wouldn't waste my knuckles on you. Just get out of my house. Get out. We—we don't need crooks on The Zodiacs. Get out. Get out . . ." Then Louie started crying again. We all pushed and pulled George to the door and somehow we managed to slam it with him on the other side.

We ran off the raffle anyway. Louie said the money that was going to go for bats and balls would be enough to get another radio—and a few hours later we left Louie's apartment. I was glad I lived in his building.

The next morning there were over two hundred people gathered around the backstop and baselines at the Parade Grounds. Izzie warmed up and he looked good. I think the new uniforms made us all play a little over our heads that day. The pitcher on the Raiders was very fast, and our only chance, we knew, was if his control was off.

When Louie cranked up his victrola before the game, most of the onlookers started laughing. We ignored them. In fact, I think hearing the National Anthem, the way we had in all our other games, made us play even harder, because in the first inning Izzie held the other team and, in our half, Kenny Murphy doubled and then I hit a single which drove him in. That was the last time we had the lead, though. The Raiders tied it up in the third inning and went ahead in the fourth, by 4–1. The final score was 7–2.

When we were picking up our gloves and stuff, and changing out of our spikes, nobody said anything. And nobody looked at Louie. We waited for each other and were walking away from the diamond when Stan spotted George.

"Uh-oh," he said, pointing. "He's got his gang with him."

We all looked and we saw about ten of them—all in motorcycle jackets and pegged pants.

"Hey," George shouted, coming nearer. "Ain't those guys got pretty uniforms."

"Yeah," said one of his guys. "And look at those jackets. They look like my mommy's underwear—"

This seemed to strike George's gang as a pretty good joke.

"Hey, you bunch of fags," George said. "Who won the game?"

Nobody answered. George and his gang had almost reached us now.

"Aw, c'mon—you don't mean you let those other fruit-boots beat you, do you? How could anybody beat a team that's got a manager like Louie? He's real smart, ain't he?"

George was in front of us now, about fifteen feet from Louie, his hands on his hips. Louie stopped.

"C'mon, smart boy. Cross my path, I dare you—"

"Don't do it, Louie!" I shouted. I looked around, hoping a policeman was nearby. Louie put down his victrola.

"I don't want any trouble," he said.

"Hey, listen to this, guys. He says he don't want no trouble. Ain't that nice. I don't want none either, see. Only I say you called me a liar and a crook and I don't take that from nobody."

"I—I didn't mean to call you that," Louie said. "Why don't we just forget the whole thing."

"I don't forget easy."

I was holding one of the bats and I gripped the handle firmly. The other guys had already let their gloves and equipment drop onto the grass. I spotted a cop about a half block away. He was moving toward us. I tried to stall.

"What's the gripe, George?" I asked. "You mad 'cause you didn't get to pitch today?"

"You keep your trap shut, Howie. Can't Louie fight his own battles—?"

"We just don't want any trouble, that's all."

The guys in George's gang began to move toward us and then George shoved Louie. I ran at him, the bat raised over my head. "We got bats, George. One of you is gonna get a bloody head."

"You don't scare us with your toothpicks!"

Somebody grabbed my arm and then the fight was on. It didn't last long—probably less than a minute—but by the time the cop got there and started bopping guys on the head with his nightstick most of us, myself included, were glad it was over. I had managed to get a leg-scissors on George and even though he was blasting me in the gut I held on long enough so he couldn't get at Louie. More cops were on the scene by then and when we were separated they asked the usual questions about who had started the fight. When they saw that nobody was going to give them any answers, they told us to beat it.

"Okay, all of you—get on home. You, kid," the cop said, pointing to Kenny. "You better get some ice on that eye in a hurry."

George's gang started to move away, and then George turned and called to us. "We'll get you guys at school—"

One of the cops ran after George and grabbed him by the front of his jacket. "Okay, tough boy," he said. "If I find out that one hair on the head of any of these kids was touched, I'll throw you and every one of your cronies in jail. You hear that?"

George nodded.

"Hey," the cop said suddenly. "I know you. You're George Santini, ain't you? Vinnie Santini's brother—"

"So what?" George tried to squirm out of the cop's grip.

"It figures," the cop laughed. "You know who Vinnie Santini is?" he said to one of the other cops. "He's that punk we had down at the station last week. I never seen a guy turn yellow so quick."

"*It's a lie!*" George shouted. He almost broke away. "You shut your damned mouth!"

George kicked at the cop and the cop whacked him across the arm with his club. Another cop held George while the first cop put his nose right up to George's face and continued. "I never seen a guy turn yellow so quick," he said. "We didn't have the light on him more than ten minutes when he started ratting on every petty thief this side of Bensonhurst. And you're probably the same."

George didn't say anything. He just sort of hung there, held up by the cop. "Get goin', punk," said the cop, shoving George. "And I better not hear that you touched these kids."

George and his gang walked away. We all picked up our stuff, Kenny and Marty carrying Louie's victrola, and then suddenly Louie started running after George. "Hey, wait a minute! Wait—"

George turned and waited till Louie caught up to him. "Yeah?" George said.

Louie stopped, as if he'd forgotten why he had told George to wait. Then he spoke, in that slow, hesitant way of his. "I was going over the records last night," he said. "And I discovered that I made a mistake yesterday. You really only owed eight dollars. I was thinking that if you gave me the eight dollars, then—then you could pitch for us against the Raiders. We play them a return game next week."

"Who'd wanna play on your sissy team?" said one of the guys in George's gang.

George looked at Louie, then at the guys in the gang, then back at Louie. "I'll let you know," he said, and walked off.

The next day he gave Louie the eight dollars. On the following Saturday, with George pitching and wearing his new uniform, we beat the Raiders, 4–0. We were the happiest group of guys in Brooklyn, George included. We won about a dozen more games that month. At the end of June, though, lots of the guys, myself included, went away to camp or to the country and the team had to break up. The next year when George was a freshman at Erasmus Hall High School he didn't play for us.

When he was a sophomore at Erasmus—I was a freshman that year—he played fullback on the football team and was starting pitcher on the baseball team. In the middle of his junior year, though, he quit school. The next time I heard about him, somebody said he had taken off for Florida with his brother.

Finkel

As THE TAXI slowed to a stop in front of the building on West 115th Street, there was suddenly a great commotion on the sidewalk. The boys and girls who had been sitting there drawing with chalk darted and scattered—some of them toward Broadway, some toward the river, some into buildings. "It's Finkel!" a small boy shouted, sounding the alarm. "Finkel! Finkel!" cried the others as they picked up their belongings and hurried to safety. From the cellar of the building, taking two steps at a time, charged Finkel, a German police dog ahead of him. The dog bounded forward, held back only by a silver leash. *"Raus mit euch!"* Finkel shouted as he reached the street level and looked about for stragglers. *"Raus, Läuse! Raus!"* The dog barked sharply and strained at the leash, the metal cutting into its neck. "I will teach you to mark up the sidewalks!" Finkel yelled, and though he could see nobody to right or left of him, he ran several yards toward the river. "Devils! If I lay my hands on you—" he threatened, shaking a fist at his invisible opponents. Across the street two boys crouched behind a row of garbage cans, terrified. The dog

struggled to get away from its master; it snarled, baring its
teeth, and with this, the two boys jumped from behind the garbage cans and streaked downhill. Finkel shouted curses after
them, his dog barked, but he did not move from in front of the
house.

The door of the taxi started to open and Finkel was there
at once, holding it, pushing his hand into that of the man who
was getting out. "Professor Perlman!" he exclaimed. "I recognize you from your pictures. I am Hyman Finkel, superintend-
ent." Professor Perlman looked at the dog and hesitated. Finkel
laughed and patted its head affectionately. "This is Sasha,
named for my oldest brother, he should rest in peace, de-
stroyed on the other side. Do not fear him. At his age, I can
assure you, the saying about the bark and the bite is true. Sasha
—say hello to Professor Perlman." At this the dog began wagging its tail furiously, rubbing its heavy body against Professor
Perlman's leg. "Sasha is almost fourteen years old," Finkel said.
The professor looked down at the dog, noticing its huge stomach, which sagged toward the gutter. He paid the driver and
then, with Finkel's help, carried his luggage inside. The lobby
was dark and cool.

"Ah, Sasha," Finkel said as the dog trotted behind them.
"When will you die? When? Already this year you have cost me
in the hundreds for doctor's fees. Two tumors removed—like
honeydew melons. I'll tell you something, Professor—I am glad
you saw Sasha and I in action. Ha! Do you know why we chase
the children—?" He laughed again and pushed the professor in
front of him into the elevator. As they rose, he explained. "To
give them a sense of terror, that is why!" Cramped in the small
elevator, the professor held one valise waist-high. Sweat
trickled down his back and Finkel's stale breath annoyed him.
"Do you understand what I mean?" He pushed his face toward
the professor's. "Now I hope you won't take this personally,

Professor Perlman, but my clients in this building, so many of them, like yourself, in the academic profession—their children live in a protected world. Insulated. A world of ideas, of theories, books, abstractions. Between them and Harlem are parks, private schools, music lessons, fancy summer camps—and so it goes, if you know what I mean." The elevator stopped and the door slid open. Finkel led the way down the hall. Sasha and the professor followed him. Finkel turned back, stopping so abruptly that the professor almost knocked into him, and under his stained *Dutch Boy* painter's hat, Finkel's eyes were shining. "So I terrorize them! You see? I create for them a sense of reality, of evil. In my own time I am a legend—Finkel the former SS officer. Ha! Twenty years ago I planted the rumor, but with that one rumor—what stories they have been able to fabricate. If you could hear of the things I have done to countless women and children, Professor, it would make your hair fall out." He laughed again, to himself this time, and shook his head. "Here we are," he said. From his overalls he took a ring of keys and flipped through them, finding the right one.

Finkel showed the professor around the three rooms, pointing out the improvements he had put in, the special items —extra bookcases, a used television set, a large oak rolltop desk. Professor Perlman thanked him and handed him a ten-dollar bill. "For your troubles," he said.

"Let me tell you something, Professor," Finkel said, pocketing the money without comment. They were in the living room now and Finkel sat down in a large easy chair, Sasha at his feet. "You did the right thing. Don't let anybody tell you no. It is not easy for old men to live alone. When Professor Hafer telephoned me and explained the situation, what with the commuting, the upkeep of a large house—believe me, I know the chores that go into maintaining even a modest piece of property—I agreed with him that this was the wisest thing you could do. Give it up now." He cleared his throat. "Sit down please, Professor," he said. "Rest a little. You're entitled— you've had a long trip, your apartment is in order, what is there for you to do?" The professor sat; Finkel leaned forward, his face suddenly intent. "And before we leave the subject, I hope you will accept my condolences upon the loss of your wife. Although I did not have the good fortune to know her, I understand from Professor Hafer and others that she was a fine woman. And the years. All those years spent together, Professor. Oh, the years, the years—"

Finkel paused and, not knowing what else to do, Professor Perlman started to thank him. "Please," Finkel said, putting up his hand. "There is no need to say anything. What are we to do at times like these? When my own wife died—that was three years ago this August—did words console me? Bah! Death is death." He sat back. "Tell me, Professor, what are your plans?"

"My plans?"

"Now that you are alone. Let's face it, a young man you're not—how much longer will you teach?" The professor looked at him quizzically. "Come," Finkel said. "Talk to me. It will do you good—you and me, Professor—two old men like us, despite the difference in our vocations, we have much in common. I can tell. You're Jewish, aren't you?"

The professor nodded.

"Tell me, are you a practicing Jew?"

"No," the professor said, and as he replied he could hear the antagonism in his own voice. "No, I'm not."

Finkel smiled. "The same for me," he said. "You and me, we are psychological Jews, eh? —Like Freud, if you know what I mean. We hate the religion yet we are proud of our Jewishness. And why not? Why not, Professor Perlman?" His question was loud, belligerent—but before the professor could reply, Finkel was chuckling. "The way he was jealous of his wife before they were married—one day there was no letter in his mailbox and he was half insane! He picked her to pieces. That is Jewish. Martha, she was a good wife to him, very *bala-batish,* if you know what I mean." Finkel paused, hoping for a reaction, but there was none. "That means that she was the queen of his household," he said. "That the home was everything to her, that she was a good Jewish wife."

"I know what the word means," Professor Perlman said sharply. Finkel looked away, smoothing Sasha's fur. "Freud himself was quite *haimisheh,* you know," the professor added quickly, and as Finkel's face broke into a warm smile the professor wondered what had prompted his comment, the use of Yiddish . . .

"Ah—" Finkel said. "You are quite right, of course. The way that man loved his children, his sisters, his wife. I thank God for one thing—that he died before the war. If he had known that he had left his four old sisters behind only to have them all incinerated like Sasha—" He raised both his hands toward the ceiling, his fingers trembling, outstretched. "I thank God for that, Professor Perlman. The man had suffered enough for one lifetime—betrayed by his followers, forced to leave his beloved Vienna, the endless pain and operations! Year after year they hacked and sawed at his mouth and jaw, removing everything. As if the first operation didn't cause enough pain, eh? For how long, Professor, I ask you, for how many years did he suffer his cancer?"

"Sixteen, I believe."

"I know, I know," wailed Finkel. "And did anyone ever hear him complain? Not Freud. He was a man, Professor, I'll tell you that. A human being and a Jew, if you know what I mean. Thirty-three operations he endured. The number is significant, eh, Professor Perlman?" His voice dropped. "But why

do you think—why was such suffering brought to him? Why—?"
Finkel was leaning forward, excited. "Anyone who has read
your books would know the mystery in such a question, Professor. I ask you, did Moses get to enter the Promised Land? Why
did Freud love Moses so? Because he too was Jewish, Professor. *Moses and Monotheism*. Moses the Egyptian, Moses the
Gentile—but passionate, suffering, moral." Finkel stood up,
hovering above the professor, shaking his fist. "What does it
matter how a man is born? Like you and me, Professor, like the
great Freud himself, Moses was a *psychological* Jew—" He
laughed then and, quite suddenly, bent over and shook the professor's hand. "I must be going," he said. "Though I have certainly enjoyed our talk. We will continue it—yes? As I said, we
have a lot in common, you and me." At the door he reminded
the professor to call him the minute he had need of anything.
"For minor electrical repairs I am merely competent," Finkel
said. "But as a plumber I am first-rate—I can assure you of
that." Sasha brushed against Professor Perlman's leg, and then
he was alone.

He wanted to laugh but found that he couldn't. Had the
conversation really taken place? The professor shook his head,
to clear it. He moved around the apartment slowly, purpose-
fully—unpacking, arranging books and clothing, sorting papers
—but he tired quickly, and lay down in the bedroom to rest.
His right leg was hurting again and he massaged the calf. And
now what, Professor Perlman, he wondered. Now what?

As if in answer to the question, he heard somebody laugh.
He sat up. It was a girl's laugh, and it was followed by gig-
gling, then some words, then more giggling. When the girl
screamed, he swung his feet to the floor and listened carefully.
The giggling started again, from the bathroom. "Not now,
John," the girl said. "Stop, please . . . John . . . Oh you!
. . ." Above the toilet bowl, the professor saw, was a grat-

ing about ten inches square, and the sounds came from it. An air shaft, an exhaust? —Finkel could have told him its exact purpose. He closed the toilet and sat on the seat, listening. "I really have to study . . . John . . . I mean it . . . that tickles . . . Stop! . . ." Silence, heavy breathing, a low moan. The professor thought of his daughter, Barbara, in her senior year at Barnard. A thump against the wall. "Ow . . . watch it . . . that hurt . . ." Giggling. "I mean it, John, I have a test . . ." For the first time, words from the man "Okay, I have to go over some stuff for Perlman's course. . ." The professor stood up. "Do you still like it?" . . . "Oh, yeah—he's not too dynamic . . . I mean, you have to pay close attention, but he's good, especially when he forgets his notes and just rambles about things—music or science. You should have heard him the other day, going on about Freud's idea of the death wish!" Professor Perlman tried to place the voice, but it vanished in a sudden scraping of the wall, an "Ouch!" and furious laughter.

He walked out of the bathroom, shutting the door behind him. He telephoned his daughter and asked if she would like to have dinner with him at the faculty club, but she said no, she had a surprise for him, he was to come to her apartment. "Oh," she said. "I almost forgot. How's *your* apartment?"

"It's all right. Fine, really."

"Good," she said. "I have to do something now, okay, Daddy? Come over soon. Bye."

Downstairs, Finkel was waiting for him. Professor Perlman nodded, smiled weakly, and tried to pass, but Finkel stopped him, gripping his arm above the elbow. Sasha was at his feet, his head on his paws. The fur around his neck was gray; his eyes, the professor noticed, were outlined with a sticky white substance. "Ah, Professor," Finkel said. "I was hoping you would come by. Have you eaten dinner yet?"

"No."

"Then perhaps you would like to join me in my apartment. Roast leg of lamb!" He kissed his fingertips. "Very fine, if I must say so myself."

"Thank you very much, Mr. Finkel," the professor said. "But I already have a dinner engagement."

"Ah," Finkel said. "A dinner engagement. —Is that different from dinner?" He laughed good-naturedly. "Don't mind an old fool like me. But I mean it—when you are free some evening I will cook for us, all right?" He came closer. "Why not? Two old men like us, living in the same building, why shouldn't we be friends, companions? We are both Jews, no?"

"You'll have to excuse me," Professor Perlman said, pulling his arm from Finkel's grip and hurrying from the building. He cut across the Columbia campus, vowing to speak to Fred Hafer in the morning about moving out of the building—but Fred would ask him why, he knew, and if he tried to explain about Finkel, Fred would only suggest again that he needed to relax, that perhaps he should consider taking a leave of absence for the rest of the semester.

Barbara lived along Morningside Drive with another girl from Barnard, in one of the university-owned buildings, but when he arrived the girl was gone—to a concert, Barbara said —and in her place was a young man named David Shapiro. "I trust I'm not intruding."

"Don't be silly—take your jacket off. David's been helping me with the surprise. Guess what it is?" He said he didn't know. "Roast duck!" she exclaimed proudly. "With orange—the way you like it." She turned to go into the kitchen. "You and David talk while I get things ready. Dave, fix Father a drink— bourbon, straight. You know where everything is."

Then she was gone to prepare the dishes she had taken from her mother's recipes, and he was left with her young man. David seemed very much at home. Too much so? He sat down and lectured himself silently for the thought. Let the girl lead her own life. Don't judge. Don't advise. For God's sake, don't pressure her! Naomi's death was no easy thing to adjust to. She was an only child. They had been very close. Then too, hadn't he and Naomi lived together for two years before marriage? He smiled, remembering. She had been a student of his in a graduate seminar. The boy seemed nice enough. He asked him what he did. "Don't you remember me?" David asked. "I was in your seminar on Elizabethan poetry last year."

"Of course," he said, laughing. "You'll have to forgive me. I'm a little distracted this evening—what with moving—and—"

"That's all right," David said, and began telling the professor about his graduate courses, his ideas for papers, his projects. Professor Perlman tried to appear attentive. His lecture classes were large, but the seminar had had only twelve students. Why didn't he remember the boy?

"Are you retiring this year?"

"Am I what?"

"Retiring—I'd heard you might."

"Don't be silly."

"I'm sorry, sir," the boy said. "I know you can retire at sixty-three if you want, that's why—"

"No, no—I intend to teach to the end," he said. "To the end."

They ate quietly and the professor enjoyed listening to their gentle teasing, their intense opinions. David asked him if he had ever written about something they had discussed once in the seminar. "Eros, entropy, and the Elizabethans," David explained to Barbara. "That was the phrase your father used— the affinities between the Elizabethan notion of the love-death relationship and Freud's. Your father pointed out that just as the seventeenth-century belief in the unity of love and death was related to their belief in the decay of the world, so Freud's notion of the union of Eros and Thanatos was allied to the modern idea of entropy—" He held a fork in front of him, pieces of duck impaled on its prongs, and talked on. Professor Perlman pretended to listen but found himself annoyed. After dinner, saying he had more unpacking to do, he left. Barbara said she would call him the next day, that she wanted to make curtains for his apartment.

He walked across the campus and down Broadway to 115th Street, but once he was in the building he could not remember which floor he lived on. His name was not listed on the register above the mailboxes—but on three of the boxes—8A, 8F, and 9C—names were missing, and he assumed one of the three was his. He rode the elevator to the eighth floor and listened at the door of 8A. Voices. He tried 8F. Voices again. He walked up a flight of stairs, found 9C, and, hearing nothing, tried the key in the lock. The door opened and he turned on the light. At his feet, he saw, was an envelope. It had his name typed on it and, relieved to discover that he was in the right apartment, he opened it.

"Received from Professor Jerold M. Perlman the Sum of Ten Dollars ($10) for Services Rendered." It was signed, "Hyman Finkel, Superintendent."

In the bathroom, brushing his teeth, he looked at the grating and, as he did, the giggling resumed. "Stop! Jesus, John, I mean it . . ." Silence, then softly: "Please, John . . . please . . . oh . . ." He rinsed his mouth. At least, he thought, looking at his teeth in the mirror, he didn't have to use dentures yet. "Honest," came the boy's voice. "It'll help you relax for your test . . ." He closed the door quickly and made up his bed with clean sheets; he undressed, locked his door, tried to sleep. He thought of Naomi. Naomi and Finkel and then Sasha. In his old age, he recalled, Freud had come to love dogs, had become dreadfully attached to them. When one of them died—a chow, if he remembered correctly—he had written to Jones that he'd felt the loss more deeply than that of most human beings.

He was up at eight the next morning. To his surprise, he felt good—vigorous, fresh—and he busied himself with notes for the day's classes. At half past ten he left the apartment. Finkel was in the lobby, repairing a light fixture. He climbed down from his ladder.

"Ah, Professor," he said, stopping Perlman. "I was hoping I would catch you this morning. As you see, I am alone. Sasha is not feeling well—he spent a restless night. Very restless."

"I really must be going," Professor Perlman said, walking away. "I have a class."

Finkel caught up with him at the door. "Please. It will only be a minute—and quite useful to you, you will see. Quite useful." Finkel stopped and looked back into the lobby, to be sure they were not overheard. Professor Perlman found him particularly repulsive; he noticed the yellow teeth, long hairs protruding from the nostrils, a mole. Finkel wiped some mucus away with the back of his hand and spoke. "I meant to ask you this yesterday, when we were talking about your wife, but for some reason it slipped my mind. A slip of the mind— that is significant, no?" He laughed and came closer. "I am very curious about something, if it is not too personal, Professor. Tell me—your wife, how was she disposed of?"

Perlman pushed him away and jerked the door open. Finkel clasped his hand on the back of Perlman's and pushed on it, closing the door. "Of course, if this is very personal to you, I will respect your privacy. Let me be direct, Professor. What I am after is this—was she buried or was she cremated?"

"Buried."

"Ts, ts, ts," Finkel said. "Very bad. But," he added, shrugging, "that may have been her wish. What I am most interested in, really—what I can be of service to you for, is this—here is why I stopped you: what are your plans for yourself?"

"Mr. Finkel, if you don't mind, I must hurry to class." The professor tried to get away but Finkel barred the door with his body.

"I ask only this of an important thinker like yourself, Professor Perlman. That you give the idea of cremation your serious consideration. I have some literature in my apartment which I will leave for you in your mailbox—but is there really need for it? Bah! Did not Freud himself specify his own cremation? And do not his ashes now lie collected in one of his favorite Grecian urns?" Finkel opened the door and the professor welcomed the fresh air. "Go to your class, Professor. But I beg of you—give the matter your consideration. Death is no insignificant thing. It is something to think about."

When Professor Perlman returned from class that afternoon the literature was, as Finkel had promised, in his mailbox. He tore it to shreds without looking at it, and tried to figure out what to do. It was a convenience, living near the campus, true, near Barbara—and he did not relish returning to the empty house Naomi and he had spent the last twenty years in. Even if he did, the agent said he already had a buyer.

He had, though, to avoid Finkel. For the next few days he was successful. If, when he left the building, Finkel was in the lobby, he would go down to the basement and exit through the cellar; if he saw Finkel in front of the building when he returned home, he would go back to his office and work there. Such games made him feel ludicrous but he felt he had no choice. For perhaps a week he evaded Finkel, and Finkel, for his part, did not seem to pursue him. He felt better. One afternoon, however, he returned home to discover that he had locked himself out and forgotten the key. Such forgetfulness, he knew, was no mere accident. He sighed, went into the basement, and roused Finkel from his apartment. "Ah, Professor," Finkel said as they rode up in the elevator, Sasha nuzzling against Perlman's leg. "Have you considered the literature I gave to you? I have been so busy since the last time we spoke that I did not have a chance to get back to our discussions—first the oil burner went crazy, then there was a fire in Mrs. Gottbaum's gas range. When things begin, they do not stop, I'll tell you that." When Finkel had opened the door, he walked into the apartment and sat down. "So," he said. "What is your decision?" Perlman told him that he hadn't given the matter much thought. "All right, all right," Finkel said, wagging his finger at Perlman, "but don't say I didn't give you a chance! Time is time, Professor. It goes." Then suddenly he was on his feet, inspecting the bookcases. "A fine library," he said. "Let me ask you something—what is your opinion of the relation of art to death?"

"Of what—?"

"Forgive me. I do not always put these things well, but I have been thinking. I read your new book on Freud last week —very, very fine, Professor—and it led me to some thoughts of my own. Vague, of course. But here: the relations of pleasure and pain, love and hate, and even, as you point out so magnificently, of pleasure and death—does this not lead one to contemplate the alliance of death with art? Does—"

Perlman cut him off. "If you'll excuse me, Mr. Finkel—I have a great deal of work to do."

"Of course, of course. Why you even bother with an old fool like me, I don't know—a man like yourself!" He went to the door and opened it. "But we are old men and we are Jews. We know. We know, don't we?" Then he winked and smiled broadly. "Beyond the pleasure principle, eh, Professor Perlman? Beyond the pleasure principle!"

For about a week after that, Perlman managed to avoid Finkel; then, in the apartment, things suddenly began going wrong—the lock jammed, a fuse blew, a fire started in an electrical outlet. Every day something required Finkel's service, and Perlman was certain that, while he was teaching, Finkel was going through the apartment, arranging the accidents. Perhaps, he thought, if he could prove that Finkel was plotting, if he could embarrass him with the evidence . . . Every morning he left a matchstick standing inconspicuously against the door. When he returned home, however, the matchstick was still standing and, invariably, something was awry in the apartment —no hot water, a broken window, a jammed buzzer, another fuse blown, the toilet overflowing. Perlman remembered a movie he'd seen; he plucked a hair from his head and, with saliva, pressed it across the crack separating the door from its jamb. It remained intact. He continued to need Finkel's service.

At night he hardly slept, and when he did he dreamed and woke, one dream after the other. He kept a pad on the nighttable and wrote some of the dreams down, hoping, by analyzing them, to obtain the objectivity which would make them cease, but it was useless, and he soon gave it up. In the bathroom, between dreams, he listened to the young lovers, and each day he grew more tired, more tense, more run down. Naomi was with him more and more. He dreamt of her almost every night; in the dreams they were always young and they would kiss endlessly, sweetly, warmly.

Then, during finals week—he had been living in the apartment for almost two months—he woke up in the middle of the night, unable to breathe, terrified. He was lying on his side and behind him, he was certain, in the bed, was Naomi. He could hear her breathing. Something heavy lay on his chest; pains worked their way up his right arm. Had he been dreaming about her again? He couldn't remember. Things were confused. He only knew that he felt her in the room with him and that he would not turn to see if she was, in fact, really in the bed. He gagged on something, coughed. A hundred years from now they would be able to freeze him, he thought, to preserve his quarter inch of cortex. He felt that he was falling swiftly into a moonless black, deep in the brain, far back. The rhyme stirred him to a vague consciousness. He concentrated and after a moment placed it—from "Night Crow" by Theodore Roethke—and this seemed to help. He rose and stumbled into the bathroom, drinking hungrily from the faucet. Then he sat on the edge of the bathtub. What time was it? His young lovers were busy. "I really have to go," she said. "I mean it . . . oh, stop that . . ." Laughter, coaxing from the boy. Perlman inhaled deeply. "Naomi, Naomi," he said. "Oh, Naomi . . ."

From the grating the girl moaned, then yelped. "Don't bite . . . damn it, I told you I didn't like that . . . Oh, come on, baby . . . I'm not your baby . . . Come on, baby . . ." Was it the same boy, or a new one? He wanted to return to bed but he was desperately afraid he would find Naomi there. The laughter and moaning had been replaced by what sounded like a struggle. "Stop—you'll tear it . . . Oh, damn! See! . . . C'mon, baby, it won't hurt . . . I told you to stop . . . Oh, please don't, don't . . ." Perlman exhaled, put the plastic drinking cup down above the sink, and rubbed his arm. The pain was still there. The girl's voice was louder. "Don't . . . I don't want to. I mean it!" They thudded against a wall, the floor, the girl was crying. "Please . . . oh, my God! Stop! . . . I mean it . . . I can't . . . Oh, oh . . ." Perlman lifted himself, stepping onto the toilet seat to get closer to the grating. The girl was crying hysterically. Then she was screaming. "You're hurting me . . . stop . . . please, for God's sake, please . . ." He heard something that sounded like slapping, then heavy breathing, then the girl's tears, and a sudden scream which tore through his skull. He had to do something, but which apartment was the sound coming from—above? below? next door? Finkel would know. "Please . . . please, please

. . . Oh, God, stop . . . Stop!" He walked back to the bed-room and, looking at the bed, he felt his heart jump—the clut-tered blankets, he realized, looked like the shape of a woman. He switched on the light. The room was empty. He put on his robe and slippers and raced from the room into the hallway. He heard his heart galloping. The elevator was waiting for him and he took it to the basement. He rushed down the corridor, pushing against the wall to support himself. His legs were ter-ribly weak and he realized that he could not see well. He had forgotten his glasses. The floor and walls seemed to pulsate for-ward and back, forward and back. He turned the corner. Finkel's apartment was at the end of the corridor, near the gar-bage cans. He heard a low sound, a growling. He stopped, then continued. A shape rose up from behind the garbage cans. It was Sasha, but he seemed neither old nor friendly nor feeble. Did he think Perlman was a prowler? He snarled viciously—then he streaked toward the professor and, his eyes blazing with fire, leapt for the throat.

When Perlman opened his eyes, Barbara was sitting on the bed next to him, rubbing her hand gently across his fore-head. Finkel stood behind her, his brow wrinkled with worry. Perlman was in his own room. "Naomi was here with me," he said to Barbara. She told him to lie quietly, to rest. "Not really, of course, but I felt her here, in the room with me—"

"And who is to say she wasn't here?" Finkel said. "Why not? Who is—"

Perlman sat up. "Get out," he said. "Get out—"

"But, Daddy, it was Mr. Finkel who found you lying in the basement and telephoned me."

"Not me—Sasha. He came for me," Finkel said. "He is old—but he is a good dog. Who knows how long he licked your face and watched over you?"

"Get out—!" Perlman repeated.

"But, Daddy—"

"Shah!" Finkel said to her. "I will go. He is not himself, but he will be all right. It is nothing. Why, the great Freud himself was subject to periodic fainting spells."

"Get out!" Perlman was screaming. "Get out! Get out!"

Finkel stood at the door, Sasha with him, looking old, mournful. "Still, we must make plans, Professor. We—"

Perlman started from the bed, but he was weak and Barbara held him back. "Out!" he screamed. "Out, out, out . . ."

The door closed. "If not for Mr. Finkel, you might be dead by now," Barbara said. "Sometimes I don't understand you, Daddy. Honestly." She paused. "And the man admires you so much, the least you could do—"

"All right, all right," Perlman said, closing his eyes. "Peace, Barbara. Some peace."

He stayed in bed the next day. Barbara made his meals and insisted on being with him. She slept in the living room and studied for her examinations. The following day Perlman resumed his activities and, strangely enough, he felt better than he had at any time since Naomi's illness had begun the year before. He did not try to avoid Finkel, but he did not see him either. Was Finkel avoiding him? Once, when he met him at the mailbox at noon, Finkel merely said hello and asked how he was feeling. He was quiet. He told Perlman that Sasha was very ill. "The end is in sight, Professor."

Two afternoons later, returning from a committee meeting, Perlman saw a truck in front of the building. Two men in white carried a stretcher into it. Finkel leaned against the gray concrete. He wore no hat. Perlman watched him from across the street. The men closed the door of the truck and drove away. Finkel did not move. Then Perlman saw the children approaching. They seemed to come from everywhere—from up and down the street, from the building, the cellar—there must have been twenty to thirty of them, and they came cautiously. Finkel's chin was at his chest. He looked at the children and smiled. They moved closer. An instant later, following the lead of the older ones, they had formed a ring around him, and as they skipped in the circle, holding hands, they sang:

> *"Finkel's dog is dead . . . Finkel's dog is dead . . .*
> *Hi-ho the cherrio . . . Finkel's dog is dead . . ."*

Perlman watched for a few minutes, unable to move. Then he crossed the street, pushed the children aside, and entered the circle. "Mr. Finkel," he began. "Let—"

"Ah, Professor—what are words at times like these? Bah! Death is death. They will return the ashes to me tomorrow."

Perlman felt his stomach turn, but he did not move away. The children continued around the two men, chanting. *"Finkel's dog is dead . . . Finkel's dog is dead . . ."* A crowd was gathering—students, mothers with baby carriages, people from the building.

"Now that school is over," Perlman said, "I'll be leaving for the summer. To Italy—Florence, Venice . . . Barbara is coming with me." Finkel nodded. The voices of the children grew louder, entering Perlman's brain and resting there. Perlman considered, but it did not matter. Finkel was right. "I'll send the rent checks by mail." Finkel looked at him from his old face, puzzled. "And I'll see you again in the fall, I hope."

Finkel gazed at him intensely, his eyes screwed up, searching the professor's face; Perlman could not bear it, he realized, and he moved away quickly. Finkel followed him from the circle, pushing the children aside roughly. "I will look forward to it," he called. His voice was strong. "Have a pleasant trip, Professor Perlman! —Have a pleasant trip!"

A Family Trip

IF PA HADN'T of been such a stickler on money, we might of got away with the whole thing and I wouldn't of got my picture in the papers so that all the kids teased the life out of me in the schoolyard for two weeks afterwards. But maybe it didn't matter about the money, because Pa said if that was what his mother wanted, that was what he was gonna do and there wasn't any man could stop him. I agreed. When Pa set his mind to doin' something, nobody could stop him. And if he promised you he'd do something for you, he did it.

Ma always tells how that's how they got married, on account of Pa's promise. When he was almost thirty and she wasn't even as old as I am now and she was Tom Wilkins' kid sister (Tom's my Pa's oldest and best friend), Pa used to bounce her up and down on his knee and she used to make him promise not to get married till she grew up. So he waited. Ma thinks it's real funny he did and she always tells the story in front of Pa but he don't laugh much. Sometimes he'll smile a bit, but most of the time he just sort of grunts. He's never once broken a promise he made to me either, and that includes gettin' strapped.

So I guess it wasn't really the money but the principle of the thing. Pa's a big one on principles. He's got lots. I don't understand most of them that have to do with politics and religion, but I knew that his principle this time was a good one. I would of told him that too if he'd asked me, but Pa, he don't need no encouragement.

Ma, she didn't say anything either. When the time come she just packed up a lunch for the three of us, put on her Sunday clothes, and told me to wash and comb my hair. I didn't feel like arguin', so I did.

"Now go help your Pa."

So I did that, too—I was meaning to the first thing when it happened. Grandma wasn't a very big lady—not even as tall as I am now. I'm twelve and Grandma was eighty something. I'm not sure how much. I didn't like to kiss her. Her skin sort of hung from her face so that I was always afraid it was just all gonna fall off sometime, or stick to my lips. She lived in the room in back of the kitchen. Nobody ever went in there until she died, and she just used to show up three times a day for meals, once a day after school so I could give her her kiss and she could ask me if I knew my multiplication tables (I couldn't understand that too well, 'cause I'd known my tables ever since third grade, and she always asked for the same ones— seven and nine—and she always stopped me before I finished anyway), and once every night she'd come into the living room and talk with my Ma while they watched TV together.

They got along real well, laughing and stuff, but Pa never did say much to her, except to ask what he could do for her. It didn't even seem like she needed much done for her, really. She hardly ate a peck and always wore the same dress and I guess that was why Pa figured the least he could do for her was to do the one thing she'd asked him to do.

Me, I didn't argue. When she died that morning, Pa just

said, "Let's go," and he didn't have to say any more. Ma's butting in about washing and stuff just wasted time from getting things done quick and proper, the way Pa always does things. "Quick and proper," he always says, "that's the only way to get things done."

"You get the feet."

Pa carried her under the shoulders and it hardly felt like she weighed anything. Getting her into the back seat, I had to let go of one of her legs to open the door, and it bumped on the ground. I knew how careful and respectful you're supposed to be to dead people, and I looked up quick at Pa.

"What are you waiting for?"

"Nothin'," I said.

We propped her up in the back seat and Ma locked the front door and walked down the steps past the garden.

"Grandma always loved my roses," Ma said, picking one. She fixed it between Grandma's hands.

Pa nodded. "Get in," he said.

Ma got in the front seat and I got in the back next to Grandma and leaned up against the front seat and watched Pa drive. He's the best driver I ever seen. When the speed limit's sixty-five he keeps the car at a steady seventy the whole time. It never goes more'n a mile over or under. Ma doesn't like him to drive fast, but she didn't say anything this time. She knew better. I kept my eyes on Pa's foot to watch how he regulates it to keep the speed so even. I bet if you put a feather on Pa's foot it'd stay there for a thousand miles. Except sometimes when he really lets her rip—that's when we go for rides together, just the two of us. Boy, do we have fun then. Sometimes when we're on a straightaway he keeps his foot on the gas and even lets me turn the wheel. You ought to read the speedometer then—Ma'd have fits if she ever saw how fast we go.

He's never even got one ticket in his whole life. You

ought to hear him talk to a cop—it's like with the argument over the money. He's like that over everything. Around our way he's known as Loghead Harris. Not to his face, of course, but I never seen a man could beat him in an argument.

He's almost always right about who's gonna win the football and baseball games, and even though he belongs to the Electrical Workers Union and always talks about how the Depression wouldn't of come if Al Smith had been President, he's got some Republican friends, and he always predicts who's gonna win for President and things. Even when Truman won, he knew it. And nobody's more loyal to his friends than my Pa. He coached our baseball team last spring and helped Jim Evans' father put on his new roof and last winter during the big snowstorm when nobody knew what to do he delivered Mary Burns' baby right in her bedroom with everybody yelling and screaming. I don't think anybody even realized he'd done it all till him and me (I helped bring him hot water and blankets and stuff) were back in our own house. He didn't say anything then either but just flicked on the TV and told the weatherman off. That was when the phone rang and they thanked him. He was right then, too—I mean about the weather, 'cause the weatherman said it would stop by the morning and my Pa told him he was full of it, that it would go until the next night and then some.

I like Pa. Even though he don't talk to me much the way he used to. I think that's 'cause he wishes he were younger (he married my Ma when he was past forty) and he thinks about what he's gonna do when he retires from working in a few years. There's lots to do around the house, but I know there's not really enough and even a good argument with Tom Wilkins every day won't really keep him busy and I'm kind of scared, 'cause he has some temper and I'm afraid if he's around all the time he'll find out about my smoking and even if he don't he'll find something to get after me for.

Anyway, after a while Ma give me a sandwich and a plum. The sandwich was peanut butter without much jelly. It was real dry and I wanted a Coke but Pa didn't want to stop. He said he wanted to get to the funeral parlor before five o'clock. So we just kept driving on down toward Kentucky. The car radio was busted and I was getting bored so I counted the number of silos I could see going by and then I asked some questions about Grandma when she was young and with my Grandpa and Ma answered me. I was only leading up to the big question, though, and when I asked that one, Pa answered.

"Because she wanted to be buried in Kentucky next to Grandpa on the same day she died."

He said it so gruff-like that I just shut up and counted silos again. He wasn't angry, though. I could tell that. Just doing what he felt he had to do. Which I guess I can understand, since some day when my Ma dies I'd like to do something nice for her, too—not nice only, but something special that she'd like and be proud of me for. I'll have a lot of money by then and make her a real good funeral, maybe like the one they gave Bill Rooney's dad last year, with all these black Cadillac limousines. Unless she wants it in our own house. I'd even do it there, if that's what she wants.

I could tell when we were getting near Louisville because I'd gone there once two years ago when Pa went to a union convention, and I remembered especially the bridge going across the state line, because I thought it would be all modern, only it was more like a wood bridge made out of old gray steel girders and I remembered how it was metal underneath too and I was scared the trucks coming the other way would slide into our lane. I should of been scared of other things, 'cause that was when Pa began to stick up for his principles.

"That's a dollar, mister," the policeman at the tollbooth said when we'd drove up and stopped. Pa had handed him seventy-five cents. "There's four of you."

"She don't count," Pa said, pointing to Grandma. "She's dead."

"Look, mister, quit the kiddin' and fork over another quarter. There's cars behind you."

But Pa wouldn't pay for anyone he didn't have to and the policeman finally got out of his booth and peered into the back seat, straight at Grandma. He looked at me too with a funny kind of smile, like he was half mad and half sick. I didn't smile back at him, though, seeing the way he talked to Pa. The policeman, he got all excited, yellin' at Pa and goin' back and forth to the tollbooth, making telephone calls. My Pa and the policeman argued quite a bit, Pa standin' his ground. He wouldn't back down. Me, I looked out the back window at all the cars lined up behind us. They were honkin' away and I felt pretty important, being in the car that was holding everything up.

Ma just sat there and looked straight ahead. I guess she was proud of Pa, too. He sure did his damndest to save that quarter. He told the guy all kinds of reasons about how hearses didn't pay and how if dead people counted, why weren't they included in censuses, and then the policeman started talking about it being illegal to transport a dead body without a certificate. But Pa argued about that, too. He told him how it was his mother and he could do what he wanted with her, especially since what he wanted was only what she wanted him to do. He didn't see how it was anybody else's business. I agreed. Nobody's gonna be able to tell me what to do with my Ma when she dies.

Pa kept talkin' to the man in the tollbooth and before long more police cars were there and we had to turn around and go to this little town a mile or two away and I stood around in this doctor's waiting room while Pa kept insisting he was only letting them do it to save time (he didn't flinch a bit when they spoke about being able to put him in jail for what he did). Ma stayed in the car. I tried to duck the first time a guy took a picture.but the second flashbulb went off before I even saw the sneaky guy, and then when Pa had the certificate and they'd switched Grandma into a pine box and put her into the trunk they got another picture. If I knew it was gonna get into the papers that the kids from school's parents read, I would of punched the guy.

But the main thing was that we got away without Pa going to jail and that we got into Kentucky to Grandma's funeral parlor before five o'clock. It wasn't much of a funeral— just the three of us and an old friend of Grandpa's who looked like he was at least a hundred years old and the minister and this nice old man who owned the parlor and give me some candy. I never saw Pa so serious. Ma neither. I guess she knew Pa done right.

Even when the kids teased me and showed the picture around I didn't mind too much, 'cause I remembered how proud Pa was all the way home. Kind of relaxed too—I haven't seen him like that for a long time. He let me sit in the front seat and we stopped once outside of Greenfield and I had fried shrimp and a Coke and Pa kept winkin' at Ma—not really smiling, but just proud, and repeating what he said to the policeman at the tollbooth the second time when he handed him seventy-five cents: that he guessed that was the right amount unless they were gonna stop the line again and look in the trunk.

Pa was right. Nobody looked in the trunk.

Ebbets Field

EDDIE GOTTLIEB moved into my neighborhood in the fall of 1955 and I knew right away we were going to become pretty good friends. I was in the eighth grade then, at P.S. 92, and Eddie was brought into my official class about two weeks after school had started. At that time I was going through what my parents called one of my "growing periods"— always talking out in class, making some wiseacre remark, or doing something stupid to get attention, and for this I'd been rewarded with a seat right in front of the teacher's desk, with nobody allowed to sit next to me.

There were no other empty seats in the room, so when our teacher, Mrs. Demetri, told us that we were going to get a new boy in our class I figured he'd be sitting next to me. Our official class hadn't changed much since first grade and it was always a big event when somebody new came into it. When I saw Eddie walk through the door behind Mr. Weiner, the assistant principal, though, my heart jumped. I could tell right away he was a good ballplayer. He was very tall and lanky —about six two then—with thick curly hair that reached down into the collar of his shirt. He sort of shuffled into the room, moving very slowly, his body swaying from side to side, his arms swinging freely. They were real long, coming down just about to his kneecaps. He kept staring at the floor, and when we all started laughing and giggling he must have thought we were laughing at him, because he blushed and fidgeted with his hands and feet a lot—what we were laughing at, though, was not the way Eddie looked but at the way he looked coming in *behind* Mr. Weiner, and I think Mr. Weiner knew it, because his face got red and angry. He was only about five foot one or two and when he walked he took huge steps, almost as if he were goose-stepping. At lunchtime we would always prance around the schoolyard or the lunchroom, mimicking him, and the teachers would never try very hard to make us stop. He was already at Mrs. Demetri's desk, right in front of me, and Eddie was only a couple of steps away from the door when he whirled around and glared at him.

"What's taking you so long?" he demanded. "Come here!"

Then, I remember, Eddie grinned broadly and in two giant steps he was in front of Mr. Weiner, towering over him, standing at attention, still grinning. We broke into hysterics. Mr. Weiner glared at us and we stopped. "Now, young man," he said to Eddie, "wipe that grin off your face. What are you— some kind of gangling idiot?"

Eddie shrugged. "I don't know," he said.

We laughed again and Mr. Weiner turned on us. "All right then. Who wants to be the first to have a private conference in my office today?" he asked.

We shut up. Eddie was staring at the floor again. I could tell that he knew he had done something wrong—but it was obvious he didn't know what it was.

"What's that in your pocket?" Mr. Weiner asked him, pointing.

"A baseball."

"Let me see it."

Eddie put his lunchbag on my desk and twisted the ball out of his side pocket. He showed it to Mr. Weiner. When Mr. Weiner reached for it, though, Eddie pulled his hand away.

"Let me have it," Mr. Weiner demanded.

"No," Eddie said, and he put his hand behind his back, gripping the ball tightly. I could tell from the printing that it was an Official National League ball. It looked really beautiful!

"I said let me have it!"

Eddie shook his head sideways. "It's mine," he said. Everybody was perfectly quiet. I glanced across the room at Izzie and Corky and Louie. They were on the edges of their seats.

"Young man, you will let me have it by the time I count three or I will know the reason why!"

"Do you promise you'll give it back?" Eddie asked.

Mr. Weiner blinked. "Do I *what*—?"

Eddie was looking at Mr. Weiner now, intently. "I gotta have it," he said. "I just *gotta!* I never go anywhere without it."

"We do not allow hardball playing in this school."

Eddie grinned then, as if everything were okay, and brought the ball out from behind his back. "I didn't know that," he said. "I'm sorry." He pushed the ball right in front of Mr. Weiner's face. We all gasped and Mrs. Demetri took a step toward them. "See—?" Eddie said, smiling. "It's got Campy's signature on it."

"Who?"

"*Campy!*" Eddie said.

"Who, may I ask, is Campy?"

"Campy—Roy Campanella—he catches for the Dodgers!" Eddie was excited now. "You know—"

"Of course," Mr. Weiner said. Then he smiled awkwardly. There was something about Eddie that had him mystified. You could tell. "Well, put that ball away and don't bring it to school again," he said. "This is your first day here, so I'll excuse you. But there are no second chances with me. Remember that."

When he left, Mrs. Demetri introduced Eddie to us. I applauded and most of the guys followed my lead. Mrs. Demetri didn't get too angry at me, though—in fact, after she gave Eddie the seat next to me, she put me in charge of getting him his books and making sure he knew where things were. Maybe she figured I'd be less trouble that way. At any rate, I was glad. The first thing I did was to ask him where he'd gotten the baseball.

"I won it," he said.

"Where?"

"On Happy Felton's Knothole Gang."

"Really?"

Eddie nodded and I nearly exploded out of my seat, I remember, wanting to tell all the guys. The Knothole Gang was this show they had on television then that came on before all the Dodger games. Three or four guys who played the same position would get together with Happy Felton and one of the Dodgers down the right-field line and they'd be tested on different things. Then, at the end, the Dodger would pick one of the guys as a winner and give the reasons he'd picked him.

I asked Eddie a few more questions and then I began telling him about our baseball team, The Zodiacs. He said he'd read about us in Jimmy O'Brien's column in the *Brooklyn Eagle*.

"You got that good pitcher, don't you—and that crazy kid who brings a victrola to the games and plays the Star-Spangled Banner on it—right?"

"That's Louie," I said, pointing across the room. "He lives in my building. But we don't have the pitcher any more. He's in high school now. Izzie pitches for us most of the time this year."

We talked some more and I asked him if he wanted to play with us, as long as he was in our class now, and he said he'd love to, if we'd let him. Then I wrote out a note, telling all the guys that Eddie had won the baseball on Happy Felton's show and that he'd agreed to play on our team, and I passed it across the room to Louie. His face lit up, and he passed it on to Corky. By the time we got into the yard for lunch that day, Eddie was a hero, and the guys all crowded around him, asking about what Campy had said to him and about what team he had played on before and things like that.

I got to know Eddie pretty well during the next few weeks. He wasn't very bright—this was pretty obvious the first time Mrs. Demetri called on him to read something—and he was very quiet, but he would have done anything for you if you were his friend. All the guys liked him and we were pretty happy he had moved into our neighborhood. He was the kind of guy you wished you had for a brother. His father had died a couple of years before, and until he moved he'd been living in Boro Park with his mother. He never talked much about her or his home or what it had been like living in Boro Park, but we all knew the most important thing—that his family was *Orthodox*. The first time one of us said something to him about making the big leagues some day, he shook his head and said that he didn't think he ever would because he couldn't play or travel on Saturdays. When we brought up the names of other Jewish ballplayers who'd played—Hank Greenberg, Cal Abrams, Sol Rogovin, Sid Gordon, Al Rosen—he said that they hadn't come from families like his. He said it would kill his mother if any of his relatives ever found out about the things he did on Saturday

—that he could hide most things as long as he wasn't living near them, but if he ever got his picture in the papers for doing something on Saturday, they'd know about it.

Eddie himself wasn't very religious—he played ball with us at the Parade Grounds on Saturdays—but he was determined not to hurt his mother, and I guess I could understand why at the time. I knew she worked to support the two of them, and that Eddie felt pretty bad toward her about moving from their old neighborhood. I guess he felt she had moved because of him. Still, even though he may have felt obligated to her in a lot of ways, it didn't stop him from *wanting* to be a big-league ballplayer. That was obvious.

1955 was the year the Dodgers beat the Yankees in the World Series, and Eddie came over to my house to watch the games on television. I don't think I've ever seen a guy get more excited than he did during the last game of that series. The Dodgers had one of their great teams then—Campy, Furillo, Robinson, Reese, Snider, Hodges, Newcombe, Erskine—but the heroes of that last game were two other guys, Sandy Amoros and Johnny Podres. When Amoros made his famous catch of Yogi Berra's fly ball in the sixth inning and without hesitating turned and threw to Reese, who doubled up McDougald at first base, Eddie went wild. He couldn't sit down after that. He just kept walking around the room, pounding guys on the back, shaking our hands, and repeating again and again: "Did you see that catch? Boy, did you see that catch?"

We must have relived each inning of that series a hundred times during the rest of that year. I kept telling Eddie that since Podres—who had won the third and last games of the series—was only twenty-three years old, he'd still have plenty of years to pitch to Eddie when Eddie got to the Dodgers. Eddie always insisted it was an impossibility, but then Louie came up with another one of his bright ideas—if Eddie changed his name and grew a mustache some day, how would his relatives ever find out? Eddie liked the idea and that spring, for practice, Eddie used the name Johnny Campy when he played with our team.

We played in the Ice Cream League at the Parade Grounds and we did pretty well, even though we didn't win the championship. Eddie was fantastic. He batted over .400, was lightning on the bases, only made about two or three errors, threw out ten guys stealing, and did the one thing he did in no other place—he talked all the time. He'd be quiet until we got to the field, but the minute he put on his shin guards, protector, and mask, his mouth began moving a mile a minute, and he'd keep up the chatter the whole game. I loved to listen to him. "C'mon, Izzie babe," he'd yell, crouched behind the plate. "Chuck it here, chuck it here. Plunk it home to Campy, honey babe. Show 'em how, show 'em how. Plunk it home to Campy! This batter's just posin' for pictures. Let's go, babe. Plunk it home to Campy . . ."

He was one of the greatest natural athletes I've ever seen —and not just in baseball, as we soon found out. Until he came to our school Izzie and I were generally considered the best basketball players of all the guys, but Eddie made us look like amateurs. We were only in the eighth grade then, but when we'd play in the schoolyard on weekends Eddie could hold his own with the high school and college boys.

He was skinny and got banged around a lot under the boards, but he was the most fantastic leaper I've ever seen. Lots of times, even when he was boxed out, he'd just glide up in the air, over everybody else, and pluck the ball out of the sky with those big hands of his. He could dunk the ball with either hand.

My parents knew how much I loved basketball and that summer, for the second straight year, they sent me to Camp

Wanatoo, where Abe Goldstein, the Erasmus coach, was head counselor. I remember he got pretty upset when I told him that Eddie was supposed to go to Westinghouse—a vocational high school—instead of to Erasmus. Schoolyard reputations spread pretty fast in our neighborhood and he'd already heard about Eddie from a lot of the guys on his team. I explained to him about how Eddie's grades weren't too good, and about his mother.

When I got back from camp and saw Eddie, the first thing he told me was that he'd decided to go to Erasmus. He said that Mr. Goldstein had visited him and promised him and his mother that Eddie would get through high school—and that he could get him a scholarship to college. We spent a lot of time that fall playing in the schoolyard together, and Eddie got better and better. He'd spent the summer in the city, working as a delivery boy and helper in his uncle's butcher shop in Boro Park, and he'd developed a gorgeous fade-away jump shot that was impossible to stop. When we weren't playing, we'd sit by the fence in the schoolyard and talk about the guys on the Erasmus team or about the Dodgers—and we'd have long debates on whether it was better to get a college education and then play pro basketball or to forget about college and take a big bonus from a major-league baseball team.

That winter we played on a basketball team together in the *Daily Mirror* tournament and we probably would have won the championship, only in the big game for the Brooklyn title Eddie didn't show up until the last quarter. He went wild then, putting in shots from crazy angles, rebounding like a madman, stealing the ball, and playing his heart out—but we were fifteen points behind when he arrived and when the clock ran out we were still down by four. For weeks afterwards you could hardly talk to him, he was so upset. All of us told him to forget it, that we understood about his mother getting sick and him

having to stay with her until the doctor came, but he still felt
he'd let us down.

His mother got better, spring came, the baseball season
started, and Eddie stopped coming to school almost completely. Any time the Dodgers were in town—except for the
days our baseball team had a game or the afternoons he
worked as a delivery boy for his uncle—Eddie would be at
Ebbets Field. He was always trying to get me to come along
with him, but I usually found one excuse or another not to. He
kept telling me there was nothing to worry about. He said he
knew somebody in the attendance office and that all we had to
do was give him our programs and show up for homeroom period in the morning—the guy in the office would write in our
names as absent on the sheets that went to the teachers whose
classes we'd be cutting. He never seemed to get into any trouble and finally, in the middle of June, I told him I'd go with
him.

We made up to meet in front of Garfield's Cafeteria, at
the corner of Flatbush and Church, at 10:30, after second period. Eddie was there ahead of me and we got on the Flatbush
Avenue bus and paid our fares. I kept looking around, expect-
ing to see a teacher or a cop.

"Just act normal," Eddie told me. "And if anybody stops
us, just put one of these on your head—" he reached into a
pocket and pulled out two *yamulkas*—"and tell whoever asks
you it's a Jewish holiday and that we go to Yeshiva. That always works."

When we got off the bus at Empire Boulevard, where the
Botanic Gardens begin, we still had a couple of hours until the
game started and I asked Eddie what we were going to do
until then.

He smiled. "Follow me," he said.

I followed. I saw a few cops along the street, but none of

them bothered us. Some old men were getting their boards ready, with buttons and pennants and souvenirs, and when we got to McKeever and Sullivan Place, where the main entrance was, a few guys were selling programs and yearbooks. We walked along Sullivan Place and Eddie stopped about halfway down the block, where the players' entrance was.

A minute later a taxi stopped at the curb and two big guys got out—I recognized them right away as Gil Hodges and Duke Snider. It really surprised me, I remember, to discover that we were as tall as both of them—taller than Snider.

"Any extra tickets?" Eddie asked.

"Sorry—not today, Eddie," the Duke said, and the two of them disappeared into the clubhouse.

I nearly died. "You mean you actually *know* them?" I asked.

"Sure," Eddie said. "Hell—I've been out here like this for three years now." He scratched at his cheek and tried to act nonchalant, but I could tell how proud he was that a Dodger had called him by name with me there. "I don't think they'll have any extras today, though—Milwaukee has a good team this year and there were probably lots of their friends wanting tickets."

"It's okay," I said, still flabbergasted. "I got a couple of bucks for tickets."

"We won't need 'em, I hope," he said. "If nobody has extras, we can try waiting in the gas station on Bedford Avenue. There's always a bunch of kids there, hoping to catch a ball, but they usually hit four or five out in batting practice. If we can get just one, the guy at the gate will let us both in—he knows me."

"If not?"

He shrugged. "The bleachers. It's only seventy-five cents, and after about the second inning you can sneak into the grandstands."

Some more Dodgers came by and they all smiled and said hello to Eddie, but none of them had any extra tickets. It didn't bother me. After a while I just followed Eddie's lead and said hello to the players also, saying things like "How're you doing, Carl? We're rooting for you!" to Furillo, or "How're you feeling today, Campy?" and I hardly believed it when some of the players would actually answer me. As I got more confidence I got braver—telling Pee Wee to watch out for guys sliding into second base, telling Karl Spooner that if he pitched he should keep the ball low and outside to Aaron—and after each group of guys would go into the clubhouse I'd slam Eddie on the back and punch him in the arm. "C'mon," I'd say to him, "pinch me right on the ass, buddy. Then I'll know it's true!" Eddie just kept grinning and telling me how stupid I'd been to wait this long to come to a game with him.

By 11:30, though, we still didn't have any tickets.

"We should of waited by the visiting team's entrance," Eddie said. "They hardly ever use up their passes—"

Then, as we started to walk toward Bedford Avenue, we saw this little guy come trotting up the street toward us. Eddie squinted.

"It's Amoros," he said. "Hey, Sandy—any tickets?" he called.

"Oh, man, I late today," Amoros said when he got to us, shaking his head back and forth. He reached into his wallet, handed us two tickets, and we wished him luck. Then he continued toward the players' entrance, running.

"Whooppee!" I shouted as soon as he was gone. "Amoros for Most Valuable Player!" I threw my arm around Eddie's shoulder and we ran down the street together, half dragging each other, until we got to the turnstile entrance. Then we stopped and strutted inside together, handing the guard the tickets as if it was something we did every day of the week. As soon as we were inside, Eddie yelled "Let's go!" and we raced under the arcade, laughing and giggling. The instant we saw the field, though, we stopped. The groundkeepers had just finished hosing down the base paths and the visiting team hadn't come out yet for batting practice. There was hardly anybody in the stands and the sight of the empty ball park seemed to sober us both up. To this day I don't think there's any sight that's prettier than a ball park before a game's been played. Watching on television all the time, you forget how green and peaceful the field looks.

We had great seats that day, right over the Dodger dugout. They blasted the Braves, 9–1, with fourteen or fifteen hits, and we cheered and shouted like mad, especially when Amoros came to bat. I remember everything about the ball park that day, and I think I remember the things that happened off the field more than I do the actual game. I remember the Dodger Symphony marching around the stands, and Mabel swinging her cowbell, and Gladys Gooding singing the National Anthem and playing "Follow the Dodgers" on the organ, and the groundkeepers wheeling the batting cage back out to center field, and the people across Bedford Avenue watching from their roofs. I remember being surprised at how many guys our age—and even younger—had come to the game, and I remember how great I felt when I heard somebody calling my name and I turned around and saw Mr. Hager wave to me. I waved back at him and then told Eddie about him. Mr. Hager was a retired fireman who lived on my block. He went to every Dodger game and when they lost he always wore a black armband. When the Giants beat the Dodgers in the playoff in '51, nobody saw him for weeks afterwards, and then he wore the same black suit day in and day out until they won back the pennant in '52. Everybody in our neighborhood knew him and it was said that he got into at least two or three fights a week at

Hugh Casey's bar on Flatbush Avenue. There were a lot of Dodger fans like him in those days.

Most of all, though, I remember how *good* I felt that day —just sitting with Eddie, eating peanuts and cheering and talking baseball. As it turned out, that was the last time I ever got to see a Dodger game. At the end of the season they announced that they were moving to Los Angeles.

I went to Camp Wanatoo again that summer and Eddie stayed in the city. His uncle had gotten him a job loading sides of beef into refrigerator cars and this helped build up his chest and shoulders and arms. In the fall everybody was predicting he'd be the next great basketball star at Erasmus—maybe even All-City in his sophomore year.

When the time came for varsity tryouts, though, he didn't show up. Nobody could figure it out. Two days later he stopped by my house at night and asked if I wanted to go for a walk. He looked terrible—his face was long and he seemed to have lost a lot of weight. At first I figured it had something to do with his mother, but when I asked him he shook his head.

"Nah," he said when we were downstairs. He sighed. "I guess you were wondering why I didn't try out for the team, huh?"

"Everybody was—" I said.

"I know. Mr. Goldstein called my house tonight and I had to tell him—that's why I came by your house. I wanted you to know before the other guys. Maybe you could tell them, so I don't have to keep repeating the story."

"Sure," I said. "What is it?"

"It's my damn heart," he said. I looked at him and he was biting the corner of his lower lip. Then he shook his head back and forth and cursed. "I can't play any more," he said. "The doctor said so." He stopped. "Jesus, Howie, what am

I gonna *do?* What am I gonna *do?*" he pleaded. I didn't know what to say. "Shit," he said. "Just shit!" Then his body seemed to go limp. "C'mon, let's walk."

"How'd you find out?" I asked.

"Ah, since the summer I've had this pain in my chest and when it didn't go away I went to our family doctor. My mother telephoned him about a week ago and he told her. It's only a murmur—nothing really dangerous—but it means no varsity."

"Can't you play at all?"

"Oh, yeah—as long as I take it easy. I just have to get a lot of sleep, and whenever I feel any of this pressure building up in my chest I have to be sure to stop."

We walked for a long time that night—up Bedford Avenue all the way past Ebbets Field to Eastern Parkway, then back home along Flatbush Avenue, and most of the time neither of us said anything. What could you say?

I made the varsity that year and Eddie came to all the games, home and away. He worked five afternoons a week at his uncle's butcher shop now, but on Saturdays, when it was closed, he'd come down to the schoolyard and play a few games. He kidded around a lot, telling everybody to take it easy against him because of his heart, but he was still tremendous. I was already about an inch taller than he was, and a pretty good jumper, but he'd go up over me as if I had lead in my sneakers.

In about the middle of our junior year he quit school and went to work full-time as an assistant to his uncle. He kept coming to all the Friday night games, though, and sometimes when I didn't have a date, we'd go to Garfield's afterwards and then walk home together.

Eddie and I lost touch with each other during my first two years of college—I don't think I saw him even once—but when I was home for spring vacation during my junior year my

mother told me he'd bought a half interest in Mr. Klein's kosher
butcher shop on Rogers Avenue. I went over to see him the
next morning and there he was, behind the counter. I stood
outside for a while, watching him wait on customers, and then
when the store was empty I went inside.

"Hey, Campy—!" I called. He was at the far end of the
counter, cutting up some meat.

He turned around. "Jesus, Howie!" He wiped his hands
on his apron and then we shook hands and pounded each other
on the back. "Boy, it's good to see you. How've you been?"

"Pretty good," I said. "When did all this happen?" I asked,
motioning around the store.

"C'mon next door to the candy store," he said, taking off
his apron. "I'll get you a Coke—boy, it's been a long time!"

He got Mr. Klein out of the big walk-in freezer in the
back and then we went next door and Eddie told me about
how he'd saved up money while he was working for his uncle—
with that and some insurance money his mother had put away
after his father's death, he was able to buy a half interest from
Mr. Klein, who was getting old and wanted to retire soon. By
then Eddie could buy out the other half and the store would be
his.

"How about you?" he asked. "How do you like college?"

"It's okay," I said.

"What're you studying?"

"Liberal arts."

"Oh, yeah? —What subjects?"

I laughed. "You don't have to sound interested," I said.

He shrugged, embarrassed. "Anyway, I follow your team
in the papers all the time—the *Times* always prints box scores
of your games. You did real well this year—second high scorer
on your team, weren't you?" When I didn't answer, he punched
me in the arm. "Ah, don't be modest—you're a good ballplayer,

Howie. Bet you got all those pretty girls running after you, too—"

"We'll be playing in the Garden against N.Y.U. next year," I said. "I'll get you some tickets—you can bring a girl and maybe we'll double after or something—"

"Sure," he said. "I'm going with a girl now—real nice, you'd like her." He shrugged, then grinned. "I'll probably be a married man by this time next year—"

When we played in the Garden the next year I sent him two passes, but I had to leave right after the game to get the bus that was taking us back to school that night. I got an invitation to his wedding right after that. It was scheduled for Christmas week, but I couldn't go because of a holiday tournament our team was playing in at Evansville, Indiana. I called him when I came in for spring vacation and told him how sorry I was that I hadn't been there.

"Jesus, Howie," he said. "Forget it. How could you have been? You were in that tournament in Indiana. I followed the whole thing." He laughed. "My wife nearly slammed me because on the first day of our honeymoon I rushed out in the morning to get the papers to see how many points you'd scored."

We talked some more and then he asked me over to dinner. I accepted the invitation, but I felt funny about it. I suppose I was afraid we wouldn't have anything to talk about —or, what seemed worse, that we'd spend the entire evening reminiscing about things we'd done when we were thirteen or fourteen.

I was partially right—we did spend a lot of time reminiscing, but I didn't mind. Eddie and I filled each other in on what had happened to guys we'd grown up with—who was getting married, who had finished college, who had moved out of the neighborhood—and I had a good time. Susie was, as Eddie promised, a great cook. She'd graduated from high school and was in her last year of nurse's training—just right for Eddie, I thought. After supper, while she did the dishes, Eddie and I sat in the living room and talked. I told him how much I liked her and he smiled.

"She's good for me," he said, nodding. "I'll tell you something—because of her I'm even thinking of going back to high school evenings to finish up."

"Does she want you to?"

"She'd never say so, even if she did—she lets me make up my own mind. But I think she'd like it."

"Sounds like a good idea," I offered.

"Yeah—but when do I have time? Running the store by myself now, there's a lot of work—books—I have to bring home, and then I'm so tired after being on my feet all day, about all I can do in the evening is turn on the TV and watch the Yanks or the Mets." He sighed. "But we'll see. I'd like to finish up."

"How's your health been?" I asked.

"Fine," he said, shrugging. Then his eyes opened wide. "Jesus!" he exclaimed. "You don't know, do you?"

"Know what?"

"About my heart—" I must have looked scared then, because he started laughing at me. "Thank God Kennedy put through that draft exemption for married men," he said. "Otherwise I'd be carrying a rifle—"

"I don't understand. I thought—"

"It's a long story," he said, "but the short of it is there was never anything wrong with my heart." He stood up and paced around the room. "When I went for my army physical about a year and a half ago, they didn't find anything wrong with me. That's how I found out."

"But what about—?"

"Ah, that was just a thing my mother told me that the family doctor went along with," he said, stopping my question.

"He was religious or something, I guess. I don't know. What's the difference now? Thinking back, I guess he *himself* never really told me outright I had a murmur—"

Susie came back into the room and I could tell she knew what Eddie had been telling me. She put her arms around his waist and hugged him.

"My God!" I exclaimed. "How could she—?"

He was about to say something, but then Susie looked at him and he changed his mind. "That's the way the ball bounces, I guess," he said, shrugging his shoulders, and I could tell he'd used the same expression before in similar situations. He kissed Susie on the forehead and held her close to him. "Anyway," he laughed, "if you're in pro ball you got to be away from your wife and kids half the year."

"But Christ, Eddie," I began. Susie glared at me and I stopped. Eddie sat down and nobody said anything for a while —then suddenly he started talking. "You know something," he said. "My business is pretty good. I mean, I'm making a good living and at least I'm not working for somebody else—but you know what I'd *really* like to do?" He leaned forward and rubbed his hands together. He looked at Susie and she smiled. "I'd like to coach kids. No kidding."

"He's terrific with them, Howie," Susie said. "Really—"

"I love it—I help out at the center sometimes, and with this team of kids from our block. Guess what they call themselves? —The Zodiacs!" We both laughed. "It's something how these things get passed down—"

We began reminiscing again and soon we were both telling Susie about the day we'd played hooky together and gone to Ebbets Field.

"Have you seen it since it's torn down?" Eddie asked. "They got these big apartment houses—"

"I've been there," I said.

"I have a girlfriend who lives in right field," Susie said. I glanced at her, puzzled. "The people all give their section of the development names according to the way the field used to be laid out," she explained. Then she laughed, but the laugh was forced and we knew it. Eddie and I tried to get up a conversation about the old ballplayers and what they were doing then—Hodges managing the Senators, the Duke still hanging on as a pinch hitter, poor Campy in a wheelchair since his crash, conducting interviews on TV between Yankee doubleheaders—but our hearts weren't in it anymore and there were a lot of long silences. After a while I said I had to get up early the next morning for a job interview. It wasn't even midnight. I thanked them for the dinner and I said I'd be in touch when I got back from school in June. Then, when I was at the door, Eddie put his arm around my shoulder.

"I been thinking," he said. "How about you playing some three-man ball with an old married man before you go back to school?"

"Sure," I said.

I met Eddie at the schoolyard on Saturday morning and we played for a couple of hours. He wasn't as graceful as I'd remembered him, but he could still jump—only now he knew how to throw his weight around and use his elbows and body and shoulders. He was murder under the boards and deadly with his jump shot and rough on defense. We played against some pretty tough high school and college and ex-college ballplayers that day and Eddie was the best of us all. Between games we'd rest next to the fence together and Eddie would talk and joke and kid about the potbelly he was putting on. When we played, though, he didn't smile and he didn't talk. He played hard and he played to win.

The Campaign of
Hector Rodriguez

WE RACE down the stairs, two at a time, loyal friends behind us, spreading the word. "Vote for Birnbaum and Rodriguez! ¡Viva Sam! ¡Viva Hector! ¡Viva Louise!" Carlos is standing in the doorway of his room on the second floor, looking at the girls with the others from his class. "¡Mira! ¡Mira!" cries one of his classmates. "Hey, chica—Carlos likes you!" They lean on each other as the crowds go by, drool on their lips, but Carlos says nothing. He's real little, a stringy guy, but he is my best friend. We come on the boat together from Puerto Rico.

I push the others aside and give him my hand to shake. "We made it," I say. "A fusion ticket—Sam, the black girl Louise, and me." Carlos smiles with his yellow teeth. His eyelids hang down. "Look," says Sam, slapping Carlos on the arm. "Can we count on you to swing the C.R.M.D. vote our way?"

Carlos shrugs. "It's okay," I say, and Carlos says he will get the C.R.M.D. vote in line. C.R.M.D. is for Children with Retarded Mental Development, but do not believe it. Carlos is quick at arithmetic, he knows the lifetime batting averages of every Spanish baseball player. Behind his droopy eyelids there is fire. He wins medals in running. He is as smart as half the school. Only he cannot read. So they put him in C.R.M.D. But he does not care. In C.R.M.D. nobody bothers you. There is a television set and shoeshine kits and knock-hockey. He makes much money shining the teachers' shoes. In his class he is the leader, and now that he is in C.R.M.D. nobody makes fun of the others the way they used to.

Except Carmen. *Carmen de las tetas grandes,* as she is known on our street. Carmen Quiñones, five foot two, fourteen years old, in the seventh grade, guided missiles on her chest. She comes down the hall now, her friends with her, chattering and chewing, swinging their asses to the music from Carmen's radio. Carmen stops when she sees me, and tosses her head back like she is Sophia Loren. "*¡Qué tetas grandes!*" I exclaim. She sneers at me. Benito Lopez, from Carlos' class, his eyes are spinning. "Hey, Benito," Carmen says. "You like me?"

Benito nods, his mouth open, happy.

Carmen throws her head back and laughs. "Well, I no like you!"

This causes great laughter from the other girls, and as they pass down the hall Carlos spits in their direction. "*¡Puta! ¡Puta!*" he shouts, above the noise.

Carmen shakes her oil-black hair and turns on Carlos. "*¡Su madre es una negra!*"

Carlos gives her the sign. She laughs and walks on, around the corner.

"How about her?" Sam asks. "She controls a big bloc of the female Puerto Rican vote—"

"You leave her to me," I say. "*Adios,* Carlos. I have a class. After school, meet me—we have a campaign to plan."

I am the leader of my people—Hector Rodriguez, running for vice-president of Junior High School Number 54,

Manhattan, on the Green Party. Everything has gone according to our plans. We are unbeatable. Sam Birnbaum of the ninth grade for president—white and Jewish; Hector Rodriguez of the eighth grade for vice-president—Catholic and Puerto Rican; Louise Carr of the seventh grade for secretary—black and Protestant. "I'm counting on you to bring in the Puerto Rican vote," Sam says to me, his arm around my shoulder as we make our way downstairs. "Do not fear," I say to him. "You are my good friend, Sam." I pound him on the back while all around us students give congratulations. "¡Viva Rodriguez!" they shout. "¡Viva Birnbaum!"

In the lunchroom I get Carmen in the corner. "I like you, Carmen," I say. She chews on an egg-salad sandwich and presses the radio to her ear. Lesley Gore is singing. "I mean it," I say. "I go for you."

"Yeah?" she says. "Well, I no go for you. You better watch out how you get fresh or I get my boyfriend after you." She telling the truth about that. Her boyfriend, he is the star pitcher for the Camaradas, a windmill delivery, a true strike-out king. On Saturday in Central Park I see them play. Carmen is there, and when he is not pitching he and Carmen are against a tree, loving each other up with passion. He is mean-looking, with a mustache, at least nineteen years old. All the men on his team have women, and all day in Central Park they love them up and drink beer and play baseball.

"You going to vote for me, Carmen?" I say. I let my hand fall against *la teta grande*. She chews her gum and listens to the radio as if I am doing nothing to her. "I like you, Carmen. I mean it. I go for you."

"What you give me if I vote for you?" she asks.

"I make a big party in your honor," I say. "For you and all your friends—a party like you have never been to. Better than the fiestas in San Juan!"

"Oh, yeah? How you do that—?"

"Sam," I say. "His parents are rich Jews who live on Central Park West. At election time they will be gone, cruising to Puerto Rico with the other rich Jews, and we can use his house, his liquor. I promise you, Carmen—you get your friends to vote for us and I will show you a good time—"

She comes closer, smiling. "For me you make the party? In my honor?"

"Only for you, Carmen. You know that. Only for you."

She laughs with passion. "Hector!" she says, grabbing me under the mouth. She flashes her teeth and shakes my head from side to side, holding me strong by the chin. "What a man you will be some day! Aiee, what you do to me!" She gives me my hand back. The door to the outside opens and the students charge to it. I walk into the yard and go around to the side with Carmen. With nobody around, I do things she likes.

"Okay," she says. "You make a party for me and I vote for you."

"What about your boyfriend?" I say.

She bites my neck. "Ha! What you think—while I am in school he waits only for me? I know him—¡bastardo! ¡Bastardo barroso!"

I press her against the bricks. "I tell you something, Carmen," I say. "He is old now and I am young, but some day I am going to be somebody. This is the beginning. Vice-president this year, president next year. I have it planned. In high school and then in college. You stick with me, Carmen, you do okay."

"You are smart Hector," she says. "You in the class with all the Jews."

"Some day I will have a mansion on Riverside Drive and an estate in Puerto Rico—servants, yachts, a swimming pool, my own airplane. You think I going to be a dumb spic all my life, you crazy." I visit *la teta grande* for the last time. "This is only the beginning, Carmen."

After school, in Sam's house, we begin our work. The smart kids from the Special Progress classes, they are making posters and tags, telephoning their friends. I tell them what to put on the signs: VOTE FOR THE GREEN PARTY—THE PARTY OF ALL THE STUDENTS! In English and in Spanish: ¡EL PARTIDO DE TODOS LOS ESTUDIANTES! The good artists draw pictures of us—black, Spanish, white; on the floor in the bedroom, I put Louise in charge of the tags—VOTE FOR SAM! . . . I LIKE HECTOR! . . . GO FOR GREEN . . . cutting them out of paper, punching holes, stringing them for distribution.

"Louise is O.K.," Sam says. Then he asks if I want to take a drink from his father's supply. Sam is all right. He is my good friend. Some day he will be a famous man—he is a scholar and an athlete. In the lavatories of our school, he is the man to come to for a cigarette. We toast to our victory. "C'mere," he says. "I got something to show you."

In his father's room, from a dresser, boxes of prophylactics. "Votes," he says, striking a match on his heel and lighting a cigar. I take one. Two girls come in, white and clean, and he issues instructions to them. A new idea for a poster: THIS STUDENT VOTES FOR SAM, HECTOR, AND LOUISE! We will tape mirrors to the posters. Sam starts to take money from his wallet to buy the mirrors, but Carlos stops him. He says he will get mirrors for nothing.

During the next week, we move our campaign into high gear. Every day more and more voters swing to the Green Party. Sam is cheered by the students when he enters the schoolyard, I am hoisted on shoulders and carried about, Louise is queen of the seventh grade. Everyone wears our tags. We start a blackboard campaign, workers assigned to every room in the school. I give speeches in the lunchroom—we promise them everything: dances, boat rides, tournaments, picnics. And all the while Carlos is blazing the path to victory with his own campaign. Every day he has new gifts for the students.

One day it is lipsticks for the girls, the next day combs for the boys: ballpoint pens, boxes of gold stars, candles, thumbtacks, cans of hair spray, golf balls—his resources are endless, his sheepish smile dazzling. Where does one get a friend like Carlos?

In their desperation the other party spreads a rumor—Sam and I, they say, we are too close, like little birds. In the bathrooms it is written: *Sam Loves Hector.* We call a council and I decide quickly. "There is only one thing to do," I say. "You've got a head on your shoulders, Hector," Sam says, and the next day we walk through the schoolyard holding hands. Boys and girls roar with laughter. At the gates at three o'clock, Sam's friends from the S.P. classes stop one of every five students and ask them who they expect to vote for. The polls show us leading by a three-to-one margin, and we publish the results. "Nobody likes to back a loser," I say. "It shames them."

When I return to West 80th Street at night, I am a hero. The Latin-American music I love fills the air. The naked babies run under my feet, the girls grab for my muscles, I am asked to play stickball by the younger boys. My grandmother, proud, sits in the window behind the fire escape and compares me to Roosevelt, Kennedy, Marin. The old men in their undershirts, playing cards and shooting craps, they ask when I am running for mayor. Carmen traps me in the hallway.

"You so famous now, you forget about Carmen?" she asks.

"I never forget you, Carmen," I say, moving in. She shoves me back.

"I get all my friends to vote for you and now, in the halls, you hardly see me." She spits at my feet. "Always with the blond-haired girls!"

"You are the only girl for me—*¡querida* Carmen!" I breathe on her neck and hold her to me from behind. "This is only politics, Carmen. A dirty business. When the election is over and I am vice-president, we will have good times. Do you forgive me?"

"I am Spanish and I am proud of it!" she says. Her chest expands with pride. My pride matches hers. "There is no one like you, Carmen," I say.

She grabs the hair in back of my head with both hands. "¡Hector! ¡Aiee! ¡Hector!" she cries. A minute later she runs for the door. "My boyfriend will see—" Then, eyes laughing, she is gone into the street. A bottle crashes down from a window and she screams marvelous curses, her head thrown back, her fist raised.

At school Carmen tells everybody about the party I am making in her honor. When Carlos hears, he broods. "She always make fun of us," he says. I console him, spending my lunch period in his classroom, letting him beat me at knock-hockey. The other boys fight each other for the chance to shine my shoes. The teacher leaves me in charge and goes to the lounge to sleep. Everybody knows about him. He was a boxer in the Marines. He has no discipline problems. On the first day of the year, he takes the strongest boy in the class and beats him up. On the second day he makes the strongest boy beat up the next strongest. Who would believe what a C.R.M.D. boy says? Carlos has a supply of candy bars in the clothes closet. When the period ends, he goes into the hall with his chocolates, getting votes for me. Carmen comes toward us, her radio blasting, her body swaying. "Hey Hector," she says, and points to Carlos. "You let this moron vote for you?"

Then Carlos curses Carmen's mother. Carmen flies at him, her nails rip into the side of his face, and a minute later the assistant principal is tearing them apart. His eyes bulge from his face when he sees that Carmen's sweater is torn down the middle. He covers her with his jacket and she strides through the crowd with him, her jaw thrust forward. Carlos is bloody. I put my arm around his shoulder and he twists away.

"*¡Traidor!*" The words cut into my heart.

"Carlos. Please—" But my words will not reach him. The nurse is escorting him away from me. His head is bent, his body tired. When he leaves the school at three o'clock, he sneaks along the fence.

"Is this the Carlos I know?" I say to him, walking by his side. "Is this the Carlos who leaped into the giant war canoe at the Museum of Natural History?" I see a faint spark in his eyes, but it is nothing like the flash that was there when he led the charge into the canoe. I fan the spark. "Is this the Carlos who ran five miles every morning to bring the fishermen their breakfasts at Mayaguez?" His head lifts. "Is this the Carlos who received the praise of the fishermen for the way he sewed their nets?"

We go into Central Park. Sam is waiting for us and we rent a rowboat. Carlos takes the oars and heads for open waters. When we are past the bridge, Sam reveals his newest book: *Ideal Marriage, Its Physiology and Technique.* "I copped it from my father's study." He reads and Carlos and I go into a trance. The words are glorious: *vestibule of the vagina . . . phenomenon of erection . . . first intermezzo of aphorisms . . . the love-bite . . .* This is what we have been waiting for. The chapters: *Positions, Converse and Averse . . . Communion and After-Glow . . . Contraception . . .*

From the corner of my eye I see Carmen and two friends coming toward us in a boat. Carlos sees them also, and he rows furiously. We ram their boat at full speed, and as they work to steady themselves Carlos laughs. Then Carmen laughs also. "Hey, Carlos—you mad at me?" Carlos sulks. "Rafaela say she like you. You like her?" From behind Carmen, Rafaela smiles shyly. "I got something for you, Carmen," I say, and hold up the book. Sam laughs. I suggest that we switch boats. The girls say they don't know, but Carmen's eyes dance and Rafaela blushes. We line our boat up alongside theirs. "Come on," I say. "I give you a good time—we race our boats and ram each other and things." They agree. Carmen will come in our boat and Carlos will go into theirs with Rafaela. "I help you," I say. Carmen stands up. Sam holds onto their boat. I give her my hand and she steps toward us. Then Carlos' eyes blaze, he shrieks into the air—"*¡Aiee! ¡Puta! ¡Ramera!*"—and with superhuman strength he shoves his oar against the side of their boat. For a second I hold onto Carmen's hand. Her eyes and mouth open wide, her skirt flares out, space appears between our boats, and then, her legs spread wide like the sides of a triangle, she descends with a great splash into the water of the Central Park Lake.

Carlos rows like ten men, his eyes sparkling. Carmen rises to the surface, screaming curses. "*¡Bastardo! ¡Idiota barroso!*" Even from a great distance, as boats speed to her rescue, I can see the fire in her eyes. "I get you!" she yells. "I get you!"

Carlos' grin will not leave. But Sam does not smile. "Couldn't you wait till after the election?" he asks. I sit next to him in the rear of the boat, my arm over his shoulder. I tell him there is nothing to worry about. I have calculated. Even without all of Carmen's votes, we will win by a handsome margin. "What is important now," I say, "is not the election—but the victory party." My heart swells. "It will be a party no one will ever forget." I take the book from Sam. "Is it not for us to see to the educational needs of our students?"

I explain my idea and his face is alive again. He pounds me on the back and praises my imagination. He is prepared to take risks, he says. We bring our boat in and sit at the café which overlooks the lake, eating hot dogs and plotting our adventure on Department of Parks napkins. Sam smokes a cigar,

Carlos looks at the illustrations in the book, and I lean back, satisfied.

At school we let it be known that we are the educational party, and when I reveal our plans to Carmen she says she will swing her girls back to our side. She says she does not hold us responsible for Carlos' actions.

We proceed with our plans. At four o'clock we meet outside Mr. Weiss' pharmacy. Sam has the rubber masks—Kennedy, Ringo, Fidel. When the store is empty, we slip inside and I put the sign on the window: STORE CLOSED. WILL OPEN AGAIN AT 5. Carlos is lookout. I draw the shades. Mr. Weiss laughs when he sees our masks. "What can I do for you boys?" We tell him what we want and he laughs again. With one sweep of my arm I clear a counter of its merchandise. I show him our briefcases, open and empty. He goes for the phone, but Sam is ready and cuts the cord with his scissors. "The pills," I say. His eyes dart this way and that. I show him in the book. "The pills!" I repeat. "Your daughter, she in my class—you want her safe?"

"My God!" he says. "Who *are* you?"

"The pills!" Sam says in his most vicious voice. He splatters bottles of perfume against a wall. I reason with Mr. Weiss, telling him he will help the population problem, keep innocent girls out of trouble, prevent half-breeds. He fills our briefcases with pills. We head for the door. "There are men planted across the street," I say. "If you leave here during the next hour, you will pay."

"I want diagrams," Carlos says. "I don't trust pills.

"Give him what he wants," Sam says. "All sizes."

We stay at the door while Carlos gets what he wants. Behind the face of John F. Kennedy there are happy eyes. "Let's beat it," Sam says.

We leave the store and take our masks off, stuffing them

into a garbage can. We proceed up Columbus Avenue. Then, coming toward us, we see them—three cops. "Act natural," I say, but when we come to them, they stop us. "Let's see what you got in those briefcases," they say. In a doorway I see her, smiling triumphantly.

Sam looks at me. I look at Carlos. "Now!" I say, and we break from the cops and run down Columbus Avenue. Carmen grabs at Carlos but he kicks her to the curb. "Stop or we'll shoot!" I hear. We turn the corner, into a side street, streaking between cars. But it is no use. More cops are in front of us. "This way," I cry, and we head into an apartment building, knocking over the ancient doorman. Carlos stops.

"I stay here and make trouble," he says. I look into his eyes. "It's the only way, Hector. You and Sam are leaders—you must not get caught."

"Carlos—" I say.

"Go!" he says.

"Carlos—!"

He kicks at me as the cops appear in the doorway. We open the door to the courtyard. "If you shoot him, we will demonstrate. He has no knife or gun. Remember Gilligan the cop!"

"Come quietly, kid, and we won't hurt you," they say.

"C'mon!" says Sam.

I look at Carlos, my friend. "Good luck—" I call. Just as the police go for him, he turns and tosses me his briefcase. "The diagrams!" he yells, and then he has slipped between them and is running like a maniac, in circles, screeching Spanish. Sam and I leave, satchels in both my hands. The police open the door to the courtyard, but Carlos throws himself between their legs. We hurry down and journey through a network of cellars, making our way to freedom.

At night I confer with the man who protects the rights of the Puerto Rican people. He is my friend, and he says he will represent Carlos. Jail, he believes, cannot be avoided. I have my own idea, though, and we discuss it. Instructions are sent to Carlos.

In court, Carlos' teacher testifies that he is truly a C.R.M.D., Carlos attacks the court psychiatrist, he sings dirty Spanish songs while the judge speaks, his grandmother tells of a home with ten children and no father, and the man who protects the rights of the Puerto Rican people makes an eloquent speech about sickness instead of sin, help instead of punishment.

The plan works. Carlos is sent to a state hospital. The hospital is far away on Long Island and Sam and I travel there on Sunday afternoon when all the other families come, their shopping bags filled with food and clothing, their eyes glazed. Carlos is happy to see us, but he cannot shake our hands. He is tied in a strait-jacket. Around us the other patients and visitors communicate with each other. All the attendants are Negro and Puerto Rican and Carlos says they take special care of him. He asks how the election is going and we tell him that his heroic act has made our victory certain. He asks me what he should do to stay out of jail and I look at the strait-jacket and I tell him he is doing fine. I ask him if he wants anything. He says he wants to return to Puerto Rico.

We go back to the city in the hot subway. Everybody is out on my street. They ask me about Carlos. Children are playing with the garbage, the men are drinking beer, and music fills the air. Everybody is talking about Mr. Sanchez, who threw his baby against the wall that afternoon. The police have taken him away. Carmen's big sister, her hair bleached a crazy pink color, comes switching down the street, looking for business. It is too hot. Everybody is sweaty and greasy. Under a lamppost she comes to me. "When you get some money, kid," she says, "I be your first. Okay? I give you a good time."

"Carmen gives it to me for nothing," I say. "She gives it to everybody for free."

She curses me and says she will kill Carmen. I go home but I roll around on my bed in the hot room and I cannot sleep. On the next visiting day I see that Carlos is changing. He does not smile. His eyes are almost closed, his neck is stiff. We tell him that we will wait until he comes out to have the victory party. He does not listen. He says that if he cannot go back to Puerto Rico he will stay in the hospital. He says it is not so bad in the hospital. It is like C.R.M.D.

"I stay here a long time," Carlos says. "I getting to like it here."

The next Sunday we come with good news. We have won the election.

"Hector had it figured right," Sam says. "It was a landslide."

"Now we wait for you to return," I say. "So that we can have the victory party."

"If I get out, I kill Carmen," he says. "I tell my doctor that."

I talk to him about the party we are going to make—the food, the music, the girls. "We got you to thank for being where we are," Sam says.

"I din do nothing," Carlos says. We keep talking to him, building his confidence, telling him what we feel. I speak to one of the Spanish attendants and point out to him how calm Carlos has become.

"Carlos," I say. "If you say you will not make trouble, Mr. Garcia will take the jacket off."

"I no make trouble."

The jacket comes off, but Carlos continues to sulk, and I have little hope for him. He talks of only two things, the return to Puerto Rico and the murder of Carmen. When we are ready to leave, he asks if we will do his laundry for him and we say yes. He goes to his room and returns with a bundle of clothes. When we leave him, his eyes are almost shut, his thin body stiff, and I wonder if I do the right thing. Maybe he be better off in jail.

"Tomorrow in assembly they swear us in," Sam says when we are standing at the corner of Columbus Avenue and 80th Street. Downstairs in the basement my people are singing with Pastor Ayala. The neon lights blink on and off:

IGLESIA DE CRISTO MISIONERA

VIDA ETERNA, INC.

The sound of electric guitars and tambourines fills me with joy.

"Yes," I say, and finger my medallion. The music is fierce.

"It's really something," Sam says. "We have what we want—but with Carl where he is, it doesn't seem to matter, does it?"

"No," I say.

Carmen is standing against a building, in the shadows, alone. She comes to me and I spit. "Go walk the streets," I say. "Like your sister."

"Hector," she pleads. "I am sorry. Forgive me—"

Sam slaps her. "Your mother sniffs bicycle seats," he says.

"Please," says Carmen, but I turn my back on her. She walks away from us, slowly. I feel something for her—but it passes. Her old friends exit from the church and shun her. They say they have prayed for Carlos. Rafaela says she sends candy and cards to the hospital. Everybody wants to visit him. I look beyond our circle of friends and see Carmen fade into the lights and noise of Columbus Avenue, heading uptown toward Harlem, *las tetas grandes* drooping toward the ground.

Sam and I shake hands. "Some day," he says. "You and me, we're gonna own this city, Hector."

"We will always be friends," I say.

We leave each other and I carry Carlos' laundry over my shoulder, into my apartment. My grandmother says she will take care of it. She has food ready for me and we eat together, without talking. Then I go to my room and try to do homework, but I can think only of Carlos my friend, and of the party that cannot be until he returns. I open the bundle of laundry on my bed, separating the socks from the underwear, the shirts from the handkerchiefs, and then I see it. My heart leaps! I grab it and hold it in front of me, then turn it around. The lettering is stamped in black: PROPERTY OF N.Y. STATE—Carlos has sent his strait-jacket home!

I stuff it under my shirt and run down the stairs, into the hot street, waving my hand to all I pass. "Carlos will return!" I shout to the girls on the corner. "Carlos will return!" I cross Columbus Avenue and race toward Sam's house on Central Park West. In my mind I can see Carlos' sulky face as he sees me discovering what he has done, and I know that he will sleep happy tonight, a sheepish smile next to his pillow.

Sam is hysterical when I show the strait-jacket to him, and we tie each other into it and laugh and talk of the party we will have when Carlos returns. "We will show them something, Mr. President," I say. "Oh, how we will show them something." And then, with devil's eyes, the president glances at the closet where the briefcases are hidden, and offers his vice-president a cigar.

Something Is
Rotten in the
Borough of
Brooklyn

In 1951 when the first set of basketball scandals broke, Izzie and I were too young to be much interested. We were in the third grade then, at P.S. 92 in Brooklyn, and in those days basketball seemed far less important than lighting fires in alleys or knocking over the garbage cans that lined the sidewalks on our block.

By the time we were in the seventh grade, though, basketball had come to mean everything to us. Every afternoon and all day Saturday and Sunday we lived in the schoolyard, and on Friday nights Izzie's father and mine would take turns bringing us to see games at Erasmus Hall High School. Sometimes we'd chip in to buy sports magazines, and we'd cut out the full-page color photos of our heroes to scotch-tape on our walls. Once, at a Knick game at Madison Square Garden, between halves, Izzie got Cousy to sign a color picture of himself from *Sport* magazine, and he mounted it on a piece of oaktag and pasted it to his wall, by his pillow.

Izzie was really good then. Everybody thought for sure he'd be an All-American when he grew up. He had everything

—speed, drive, and the greatest shooting eye anybody in our neighborhood had ever seen. What he had that amazed everybody most was a set-shot that he let go from his forehead with a little outward flick of his wrists. The way he held the ball just above his eyes you sometimes wondered how he saw the basket. But he did. And if you came up close to try to block his shot, he'd zip right around you for an easy lay-up.

When the Erasmus team came to our public school that year, Izzie and I were excited. They came once a year and they put on a "clinic" for us—passing, dribbling, shooting, and going through patterns, while their coach, Mr. Goldstein, explained things to us, and we all sat on the floor, watching, and wishing that some day we'd be out there on the court in the blue and gold Erasmus uniforms, coming back to our school with every one of the seventh and eighth graders wishing they could be us.

"I'd like to use one of your boys for our next demonstration," Mr. Goldstein said to our gym teacher when the clinic was almost over. Mr. Goldstein was a short man, paunchy, but he dressed like a man who could have spent every weekend at the Concord Hotel if he'd wanted to. He was generally acknowledged to be the best coach in the city, and according to the guys in the schoolyard, every college team in the country had approached him at one time or another to leave Erasmus. But he'd stayed there, turning out top-notch teams for more than twenty years. I knew he didn't have to worry much about money, because over the summers he was head counselor at Camp Wanatoo. "I hear you have a boy named Izzie Cohen who's supposed to be pretty good, from what my players tell me," Mr. Goldstein said to our gym teacher. "Is he here?"

I was sure Izzie's heart was going to bounce out on the court, but he didn't seem flustered at all—he just stood up from where he was sitting beside me and walked straight over to Mr. Brown, our gym teacher. He didn't seem nervous at all. When he stood next to them, though, for the first time in my life I think I realized how short he was. He wasn't even as tall as Mr. Goldstein, and he seemed at least a foot and a half shorter than any of the Erasmus players.

"Well, well," Goldstein said, "so you're the little hot-shot I've been hearing about." He put his arm around Izzie's shoulders. "Let's see what you can do. John—throw Izzie here a ball—"

Goldstein had called to Johnny Rudy, who was the best player Erasmus had that year, and Johnny threw Izzie the ball.

"What's your favorite shot?" Goldstein asked.

"Set," Izzie said.

"Good—you just relax and let's see you take a few. When you feel loose—"

Izzie nodded and dribbled toward the foul-circle. All the Erasmus players stopped shooting and they stood around mumbling to each other and laughing. Nothing seemed to bother Izzie, though—he just went to the top of the key, put the ball over his eyebrows, flicked his wrists, and *swish!* the ball dropped through the basket.

I don't think our gym had ever heard a cheer like the one we let loose then. Izzie took the ball, picked out another spot on the floor, and shot again. He made six in a row from over twenty-five feet out before he missed one, and we didn't stop cheering the whole time.

For the rest of that year Izzie was *the* hero of our school. I'd have given anything to have been him. We still went to the schoolyard together every afternoon and on weekends, but things were different now. Before, we used to have to wait our nexts on Saturdays and Sundays, because all the guys who played were much older than us—so that we only got to play about twice all day—now, though, Izzie was getting picked all the time. The guys would set up picks for him and he'd bomb away, hardly ever missing. Once in a while—I guess because they felt sorry seeing me left out—I'd get picked too.

There was one guy who always used to pick the two of us to play with him when he came down. He was a big black guy—at least six five and he looked more like a fullback than a basketball player. His left eye crossed toward his right one a little and he had big pinkish lips that didn't seem to go right with his straight nose. When he played he was mean as the devil too, and he used to sort of snort when he dribbled. Nobody—but nobody—ever took a rebound away from him if he was planted under the boards, and when he started to drive, everybody backed out of the way or got run over. He'd been all-everything in high school, I figured, and I was sure—if I was sure of anything—that if he'd gone on to play pro ball he'd have been better than both Sweetwater Clifton and Carl Braun rolled into one.

He didn't come down too often—maybe once or twice every few months—and we used to wonder what he did the rest of the time. One day Izzie and I decided we'd find out, and that was how we first learned about the basketball scandals.

Everybody shut up as if they were dead when Izzie turned to him and asked the question. For a second, the way he looked, I thought he was going to get angry. Everybody had stopped playing—right in the middle of a game—and they all stared at us.

"Somethin' the matter?"

"No, nothin', Mack—"

"Then why'd you stop—?"

They started again real quick. Mack leaned back against the wire fence where we were sitting.

"I was in the scandals," he said.

"The what—?" I asked.

"The scandals, man—the fixes. You know—shavin' points, dumpin' games—the whole works—"

He sounded impatient and Izzie and I knew enough not to press him or say anything else. "Why I don't play for some college?" He laughed. "Because I got me a real good job now. I work at the Minit-Wash, soaping down cars, you know? That's how come I got such clean hands. Yeah, me, I got the cleanest hands of any fixer around—"

He looked at Izzie then. "You're gonna be a good ball-player some day, kid," he said. "You just don't let nobody sweet-talk you, that's all. You dump, if you want—if you're good enough to. Only be careful. That's the main thing. Ain't nothing wrong with it, far as I can see—just you gotta play it cool. Be cool, man, and you do all right."

Then Mack got up, draped his sweatshirt over his shoulder, and started to walk out of the schoolyard. He knew everybody was staring at him, but he didn't say anything. He just waved to Izzie and kept walking.

He never came back. During the rest of the year, the guys talked more about Mack and the fixes, so that after a while I understood the whole thing better. But Izzie had worshipped Mack even more than I had and he didn't like to hear any of the talk. Whenever anyone mentioned the fixes, Izzie would walk away.

That summer, for the first time I could remember, Izzie and I were separated. My father knew how much I loved basketball, and he and my mother sent me to the camp where Mr. Goldstein was head counselor. Izzie's parents couldn't afford to send him along with me—his father worked as a tailor in a cleaning store—so he stayed home. I sent him a postcard about once a week, telling him how many points I was scoring in full-court games and how I'd talked with Johnny Rudy, who was a waiter at the camp, and how he'd give me pointers, and how I called Mr. Goldstein "Uncle Abe," and things like that. When I got home at the end of August I didn't even wait to change my clothes. As soon as I'd dropped my suitcase and my glove and ball in my bedroom, I raced out of the house and ran as fast as I could to the schoolyard—and there was Izzie, playing with a bunch of kids.

It was great just watching him move around the court again, only something seemed different. He played from more of a crouch, even against kids shorter than himself, protecting the ball with his body, his back to the basket, and when he shot his set-shot now, it was from lower down—from the chin instead of the eyebrows. It didn't seem to affect his accuracy, though—he still swished the ball through. I walked into the yard, sat down, and waited.

When the game was over and his team had won, he came over to me. I stood up, smiling. "Boy—you sure did grow!" he said. They were his first words. "You must of grown six inches!"

"Five, according to the camp nurse," I said.

He hitched up his belt and looked away from me. "Well, pick two losers and let's play."

I was probably a foot taller than Izzie now and I could tell it bothered him. He didn't ask me anything about camp. He just concentrated on getting the game going. During that first time we played against each other, I didn't know what to do. Izzie was guarding me and I knew that if I took him into the pivot I could score lay-ups all day long. But I didn't want him to think I was taking it easy—

"Watch my new corner jump-shot," I called when the ball came to me. I dribbled away from the basket, Izzie next to me. "Goldstein taught it to me."

I didn't even hit the rim the first time I shot. Izzie's team got the rebound, passed it around, and Izzie started to take a set-shot. I was up on him right away and I smashed it. The next time I got the ball I hit a jump-shot from near the corner. I didn't try to block any more of Izzie's shots, but I didn't need to because he couldn't seem to hit for beans after I'd stuffed him that first time.

He was pretty quiet when we'd finished playing, but I just kept talking about everything I'd done all summer, and when I switched the subject to college and pro teams he began to loosen up a bit and pretty soon it was like old times, comparing ballplayers and predicting which teams were going to do what that year, and imitating the moves of our favorite players.

I went back to Camp Wanatoo the next summer and Izzie stayed in the city again. At the end of July his father died of cancer. Everybody knew it was going to happen and when Izzie wrote me about it he didn't seem too upset—mostly he sounded annoyed about the religious stuff that had accompanied the funeral. He said the rabbi had made a cut in the collar of his good black suit with a razor blade.

When we both entered Erasmus that September as freshmen, I was six one and Izzie wasn't much more than five feet. Five feet one or two. He never grew after that either. Maybe an inch.

He changed a lot too. We still saw each other every day and we had no trouble talking about sports and school, but he didn't come down to the schoolyard as much. He spent more time at home, taking care of his kid sister while his mother was away working. I'd stop by his house sometimes on my way home from the schoolyard for supper, and he'd be sitting on the couch, with his sister next to him, leaning on his shoulder. Her name was Miriam, and even though she was a year or so younger than we were, she was already bigger than Izzie. She wore a lot of Izzie's clothes—his shirts and his old baseball hats —and she reminded me of those refugee kids you saw in all the movies that came out after the war. I used to picture myself riding on the front of a Patton tank through a European village, with her looking up at me with big eyes, one hand in her mouth, while I'd reach into my pocket for a Hershey bar to give her. Izzie would read stories to her, and I'd stay with them for a while, drinking a Coke Izzie gave me, and listen also. Miriam hardly ever smiled, except when he read poems to her that he'd written himself. Then she'd giggle and snuggle up to him.

Their mother worked as a saleswoman at A & S's in downtown Brooklyn, near the Loew's Metropolitan and the Fox, and I'd sit in the kitchen with Izzie, talking about what the games had been like that afternoon—who was improving and which guys were going to try out for the Erasmus team that year and things like that—while he started getting supper ready for the three of them.

His poems were pretty good, I thought—they had a lot of strange words in them that he'd invented himself—and when we were sophomores he had some published in the school literary magazine, *The Erasmian.* From then on, he stopped talking with me so much about basketball and spent most of his time working on his poems and being with his sister. I played on the school team and he didn't, but we were still close friends. Not as close as we'd been, but pretty close, and even though I began spending most of my time after that with guys from the school team, I think I still thought of Izzie as my best friend. We'd meet each other at the corner every morning at 8:15 to walk to school together, and I was becoming too busy with practice sessions and games and dating girls to realize that I hardly ever stopped by his house any more and that he never came by mine to see me. Once in a while he'd come down to the schoolyard on a Sunday morning—he'd always have *The New York Times* tucked under his arm—and he'd get in a game or two of basketball, but he never stayed long.

We drifted apart during the last two years of high school. Because of his height, I guess, he didn't go out with girls too much, and most people I knew at school, especially the guys on the team, thought he was weird. He'd do crazy things— like mimeographing his own poems and handing them out in the cafeteria during lunch period—and even though I always defended him when people said how screwy he was becoming, by the time we were seniors I had to agree with them, though I never said so.

He was editor-in-chief of *The Erasmian* by then, and he had his own set of friends and hung out in Greenwich Village with them. He dressed strangely, too. He was never sloppy, but he'd wear crazy combinations—a bright-red polka-dot bow tie with a blue flannel shirt, or a vest over a T-shirt—things like that. When the yearbook ran the popularity contests that year —most likely to succeed, best-looking, class athlete—he ran for Joe Erasmus. He had big glossy pictures made of himself dressed in nothing but a bathing suit, with a beret on his head and a cigar in his mouth. He was staring at a skull he held in his right hand and under the picture he'd printed: YORICK SAYS —VOTE FOR IZZIE COHEN.

The second set of basketball scandals broke during our senior year of high school, near the end of the basketball season. By then I'd grown to about six four and was a starter on the Erasmus team. Mr. Goldstein had had a heart attack the previous spring, so he wasn't the coach any more. Instead, we had a young guy who'd been a big star at Erasmus and C.C.N.Y.—Al Newman. He was a good coach, but no Goldstein, and we were fighting just to get into the city playoffs. Mr. Goldstein had been made head of the Physical Education Department, but everybody knew that that didn't take much work. He'd sit in his office all day and talk with anyone who came by. He still came to practices and games, and he said he'd be back coaching by the following year, but his wife had told me at camp that the doctor would never allow it.

"I'm happy where he is now," she said. "And I'm grateful he has something to do with his days. You know he could stay home and live well—we have enough saved, Howie—and there's always the teachers' retirement plan waiting. But he wouldn't be happy away from Erasmus. It's part of him."

I knew that what she said was true. Even the money part. Aside from the camp job, there was a stock-brokers firm on Flatbush Avenue, about a block away from school, and Mr. Goldstein would spend his lunch hour there with some other teachers. He'd bought a brand-new Dodge after the summer, and he was still the sharpest dresser around.

A few days after two big stars from N.Y.U. and Columbia confessed to fixing games, Izzie telephoned me. He told me he had big news about the latest basketball scandal and that if I came to his house right away he'd give me the lowdown. He sounded mysterious about it all, and I told him I'd be there in a few minutes.

We sat in his bedroom and he offered me a cigar. I told him the basketball season was still on, so I wasn't smoking. He shrugged, leaned back in his swivel chair and inhaled. It was probably a year since I'd last been in his room, I realized. The room seemed smaller than it had a few years before, and it was cluttered—books and magazines stacked everywhere. On the walls he had pasted postcards of famous paintings you get from museums, and over his desk he'd painted a big hammer and sickle in red, white, and blue. There were shelves built into all the walls now, and half hidden by one over his bed, with clothes hanging over the edge across one side of it, I could see the picture of Bob Cousy. The edges were cracked and had been mended with scotch tape.

"What's the scoop?" I asked.

"This isn't easy to talk about, Howie," he began. He sipped from a glass. "Care for a drink?"

I shook my head. He leaned forward then and, even though we were just a few feet apart, he spoke in a whisper. "I have discovered, it seems, the newest of the basketball fixes." He paused and closed his eyes knowingly. "Your revered Mr. Goldstein—'Uncle Abe,' I believe you used to call him—is deeply implicated in them, I fear."

I stood up. "What—?" He smiled up at me. "Oh, come off it, huh, Izzie," I said. "He doesn't coach college—he doesn't even coach high school any more. And even if he did—"

"But Mr. Goldstein has quite an interest in the stock market, doesn't he? And you and I, Howie, we know what teachers' salaries are like . . ."

"Sure, sure—but his wife used to teach too—and he's head counselor at Wanatoo—"

"Ah yes, yes," he said. "All right. So add another thousand dollars. *Two* thousand dollars for the position of head counselor at Camp Wanatoo. Let's even add a bit more for the bonus he gets for each camper he signs up. Could all that account for his new car? His trip to Miami every Christmas? His own home on Bedford Avenue?" He knocked some ash from the end of his cigar onto the floor. "And have you ever noticed the coat that Mrs. Goldstein wears at our school's basketball games? I've been told that on chilly evenings during the summer she could be seen wearing her mink to the canteen of Camp Wanatoo. A marvelous image, I might note: mink at a canteen in a Catskill camp. I should use it. It's difficult to believe, Howie, I know, but our beloved coach—"

"Look, Izzie," I said, walking to the door. "You're really

going off the deep end. You better sober up and I'll talk to you on the way to school one day this week, okay? Or—"

"I will assuage your fears, Howard," Izzie said, rising and coming to me, his hand on my arm. "Mr. Goldstein has never conspired to prearrange the scores of high school basketball games—his dealings are far more nefarious." He returned to his desk and pulled a manila envelope from a drawer. He started to hand it to me and just as I reached for it he pulled it back. "I have in this envelope proof of the—what shall we call it?—the *finagling* Mr. Goldstein has been engaged in. In my wildest imagination I could never have invented anything more absurd —or more tragic for those of us who look to our teachers, to our boyhood heroes, for guidance, for example, for—"

"Come on," I said. "What's in the envelope—?"

"When the scandals broke last week, I found them rather ludicrous," he continued, sitting down again. "And it goes without saying that I do not at all condemn any of the players who have fixed games. For that philosophy I am still indebted to our one-time friend, Mack—if you remember him."

"I remember."

"This time I thought to myself: Izzie, I said, there is something cockeyed in all this fixing business—all this moralizing from teachers and rabbis and newspapers. Rigged quiz shows, point-shaving, payola—what's the big deal, eh?"

I sat down on the edge of his bed, leaned back, and listened as he talked on and on. I'd never felt so far away from him. The picture of Cousy was behind me and I wondered if Izzie had seen me glance at it. It was hard to remember any of the conversations we'd had when we'd been in grade school together, and it was harder to realize that the guy who was sitting across from me and talking had been the same guy I'd spent almost my whole life knowing. What I couldn't understand, I suppose, was how any guy who'd loved sports so much could have turned out this way. All of us—Corky, Louie, Eddie, Marty, Kenny, Stan—we'd all had our different ways, our own strange ideas once in a while. If I'd wanted to think about it, I guess I could have found something weird in everybody's home, including my own—you could never know everything that went on inside somebody's house, behind his doors when you weren't there. Still, if Corky had lived through all the stuff with his brother and his old man, and if Eddie could keep going, not having been able to play ball . . .

I shrugged, but Izzie didn't seem to notice. "I thought to myself," he was saying. "Izzie, I said, there must be some analogue, some microcosm in our own small Brooklyn–Jewish–Flatbush-Erasmus-world that would point up the inherent absurdity in these scandals. And so I said to myself: what honest good man in Erasmus could be tempted by the Almighty Dollar? Who could be our own Topaze? The answer came at once—Abraham Goldstein. In my mind's eyes I saw it all: the parallel to the national scandals." He spread his hand outward in an arc, as if the words he spoke were hanging in front of him. "Famous coach receives bribes from local Sporting Goods Store in return for letting them sell Erasmus boys and girls their gym suits—"

"*What*—?" I got up, then sat down again and started to laugh. I shouldn't take him so seriously, I thought to myself.

"Yes, it's funny, isn't it, Howie? Goldstein grows rich while Levy's Sporting Goods Store gets sole rights to sell us T-shirts, gym shorts, and jockstraps. Most men who are possessed by visions—Blake and Coleridge come to mind at once—rarely see them manifested in their own lives. But I have, Howie. While Levy's has been supplying five thousand boy and girls with their gym apparel, Mr. Goldstein has been getting what is known along Flatbush Avenue as a good old-fashioned kick-back."

He leaned back, somewhat breathless, obviously pleased with himself. "If you're lying," I said, "I swear to God I'll ram my fist straight through your face."

"Tomorrow New York City shall know the truth," Izzie went on. "My campaign will begin." He took a sheet of paper from his envelope and handed it to me. It was handwritten in capital letters:

WHILE MR. GOLDSTEIN GROWS RICH WE WEAR
LEVY'S JOCKSTRAPS.
HAS ANYONE COMPARED PRICES???
WHAT IS BEHIND THE LATEST EVENT IN
THE GROWING SERIES OF ATHLETIC FIXES???

It was signed, "The Shadow."

"You're out of it," I said, throwing the paper back at him. "I swear to God you are—"

"Ah, but like another famous madman, there is reason in my madness, eh? Tomorrow five hundred mimeographed copies of the sheet you have just seen will appear mysteriously in the classrooms and corridors of our school—"

I didn't bother arguing with him. I just told him again that I thought he was nuts, and I left. On the staircase going out of his house, I met his sister. She smiled at me the way she always did when I saw her in the halls at Erasmus—not able to keep her eyes straight on me—and I felt uncomfortable this time. Her arms were full of packages from the store and I fumbled a little, offering to take them upstairs for her, but she wouldn't let me and I was just as glad. She said something about my not coming by their house for a long time and I nodded. She was leaning back against the banister and I was a step below her. I could tell she wanted to talk with me, but I didn't have anything to say. She asked me about my family, and said she'd seen how well I was doing on the basketball team, and I nodded again. Her hair was long—kind of dark brown—and it wasn't combed too well. She shuffled her packages into the crook of one of her arms and brushed it back. "How's Izzie?" she asked.

I shrugged, "Okay, I guess."

She nodded. "It'd be good if you could come by more often, but—" She stopped, then sighed. "Don't mind me, Howie," she said. "I don't know sometimes—you know what I mean?" I felt a little dizzy. There was something in her face, the way she stood—kind of relaxed, yet unsure of herself— that made her seem younger and older at the same time. "Well," she said when I didn't answer—a kind of weak smile under her red cheeks. "I guess we can't hold these packages all day, huh? I'll get upstairs to Izzie—Momma's still at the store—"

I asked her if she worked there too now—at A & S's—and she said yes, and then I said I'd see her at school sometime and I ducked down the stairs.

The next day Izzie's notices were all around the school and lots of guys came to me and asked about them, figuring that only Izzie would pull a stunt like that. I played dumb. When Mrs. Goldstein telephoned me that night and asked about the notices, I told her I couldn't figure out what they meant.

Two days later Izzie had mimeographed up a new batch of sheets. On these he'd placed two lists: on the left-hand side were the prices Erasmus students paid for their gym uniforms, and on the right-hand side were the prices Davega charged for the same things. In almost every case, the Davega prices were lower.

Mr. Goldstein didn't show up for school the next day, but Izzie's notices did. This time he'd printed up a list of Mr. Goldstein's property and expenses—his house, his car, Mrs. Goldstein's mink coat, the trips to Miami, etc.—with the estimated cost of each. Then he'd listed Mr. Goldstein's salaries from school and camp. Across the bottom of the sheet he'd printed: "Something is rotten in the borough of Brooklyn."

Two days passed and there were no more messages from "The Shadow." The weekend came and we won an important game against Madison, insuring us of a spot in the playoffs. I hoped Izzie would have stopped his campaign by the time we got back to school Monday, but he hadn't. This time he'd printed leaflets which seemed to prove that Sears-Roebuck had sent a color television set to Mr. Goldstein's house and had sent the bill to Levy's Sporting Goods Store. At the bottom of this sheet was a quotation from Edmund Burke: "All that is necessary for the forces of evil to win in the world is for enough good men to do nothing." The *New York Post* carried an item about Izzie's leaflets in their evening edition that day— I figured Izzie must have mailed them the material—and on Tuesday night Mrs. Goldstein called me again. She pleaded with me to do something.

I called Izzie right after she hung up, and he was obviously excited by the fact that Mrs. Goldstein had been telephoning me. There was no talking with him, though. When I mentioned Mr. Goldstein's bad heart, he only carried on more than ever. "Our names are all written in the Book of Life, Howard. I am not moved by your plea for pity . . ." I hung up on him.

A day or two later, our coach told us that Mr. Goldstein was going to send in a letter of resignation to the Board of Education. The guys all looked at me when he said it, as if it were my responsibility to do something, but I just shrugged and ignored them. Izzie hadn't been seen in school for the previous two days. I went home for supper and took a walk along Flatbush Avenue. A little after nine I found myself knocking at Mr. Goldstein's door. I don't know what I would have said to him if he'd been there, but he wasn't. Some neighbors saw me and told me that he'd been taken to the hospital a few hours before.

If Izzie had been there right then, I think I might have killed him. I headed straight for his house. By the time I reached it, though, I'd calmed down and decided to call the hospital to see how Mr. Goldstein was.

"Greetings, greetings, my basketball-hero comrade." It was Izzie. He was leaning against a lamppost, in the shadows, puffing on a cigar. His beret was tilted to one side, so that it nearly covered his right eye.

"How long have you been watching me?" I asked.

"Forever, forever, Howie—since we were boys together, since we came in trailing those wings of glory . . . or were they clouds?"

"Mr. Goldstein's in the hospital." I said it matter-of-factly.

Izzie nodded, as if he knew already. "Cowards—cowards die many times before their—"

"Oh, shut your trap already, huh? Just can it!" I took a step toward him and drew back my fist.

"Come, come," he said calmly. "Get it over with. Hit me. Use your physical power. What else do you have, after all?"

"Forget it," I said, shoving my hands in my pockets. "There's no use talking with you—"

"Have you seen our friends down the street?" Izzie asked. I turned and looked. It was dark and I couldn't make out much. At the end of the block, though, I could see the shapes of a group of guys. "I await them in the light of the lamppost. They called a while ago and told me they were coming to *get me* . . ."

I saw them coming toward us now. There were about a dozen guys, and I could make out faces.

"Are you totally nuts?" I said. "Get inside your damned house. Those guys'll beat shit out of you."

"If that will satisfy their animal desires, then perhaps—"

"Don't be an ass—get inside, Izzie. They'll *kill* you!"

He didn't move. I whirled around. The guys were almost to us now—some of them were on the basketball team with me, and the rest were jocks from the football team. I looked back at Izzie. His eyes weren't shifting. Instead, he had this weird smile on his face, and he just kept puffing away on his cigar, blowing smoke rings.

"You're the first one here," Hank Ebel said to me. "That means you got rights to go at him first, Howie."

"Ah, lay off, huh?" I said. "You'll just get in trouble if you do anything to him—"

"I need no defenders!" Izzie shouted. His voice was strong. "Let them have their way with me. We are in the arena, Howie!"

"You're not gonna take up for him, are ya, Howie?" Stan Reiss asked. I looked at the others—Harvey Rosen, Jerry Charyn, Vic Fontani. "No," I said. "No—but I'm not—I'm not gonna let you guys get yourselves in trouble. Just leave him be."

"Bullshit."

One of the guys made a move toward Izzie and I backed up, spreading my arms out to protect him. He screamed. "Let me alone, Howie—I can fight my own battles. Let me alone! Let these boors tear me apart for telling them the truth. Let me alone. Let me alone . . ."

One of the football players grabbed at me to shove me aside, but I didn't move.

"Look, Howie," he said. "We got nothin' against you— but if you don't let us get him, we're gonna have to get you too."

"Okay," I said. I meant it—but I knew already that it didn't matter. I wasn't going to be able to help Izzie. Still, I stood my ground, more tired than defiant. Somebody grabbed at my shoulder and I shook him off. Someone came at me from the other side and I swung. Then they were on me. They didn't hit me much. Just grabbed me by the legs and arms. I fought and swung but there were too many of them. They dragged me away and a few of them sat on me while the rest took care of Izzie.

It didn't take them long. I heard him laughing, shouting something—poetry, I guess—and then I heard him scream. He really howled! You could hear windows sliding open in all the apartment houses on the block.

The guys let me up a second later and they took off down the street. Izzie was lying next to the lamppost. His lips were moving, producing a strange sound—I couldn't tell if it was whimpering or laughing. I got him under one arm and helped him into his building and up the stairs. When we got into the apartment and his mother saw him, she nearly fainted. I told her to call a doctor, but she was too paralyzed to do anything. Miriam came out of her room then, and while she got Izzie to a couch in the living room, I telephoned. Izzie'd been pretty well mashed up around his face—and his left arm hung limply. While I held a compress on his eye, Miriam coaxed her mother into the bedroom and got her to lie down. Then she came back in. I looked at her, shrugging to indicate that I was sorry—hoping she'd know I didn't have any part of it. "When it snows it pours," she said. "Where's it all gonna end, is what I want to know. You ever see anything like us?" She seemed in command and I just did what she told me to, getting Mercurochrome and Band-Aids from the bathroom. She had a ballpoint pen stuck in her hair right over her ear, and her sweater was loose. "I'm glad we weren't working tonight, is all. I just don't know sometimes, Howie, you know what I mean?" Izzie blinked and smiled at us. "You jerk," Miriam said to him, and he smiled bigger. She talked to me like my own sister. "Like, where's it all gonna end, Howie?" I shrugged again, and she seemed to take this for a good enough response. Her mother started crying from the other room, chanting in Yiddish about Izzie and Izzie's father. "See what I mean?" Miriam said, and she left me. It was crazy, in the middle of everything, but I realized that for the last few minutes my eyes had been fastened right on her chest, as if I'd noticed for the first time what an enormous pair of knockers she had.

"Well, well, Howie my friend," Izzie began. His voice cracked. "I—I suppose I cannot say *Et tu, Brute*—"

In the other room I could hear Miriam. "Shush, shush— you worked hard today, Momma—you take it easy. It's okay, Momma. I'll take care of everything. It's okay . . ."

I kept thinking that Izzie's mother was really his grandmother. His bottom lip was already swollen to twice its size and both his eyes were starting to close. I got more ice from the kitchen. When I came back, the door to Mrs. Cohen's room was closed and Miriam was washing up some blood from the couch. She shook her head, and drew in deeply on a cigarette. I kept my eyes off her chest. "There are real idiots in this world, aren't there, Howie? I mean—"

The doctor came in a little while and I was glad. He examined all of Izzie's cuts and swellings, put his arm in a sling, and told him to come to the office the next day for X-rays. When he left, Izzie and I went into his room together and Miriam left us alone. The whole time the doctor had been there, Izzie had seemed cocky. As soon as he got into his room, though, he collapsed, just sort of folding and dropping to the floor. I lifted him to his chair and he opened his eyes halfway. He was shivering and I threw a blanket over his shoulders.

"Should I call the doctor again?" I asked. "Or get Miriam?"

He shook his head from side to side. He seemed totally sober now and he gave me a long look, as if he were trying to tell me he couldn't figure out why it had turned out this way either. I got him to lay down on his bed, under the covers, and then I left. "You try to sleep," I said. "Maybe I'll stop by in a few days."

Mr. Goldstein was on critical for a week, and then he began to improve. He didn't come back to school, though. I got a Graduation card from him that June. Izzie returned to classes about a week and a half later and, to my surprise, nobody paid much attention to him. We were all too busy worrying about the playoffs and which colleges we would be going to—events passed pretty quickly in those days. Izzie got a state scholarship and was supposed to go to Columbia the next fall, but when I was home for Thanksgiving during my first year at college my mother told me that he'd dropped out of school and was living at home.

The next time I saw him was at the end of my first year of college. I'd driven home with some guys who were on the freshman team with me and I took them over to the P.S. 92 schoolyard to show them around. I'd improved during my first year of college and I didn't have much trouble with the Erasmus players. There were some other guys at the schoolyard who played college ball, and I could hold my own with them too. I'd developed a good outside shot and it surprised a lot of the guys who'd known me at Erasmus. My friends and I played a few games and then we started to leave.

"Hey, Howie—you see your friend Izzie lately?" one of the Erasmus players asked.

"No."

"There he is. Didn't you notice? He's a real star now."

The guy laughed and I looked where he'd pointed. On

the other side of the wire fence, at the far end of the playground, I could see a bunch of grade-school kids playing basketball. I had to squint at first. Then I recognized him. He was playing with a group of little kids. Some of them were already taller than he was. I turned away quickly.

"One thing you gotta admit—he's got the best set-shot of all of 'em!"

Everybody laughed.

The Child

THE CHILD had not been wanted. He said they couldn't afford it yet; she said they hadn't done all the things they had planned to do. They thought, during the second month, of giving up the child, but decided against it. They agreed that she would continue to teach until the seventh month, and they told each other that they would love the child anyway, that somehow things would work out.

As the months went by and the child began to grow inside her, Helen changed; not only did she begin to forget about the many things they had hoped to do while still not "burdened" with children, but she found that she was beginning to look forward to becoming a mother. "Maybe it was best this way, honey," Gary would say at night when they lay in bed together. "Maybe we were only kidding ourselves, maybe we would have just let the years slip by, inventing excuses, if this hadn't happened to us." After spending an evening with their friends they would take pleasure, almost secretly, it seemed, from comparing themselves to those married couples who were still without children, from noting how the child was drawing them closer to one another.

She wrote to her family and to his, and they received long letters of congratulations and sizable checks from both sets of parents. They were amazed, they told each other, at how easily they could accept the gifts, without feelings of guilt, of obligation. Helen delighted in her third-grade children as she had never done before, and he became more optimistic about their financial situation. Several times a week he would sit down on the living-room couch with her and he would go over the figures—showing her, with pencil and paper, that even if she didn't return to teaching for three years, everything would be all right. She praised him for his ability to arrange things, to foresee possibilities she would never have thought of.

What pleased them most, though, was feeling the baby, listening to it. He would lie with his ear pressed gently to her stomach, and every time he heard a sound they would experience a thrill which seemed magical. "I think I'm falling in love with you all over again," she said to him. "It's so strange."

She had never seemed more beautiful to him, and he had never loved her more. They had never, he felt, been this close. Still, as the months went by, he became increasingly uneasy. In particular, he was afraid of what would happen to her were something to go wrong. He called her doctor and the doctor told him not to worry. He did, anyway. Helen didn't, he saw, and this worried him even more. While she was making supper one evening he leafed through a copy of *Life* magazine and found an article about Thalidomide babies who were being rehabilitated through the use of artificial limbs. Had Helen seen the article? If, as he hoped, she had not seen it, what was he to do? If he threw the magazine away without telling her, and if she found out, she would think that he was treating her like a child, overprotecting her. "Have you finished with all the magazines in the rack?" he called to her. "It's getting stuffed." "I'm finished with them," she called back.

At the office, his friends told him that she would begin feeling ugly and neglected, that her eyes would turn inward, that she would begin neglecting him—he waited, but none of these things happened. Still, he was afraid for her, for the baby. He went to see their doctor, and the doctor smiled at his fears. Gary considered, and then told the doctor about the time, before they were married, when Helen had been ill. The doctor nodded; Helen had told him all about it. There was nothing to worry about. If anything, giving birth to a healthy child would, he said, serve to close the door even more securely on that period of her life. What if the child wasn't healthy, he asked. The doctor replied that something could always go wrong, of course—there were never guarantees; as things stood, though, Helen was coming along beautifully and he didn't see any cause for worry: there was more chance of a safe falling on Gary while he walked in the street, he laughed, than of something being wrong with the child.

Without telling Helen, Gary telephoned her mother and urged her to come and stay with them, but Helen's mother said that she wasn't needed yet. She thought she would come to New York after the baby was born, when she could be more helpful. Gary said all right. When it came time to give up their own pleasures, he became wary again, he waited for something to happen, but she neither neglected him nor felt neglected; if anything, she became more affectionate than she had been before, and at night her only concern was that he might go to sleep unsatisfied.

One evening he tested her by opening the middle drawer of the living-room secretary and taking out the European travel folders they had collected. She smiled. "We'll go some day," he said. "You'll see." "We'll go some day," she agreed, her hand touching his cheek. The radiance in her own cheeks disturbed him. On weekends they saw their friends, and when he would mention her "strangeness," nobody seemed to understand him. Everybody said that she was beautiful in pregnancy and would make a beautiful mother. His friends teased him about being "put off," and afterwards she would console him, more soft, more kind than ever.

Then he seized on something definitely amiss: she had not sensed his worry. There it was, he told himself. She was too placid, too understanding, much too free of all anxiety. He telephoned the doctor again and explained; wasn't it unnatural for her to have no worries whatsoever and not to sense the fact that he was worried? The doctor laughed. "Do me a favor, Gary," he said. "Tell her what you've told me and see what happens."

He did. "Oh, you're sweet," she said, cuddling to him in bed. "Of course I know you've been worried. You've been so dear—"

"You knew?"

"Of course." She laughed again. "Everybody knows. You're not very good at hiding things. But don't be glum, dear one. I like you this way. Somebody has to do the worrying for the three of us."

Three weeks before she was due, she told him that she had invited Mrs. Hart to have dinner with them. Mrs. Hart had been their landlady before they were married. "Won't she be surprised!" she exclaimed. He didn't answer. She snuggled up to him. "I just thought she would get a kick out of seeing us together—you know, as a married couple. Remember the way she used to wink at me whenever she'd see us going in and out of your apartment?" He remembered. They had not seen Mrs. Hart for over two years. She giggled: "I liked living in sin with you. Do you know that?" He tried to smile. "You don't mind if she comes, do you? When I told her I was Mrs. Fogel, she said, 'Gary's mother?' Then I said, 'No, I'm *Helen* Fogel, Mrs. Hart,' and she congratulated me and said that she'd seen the announcement in the *Times.* Do you mind if she comes?"

He said he didn't mind; he couldn't help but feel, though, that something stupid—something terrible—would happen if Mrs. Hart came. He thought, he waited. Then the day before Mrs. Hart was supposed to come, he telephoned their doctor and told him everything. The important thing was Helen and the baby, he told himself. He had been foolish to wait this long. The doctor didn't see anything particularly wrong, or antic, in what Helen was doing, but he suggested that Gary see a psychiatrist if Gary thought that would help. "I'll go," Gary said. The psychiatrist listened to Gary and agreed with him that it was natural for an expectant father to worry, but he didn't seem to find anything fearful in what had happened. Still, until the baby was born, Gary could come for sessions twice a week if he liked. Gary felt uncomfortable, silly, and said that he supposed he was just a typical nervous father-to-be; he left before the time was up.

That night Helen told him that she had telephoned Mrs. Hart and canceled the dinner arrangements. "It would have made you uncomfortable, wouldn't it?" she said. "Anyway, it was a silly idea in the first place."

Two and a half weeks later, three days ahead of schedule, she went to the hospital. She called him at his office, and by the time he arrived she was in the delivery room. When he was allowed into her room afterward, she was sleepy, but happier than ever. "I saw the whole thing," she said. "It was beautiful."

She came home from the hospital three days later, and her mother flew in from Cleveland and stayed with them for two weeks. The girl had weighed seven pounds four ounces at birth, and everyone agreed that she looked just like Helen. Gary's parents drove in from Boston, stayed for a week, and then left. As the doctor had predicted, his anxiety was gone as suddenly as it had come. The two of them spent endless, time-less hours watching their child; the hands and feet—the finger-nails, the soft wrinkles at the knuckles, the lines across the palm, under the toes—they fascinated him most: so delicate, so perfect, so miniature. Proudly, he told all their friends that whenever the baby started crying, all he had to do was lift it and she would stop. Once in a while, out of habit, he supposed, he would find himself observing Helen, noting her behavior, but she gave him no cause for worry now, and he was pleased. He had been a bit concerned at first that she had experienced no pain whatever during labor, but the doctor assured him that her experience was not abnormal. "It happens," he said.

At night they took the baby into their bed with them and watched her, talked to her. Then they would return her to the crib and talk for hours about how glad they were that they had not given her up. "I've never loved you so much," he said. "Soon," she said. "Soon." He studied their finances, showed her the results of his calculations, and they agreed that they would have to be careful. They checked with their doctor after the first month and then put up a calendar next to their bed with the probable "evil days" circled in red.

Two days later the baby broke out in a rash that covered her arms and neck. They went to the doctor, and he told them not to be alarmed. He prescribed a skin cream and said that the rash would probably disappear in a week or less. "It's summer, though," he said, "and the heat will tend to aggravate it. But don't worry. It's nothing." They asked him the other question, and he smiled and said that it was all right. Hadn't he told them so the other day? They went home, happy, relieved. The baby started crying in the car, stopped, then started again when they were in the apartment. "Poor little thing," Helen said as she smoothed the cream onto her daughter. Gary watched and felt helpless. The baby stopped, then started again a half hour later. They stayed in the bedroom, and he held her. When he offered her to Helen, she said to let her cry. "There's nothing to worry about," she said. "You heard the doctor." "But the rash is worse than before," he said. "It's spreading to her chest." "There's nothing to worry about," she repeated. "Come to bed." He rocked the baby gently against his shoulder, and she howled even more. "Come to bed," Helen said, undressing. He put the baby in its crib, and she cried in a way that terrified him; she seemed to be gagging. "Please look at her," he said. Helen got up, trailing her underclothes, letting them drop to the floor; she looked at the baby and the baby stopped crying. "See?" she said, touching his arm with her forefinger. "Now come to bed." He went with her. "I'm so tired," he said when she'd put the light out. They touched each other gently, saying that the baby would be all right in a few days, and then he kissed her and told her to get a good night's sleep. "I hope the baby sleeps until morning," he said, but just as he spoke the baby started crying again. He turned on the night lamp and got out of bed. There were large red splotches on her face. "Shouldn't we call the doctor?" he asked. "Come to bed," she said. The baby kept crying. He held his child for a while and tried to soothe her by rubbing more salve on the red spots. The baby's skin seemed red-hot to him. Gradually, the crying stopped. When he put her back in the crib, she whimpered.

A quarter of an hour later he asked Helen to get up. "Guess we'd better get the new safety valve out," he said, nodding toward the calendar. "You never know." She clung to him, her arms locked around his shoulders. "Do you want me to get it for you?" he asked. She moaned. "Do you?" he asked again. When she didn't answer, he stroked her hair and said that he would get it for her. But she wouldn't let him go. "Please," he said. "We have to, honey. I don't want to, either, but we have

to." "No," she said, clutching him. "No." "But it's an 'evil day,'"
he said, laughing. "I don't care," she said fiercely. Their child
began wailing again, and he tried, gently this time, to get away
from Helen so that he could tend to the child. She was choking
on something now, wailing, sputtering. "I don't care," Helen
said again. The baby's screaming stopped for a while. When it
started the next time—louder, more painful than before—he
tried to get away, but by then he knew that he could do nothing but agree with what she repeated endlessly in his ear, that
there was nothing to worry about.

Elijah

ONCE, I remember, Izzie tried to get up a petition for us to sign, saying that unless Hebrew school was changed to two afternoons a week instead of three, we would all get our parents to switch to another synagogue. But Mrs. Bluestone caught him with it before he'd gotten half a dozen signatures on it and by the time the rabbi got through with Izzie he wasn't in a mood to pass around any more petitions. He didn't hate Hebrew school any less. None of us did—in fact, if anybody had taken a vote in those days on what we hated most in the world, Hebrew school would have won easily. It wasn't so bad in the winter, when you couldn't do much outside, but in the fall and spring when you wanted to be playing stickball and punchball or going to the Parade Grounds for hardball, those three afternoons a week were enough to turn us all into Catholics.

While we'd wait for classes to start—or during the five-minute recess we had every day at four o'clock—we'd talk about what a lousy deal it was being Jewish, and sometimes when it was a really beautiful day outside and we felt brave,

159

we'd parade up and down outside the bathrooms, singing "On-ward Christian Soldiers." Louie would be lookout and when he'd see one of the teachers or the rabbi coming, he'd yell "Chickee!" and we'd break ranks and be sitting on the steps, making believe we'd been studying all along.

Usually, if the rabbi came, he'd lecture us about "dese-crating the Temple of God" with what he called our "vulgari-ties." I could never look into his eyes when he spoke—and the same went for most of the guys. He was a little man, short and stocky—not much bigger than we were then—but he had a way of looking at you that made you certain God was going to find some special way to punish you. "You have come to the House of God dressed like an iceman!" he said to me once, and I never came to Hebrew school without a tie again.

Probably the worst thing about Hebrew school was in the winter when it would be dark out by the time we left and these tough guys would be waiting across Bedford Avenue in the doorway to the Flatbush Boys Club or Al Roon's Health Club —they'd make fun of us for having to go to school so much. And then, when we'd hide our Hebrew books under our coats, the girls would walk next to us for protection—or they'd get the Negro janitor to come out from the synagogue and chase the guys from across the street. There was nothing we hated more than having anybody think we needed protection. It made the tough guys tease us even more about being sissy Jews, and then we could do only one of three things: feel bad, punch the girls around and throw their books in the air, or answer the tough guys back, cursing them the way they cursed us, calling them dirty Micks or Wops, and telling them they weren't such "rocks," that they talked so big because they were scared to fight. A few times they chased us down Bedford Avenue, and a few times everybody kept daring and double-daring everybody else until we had a real fight. But the fights never lasted long—

most of the time a grown-up from the Boys Club or the synagogue would break it up—and the worst anybody ever got was a bloody nose or a good shiner. Then, for a few weeks after, we'd all tell each other how tough we'd been or how many punches we'd connected on, and we'd get pretty brave in answering the Boys Club guys back. Izzie had a whole repertoire of lines about nuns and brothers and what dogs did to "rocks," and we'd stand around the steps of the synagogue cheering him on as he shouted them across the street. The thing we'd all wait for would be when he'd say, "If you're so strong, let's see you pick that up—" and then he'd rear back and let fly with a tremendous gob of spit, which, when he caught the wind right, would usually land three-quarters of the way across Bedford Avenue. Izzie could spit farther than any guy I've ever met.

About the only time all year when anybody looked forward to Hebrew school were the few weeks in the spring when we got ready for Field Day. We'd get to the Hebrew school at about 3:30 but we'd only spend a half hour, maybe less, in the classroom and then Mr. Gleicher would take all of us over to the Parade Grounds for practice. Field Day was supposed to be the celebration for Lag B'Omer, a Jewish holiday, and all the Hebrew schools in Brooklyn got together for it at George Wingate Field. There were a lot of speeches by rabbis and politicians, and some Hebrew music and pageants and dances that the girls would put on. The only thing we cared about was the track meet. Every Hebrew school in Brooklyn sent a team, and ours had come in first more than any of them. It was the only thing about the school that any of us were proud of.

Our synagogue was called Congregation Shaare Torah, and it was pretty poor. It only had two floors: an upstairs temple that was nice enough, and a downstairs part that they called the "vestry rooms." They were very dingy—in fact, they weren't rooms at all. Just a basement with a bunch of sliding doors. They used this basement for everything—classrooms, offices, the rabbi's study, the Junior Congregation Services on Saturday, dances, meetings, High Holy Day services, Sunday afternoon clubs, and even Bar Mizvahs and weddings. They were always announcing fund-raising campaigns to build a new center—but during the years we went there they never did, so that we used to be envious of the guys who went to other synagogues where they had basketball courts and swimming pools and ballrooms. The only bright spot in the whole place for us—aside from the fun we had stealing kids' books and passing them to the back row and under the sliding walls into the next classroom—was the trophy case outside the rabbi's study. There were silver and gold cups in it, inscribed, and medals, and photographs of winning track teams with the guys laughing and hanging their arms over each other's shoulders. We spent a lot of time gazing into that trophy case and there was this one photograph of a college runner, I remember, in a Columbia uniform, and he was holding his running shoes, leaning against a high hurdle and brushing his hair from his eyes while he smiled at you. I used to spend hours in front of my mirror at home, trying to get his expression on my face, imagining the day I would be able to send a picture like that back to the Hebrew school. "To Mr. Gleicher, a great coach," the inscription on it would read, "from your former student, Howie."

Next to the trophy case, on a wall with the plaques which represented trees bought in Israel, was the story we all knew by heart, about Mr. Gleicher, who had been a hero with the Haganah during the Arab–Israeli war in 1948. The story came from an old issue of *World Over*, a magazine that was given out to Hebrew school kids all over the country, and there were pictures in it of Mr. Gleicher in his Haganah uniform—and one of him in his track uniform. That was what interested us most,

I suppose—the fact that until he'd had his knee blasted in an Arab mine field, he had been known as "the world's fastest Jew" and was supposed to have been a sure bet to win all kinds of medals for Israel in the 1952 Olympics. According to the article, Mr. Gleicher had been born in Poland, but had fled to Israel with his family in 1938. Then, when his father had died in 1940, he and his mother had been brought to America by members of their family who had escaped here from the Nazis. The article had a lot of stuff about how much they'd been persecuted, and how many members of his family had died at which concentration camps—but the important thing as far as we were concerned was Mr. Gleicher's track feats—his running times and medals and records—and how, when he was going to Brooklyn College, he'd gotten the job at our school, teaching Hebrew to help support his family. It was a nice feeling to see the name of your Hebrew school in print. Except for the one year in the U. S. Army and the two years he'd spent in Israel after the war had broken out there, he'd taught at our school steadily since 1942, and we'd come in first or second at Field Day every year except for the three he was away fighting.

The year most of us were in the sixth grade at P.S. 92, though, we figured we didn't stand a chance even to place in the first five. What had happened was this: all the guys a year ahead of us in Hebrew school who were good runners had had their Bar Mizvahs by about April—and, naturally, all of them had immediately stopped coming to Hebrew school. This meant that even though Izzie, Stan, Marty, and I were pretty good runners for our age, in the major event of the day—the Senior Relay—we'd be racing against guys a year older. We knew our school would score its share of points in all the other races, but unless you came in first or second in the Senior Relay, you didn't stand much chance to win the championship and the Bar Kochba Trophy.

Still, we worshipped Mr. Gleicher, and we kept telling

each other that if we tried hard enough, we could do it. So every day, starting about the middle of April—Field Day was scheduled for the second Sunday in May—we were out at the Parade Grounds practicing. Even on days when we didn't have Hebrew school. Louie had a stop watch and a record of winning times for the last few years, and we drove ourselves until our tongues were hanging out, trying to equal them. We made progress, and you could tell from the quiet way Mr. Gleicher would encourage us that he knew how hard we were trying, but after a couple of weeks it became obvious that it was going to take a miracle for us to win.

Then Elijah appeared. One afternoon, when there was no Hebrew school and we were out at the Parade Grounds by ourselves, running laps around the baseball backstops, he suddenly appeared beside us. "C'mon, Jewboys!" he called. "Catch me, mothers!" Then he was gone, flying by us as if we were standing still. He'd slow down sometimes, but when we'd be almost up to him, he'd just laugh and take off again.

The next afternoon, while the girls were off by themselves practicing their dances and we were jogging around the field with Mr. Gleicher shouting to one of us, and then to another, to take the lead, he showed up again. "C'mon, Jewboys," he said. "Catch me, mothers—" We took after him as fast as we could, but he flew away from us as if, as Izzie put it, he had jets in his ass. Once, when we were coming around the last turn for the final fifty-yard sprint, he even turned around and ran backwards for about twenty yards, but we still couldn't catch him. "You Jewboys sure can run!" he laughed.

When we had all collapsed on the grass in front of Mr. Gleicher, Elijah hardly seemed tired. He stood away from us, at a distance of about thirty or forty yards, leaning against a tree, watching us while Mr. Gleicher talked. "You must learn to breathe in regular patterns," he said. "From down low. You must stretch your diaphragms." None of us was listening to him too much, though. We all kept glancing over at Elijah. Mr. Gleicher had seen him too, we knew, and he smiled in Elijah's direction—but he didn't say anything.

On the way home that day, most of us were pretty depressed, and some of us even began complaining that Mr. Gleicher wasn't such a great coach after all, that maybe it was his fault we weren't improving. Stan Reiss even said what I'd thought a few times—how quiet Mr. Gleicher always was, how he never *inspired* you—but Izzie got mad at this. "A guy like that's been through a lot," he said, and he reminded us about his knee getting shot up, and about his wife. We knew that he had married an Israeli girl who had died in 1949—it said so in the *World Over* article—and from the first day we entered Hebrew school and we'd heard about Mr. Gleicher from the older kids, they had also passed along rumors about her death, with some pretty gory stories about how she'd been captured by Arabs and what they had done to her before they finally killed her. Then, just as Stan was telling Izzie he was sorry he'd blamed Mr. Gleicher—we were at the corner of Caton Avenue and East 21st Street, outside the BMT station— Elijah was suddenly alongside us.

"Hey," he said. "You guys wanna buy things?"

We stopped—none of us knew quite what to do. What took us by surprise most, I suppose, was that he had come right up to us that way, as if what had happened at the Parade Grounds had never taken place. "C'mere," he said, motioning to the wall overlooking the train tracks. "Make a circle round me so the cops don't see. C'mon—you don't gotta be scared. You with the stop clock," he said, meaning Louie, "you be lookout." There were about eight of us and we followed him to the wall. He fished into his side pocket. "You want cigarettes? I got Chesterfield and Old Gold. I give 'em to you cheap—ten cents a pack."

"We're in training," Stan said.

"Yeah. I seen you," he said, and rolled his eyes. "Okay."
He put the cigarettes away. "I got some good rings—take any
one you like, a nickel each," he said, tinkling a handful in front
of us. "You go to the store to buy 'em, they cost you forty-nine
cents each. The ones with pearls cost eighty-nine, I let you have
'em for ten cents. How 'bout it?" None of us said anything, and
Elijah flashed his fingers in front of our eyes. On every one of
them except the thumbs there was a different ring. "I wear 'em,
you whiteboys can wear 'em too. Only these ain't Woolworth
rings. These the real thing I wear. This here's a genuine ruby,
and this a topaz with a 14-karat gold setting. You believe it. I
get you these too, you don't like the fake ones." He looked up.
He was a skinny kid, an inch or two shorter than most of us.
"You wear these rings, you start to run faster." He laughed, but
none of us joined in. "Okay," he said, putting the rings away. "I
show you something else. I got some necklaces you can give
your mother for her birthday." He drew out pearl necklaces,
then ankle bracelets, combs, fountain pens—but we still
couldn't speak; it was as if he had us paralyzed. Even Izzie
seemed flabbergasted. "How come you don't want nothing?
Ain't you got money? My old man says you Jews got all the
money." He rolled his eyes again. "C'mon guys, buy something
from me, huh? I got to make some money today. I come home
without money, I catch hell." He licked his lips. "I tell you what
I do for you—you give me orders, tell me what you want, and I
see if I can get it for you. Get you good prices." He took a pad
from a back pocket and spit on the end of a chewed-up pencil.
"What you want—baseball gloves? some nice ties to wear for
school? a pipe for your father—?"

"Okay," Izzie said, and we all jerked our heads toward
him. "Can you get me a Pee Wee Reese model glove?"

I gulped, but Elijah's face lit up. "Sure! That's easy,
man!" he said. "But you got to give me a deposit on it first—
fifty cents down, a buck and a half when I bring the glove."

"C'mon," Izzie said, starting away. "How dumb do you think we are?—You take our money and we'll never see you again."

Elijah grabbed Izzie's arm. "You can trust me, kid—honest. Do I look like a guy who'd fade out on you? I bring you the glove at practice tomorrow. I promise."

"Forget it," Izzie said.

"Look—I bring the glove tomorrow, you have the money?"

"Yeah—sure," Izzie said.

"Okay." He turned to the rest of us. "You guys sure you don't wanna buy a ring or a comb or something till then?" He looked down at the sidewalk. "Oh boy, I just got to get some money, guys. You tell me what to do, I do it. I do anything for money!"

People started coming out of the subway then, home from work, and Elijah dropped back against the wall, gathering us closer around him so nobody would see him. When the train below had clattered out of the station and he told us again how he would do anything for money, I offered to buy a comb for a nickel. The other guys followed my lead and inside of a minute Elijah had sold us a bunch of combs and rings and some candy. He seemed happy again—the way he had when he'd been running in front of us at the Parade Grounds.

"You guys saved my life!" he said when we'd finished our transactions. "Fifty-five cents I got now. At least my old man won't lay into me." He walked us to Flatbush Avenue, then waved goodbye. "I see you guys tomorrow. You bring the money, Shorty, and I'll have the glove. I got to split now."

Izzie acted as if he was mad that Elijah had called him Shorty—even though Elijah was no taller than Izzie—but you could tell that he really felt pretty good that he'd been the only one with enough nerve to order something. "Holy mackerel!"

he kept saying. "Two bucks for a Pee Wee Reese model glove. Holy mackerel!"

The next afternoon, about twenty minutes after we'd started practice, Elijah came running by us, waving a baseball glove in his hand. "C'mon, Jewboys," he said. "You catch me, I give you the glove for nothing." He took off and we took off after him, Izzie giving it all he had, but it was no use. No matter how hard we ran, we couldn't come close to him—and he hardly seemed to be trying. Mr. Gleicher watched what was happening, and he seemed to enjoy it. For the first time since we'd begun practice, he was smiling.

"*Ma-hare! Ma-hare!*" he shouted to us in Hebrew, and when we had finished our laps and lay stretched out on the ground in front of him, exhausted, he praised us, telling us he had never seen us run faster, that if we kept it up we would do well on Field Day. Elijah remained at a distance, near where the girls were practicing. After we'd rested for five minutes, we started running again, practicing passing the baton this time, and Mr. Gleicher shouted at us the whole time. "On your toes! On your toes! *Ma-hare!* . . . Pump the arms, *bevakasha! Mahare,* Izzie!" Izzie was the anchor man for the relay team, and as he came around the last turn this time, after Stan had passed him the baton, Elijah joined him, running a few yards in front and tossing the baseball glove up and down in the air. "*Ma-hare!*" Mr. Gleicher yelled, and we all joined in. "*Mahare,* Izzie. *Ma-hare!*"

Elijah kept laughing, his legs flying under him, and as they came by us, a few yards apart, you could hear Izzie muttering, "Black bastard . . . I'll catch him . . . black bastard . . ." Then there were suddenly three men running, and within five strides, busted knee and all, Mr. Gleicher had caught Izzie and pulled him up short, grabbing him by his sweatshirt. He looked as if he were going to kill him, he was so angry. He shook him with both hands and lifted him up in front of him, gritting his teeth and hissing rapidly in Hebrew. Then he threw him down on the ground and we all ran over. For a minute I even thought he was going to kick him, but he didn't. He just clenched his fists and glared.

"Hey, man," Elijah said to Mr. Gleicher, wandering over to our group for the first time. "Why don't you pick on somebody your own size?"

Izzie brushed himself off and looked up at Mr. Gleicher.

"What—what was that—?" Mr. Gleicher said, turning to Elijah.

Elijah backed away now. "Hey, Shorty," he said to Izzie. "I'll give you your glove later—by the subway stop. This guy's out of it—"

Mr. Gleicher looked down as if he had just woken up and was wondering how Izzie had gotten there. He looked at his hands, then back at Izzie. "Come here," he commanded Elijah. Elijah looked away. "I said to come here!" he repeated, raising his voice, and Elijah shrugged and came toward him obediently, hanging his head. "What you want, man—?" he asked, but there was little defiance in his voice.

Izzie rose from the ground and took a step toward our group of guys, but Mr. Gleicher whirled on him, grabbed him by the arm, right on the muscle, and pulled him to his side. "You apologize to this boy," he said to Izzie. He put his arm around Elijah's shoulder, very gently, and bent down and whispered in his ear. Elijah whispered something back, and he stayed at Mr. Gleicher's side, sort of leaning against him. "You apologize to Elijah," he said to Izzie.

"What for?" Izzie said, and Mr. Gleicher squeezed his arm so hard that he howled.

"Apologize for what you called him. I won't have it!"

"Okay. I'm sorry, I guess—"

"He has a name," Mr. Gleicher said.

"I'm sorry, *Elijah*," Izzie said, and Mr. Gleicher let go of him. He stayed next to Elijah, though. It was really strange, the two of them next to each other, Mr. Gleicher running his hand over Elijah's head, and Elijah looking smaller than ever.

"Where do you live?" Mr. Gleicher asked Elijah.

"With my father," Elijah said, but he didn't look up.

"And where is that?"

Elijah shrugged. "Away from around here. You don't know."

"Don't be afraid," Mr. Gleicher said. "We are all your friends—isn't that right, boys?"

We mumbled that it was, and then Mr. Gleicher began going into this long lecture to us about brotherhood and prejudice. It was crazy—you never would have expected it from him, it was the kind of speech the rabbi might have made, only less stern—and the longer he went on, the more Elijah smiled out at all of us from under his arm. A few times some of us started to interrupt him to tell him we didn't dislike Elijah at all—but I think we all knew it was useless to try to explain. "I didn't mean anything," Izzie blurted out once. "I just wanted to catch him—" But Mr. Gleicher ignored him and went on about how as Jewish boys we had a special responsibility to befriend those others of the world who had suffered as the Jewish people had. I don't think anybody had ever heard him talk so much. And just when we thought he'd finished and was going to let us go, he reached into his pocket and took a photograph from his wallet. He looked at the picture for a while and it seemed to change his mood, to soften his features.

"Sit down, boys. Sit down. I want to tell you a story." There were about twenty or thirty of us altogether, not counting the girls, and Mr. Gleicher sat down in the middle of us, suit and all, Elijah sitting cross-legged by his side, still leaning against him, and he passed the photograph around. It was a picture of an old-looking Negro man in an Arab-style costume, with scar marks on his face like you used to find of Africans in the *National Geographic*. "This story was not in the *World Over*," he began, and then, as we sat there in absolute silence, for a good half hour he told us how two days after he had had his knee blasted and had been left for dead on the desert with all the other men in his unit killed, he had been rescued by a group of wandering black men. I forget what he called them— some tribe of nomads. At any rate, the important part of the story was that these black men had hidden him and nursed him back to health, transporting him across Israel with them, even though they were risking their lives whenever Egyptian or Syrian or Arab patrols came to check their camp. Mr. Gleicher went on about how the chief of these wandering black men was one of the wisest men he'd ever met—like a rabbi from the time of the Temple, he said—but the parts we were most interested in, of course, had to do with the adventures and the close calls he'd had while being taken across the country to Jerusalem. Then, when he'd finished, he made each of us go up to Elijah and shake his hand. The thing I remember most was the strange look on Mr. Gleicher's face, and the gentle way he kept running his hand over Elijah's head, with his eyes shining the way they did in the *World Over* picture when he was wearing his Haganah uniform. And I remember thinking, because of the way he treated Elijah, that it would be nice if he married again and had kids of his own—maybe with a Hebrew school teacher like Miss Berg, who taught us music on Sundays.

"Hey, listen," Elijah said to Mr. Gleicher when we'd all finished shaking his hand. For a second, from the way he was eyeing Mr. Gleicher, I got scared he was going to ask him if he wanted to order anything. But he didn't. "I got a question for you," he said. "How come you practicing running with all these Jew kids—?"

Mr. Gleicher smiled and told Elijah it was for Field Day —and then he started to explain why we celebrated Lag B'Omer the way we did, with races and dances. At first all of us sighed and got ready for the religious stuff we expected to hear —but instead Mr. Gleicher began to talk about the way the Jews had fought against the Roman armies eighteen hundred years ago, and about how, as in the Arab War, even though they'd been outnumbered ten to one, they had been victorious. He mentioned Rabbi Akiba also, and the ending of the plague that Lag B'Omer commemorated, but mostly he spoke about the army of Jewish rebels led by Bar Kochba—the hero the trophy was named after. He told us how Bar Kochba lived in the hills, with bands of raiders made up not only of Jews, but of volunteers and outcasts and outlaws of all kinds—maybe even black people, he told Elijah. He described how, striking mostly at night, using bows and arrows and homemade weapons, Bar Kochba had conquered village after village, town after town, until the rebels had retaken the holy city of Jerusalem from the great Roman army—he made Bar Kochba seem like some kind of Jewish Jesse James or Robin Hood. I don't think there was a single one of us who walked home that afternoon not feeling good about being Jewish—and not feeling that having to go to Hebrew school wouldn't have been half bad if there were more holidays like Lag B'Omer and more Jewish heroes to study like Bar Kochba.

Elijah walked along with our group of guys, talking about Mr. Gleicher. "That guy's got cool stories," he said. "He's okay." When we got to the subway stop, he gave Izzie the glove and Izzie gave him the two dollars. Then he asked us what else we were going to buy. "You want some of them Jewish stars to hang around your neck?" he asked. "Or some official

Major League baseballs? How 'bout a wallet for your fathers?"
We were feeling good and a few of us ordered things from
him. He seemed to like it more if you bargained with him
—I remember I was able to get him down from sixty cents
to a quarter for a baseball—and when we were done and he'd
put his pad away, he gave each of us a ballpoint pen, free.
"That's for good will," he explained, "cause you guys are my
good customers." He giggled. "—Even if you do try to Jew me
down." He left then, waving to us. "I see you guys tomorrow. I
have the goods."

Elijah showed up for practice the next day, loaded down
with the stuff we'd ordered, and he showed up the day after
that, too. In fact, for the next two weeks, he was there every
afternoon, running in front of us, saying the same thing, again
and again: "C'mon, Jewboys—catch me, mothers—" And the
more we tried to catch him, the more he'd laugh.

"You Jewboys are getting faster, though," he said at the
end of the first week, while he walked us home. "Must be those
rings I been selling you."

"I don't know if it's the rings, or what," Louie said. "All I
know is, since you started running with us we've cut our relay
time by twelve seconds. If we can cut it down another eight or
nine, we might still have a chance on Field Day."

"If you give me some money, I come to that race next
week, run in front of you," Elijah said. "If it make you run
faster, I call you worst things than Jewboy. I know some good
words for Jews."

"We'll see," Izzie said, but from the way he was looking
at Elijah, I could tell he was beginning to think about something else, cooking up one of his wild ideas. "We gonna see you
at the movies tomorrow afternoon?"

"Sure," Elijah said. "I promise you, didn't I? I keep my
word, you can count on that." He put his arm around Izzie's

shoulder. "You guys my friends, like Mr. Gleicher says. Since you buying stuff from me, my old man treat me good."

"What's your old man do?" Louie asked.

Elijah smiled and looked straight at Louie. "Okay. So long as we been friends a while now, I can tell you." He paused, and then told us, real proud. "He's a man of the Lord!" He shook his head up and down and puffed out his chest. "He's a minister of the church, the Lord spoken to him direct. Everybody in our neighborhood scared of him—he make you scared blue if you meet him."

"A black rabbi!" Izzie exclaimed, and when we laughed— thinking of our own rabbi, I guess—Elijah laughed too.

"That's pretty good," he said. "We got a real black rabbi, though, lives a few blocks away. My old man hates him, says the Lord gonna strike him down. All his congregation too. Old nigger men, reading Jew newspapers—"

Izzie's eyes lit up, and he began asking Elijah about the black Jews. It was true, Elijah swore—you could ask Mr. Gleicher. In fact, he said, Mr. Gleicher had been talking to him about the black Jews two afternoons ago, when they'd taken their walk. Every afternoon that week, while we went through our exercises, Mr. Gleicher had taken a walk with Elijah down to the end of the Parade Grounds, where the good ballfields were, the ones that were fenced in all around, and had grandstands. Elijah swore to us that Mr. Gleicher knew about the black rabbi who lived near him—and had asked him all about the black Jews of the Tompkins Park synagogue.

"My old man," Elijah said, "he got nine wives, too. I told Mr. Gleicher all about them. I come from the first one, though —so I gonna be head of the church when he dies." He suddenly stopped and looked around. "You guys wanna hear me talk in tongue?"

"Do what—?" I asked.

"You never heard nobody talk in tongue?" he asked, and when we all said we hadn't, he seemed surprised. "I tell you what, I do it the first time for you, I don't charge you nothing. Then if you like it, we make up a price for after."

"Okay," Izzie said, and we stood around Elijah in a circle. "Talk in tongue."

"Can't do it here," he said. We were on Bedford Avenue, near Lenox Road. "Too many people around."

"Nobody's home at my house—" I offered.

When the guys piled into my living room a few minutes later I got out some milk, and the candy from my mother's breakfront, and then Elijah told us to sit down around him and that we could help him by repeating what he said sometimes, or clapping our hands. He said he wasn't sure he could do it without his father's presence but that he would try—and then he started in. At first he just said some crazy sayings about Jesus Christ and the blood of the lamb and about the Lord coming into him. None of us was brave enough to repeat the stuff about Christ—not in my living room, anyway—but I remember clapping and saying things like "Come into my heart, Lord!" and "Fill my spirit with the love of everlasting," and short things like "Oh yes, Lord!" and "Hallelujah!" We were enjoying it, clapping and watching and repeating what Elijah said—and then he suddenly seemed to go crazy, jerking his body every which way, moaning like a wild man, and shaking his head back and forth as if it were attached to a pneumatic drill. He didn't need our clapping after that. The only thing he needed was our hands. He went around to each of us, falling on his knees, taking our hands and making us press them into his forehead and his eye sockets. After a while he started rolling around on the floor, saying he was seeing God, and God was working in him, driving out the devil—but now he was talking a lot about his father, too, and the money he was bringing home for the Lord, and I kept glancing at the door, praying that my mother wouldn't suddenly show up.

The more frantic he got, the quieter we got. After he'd stood up and shouted, with just the whites showing in his eyes, he suddenly seemed to go completely berserk, spouting stuff in a language none of us could understand, never seeming to take a breath. Then he shrieked and fell to the floor, rolled over once, and lay there. I was sure he was dead.

We sat on the edges of our seats, staring. "Holy mackerel!" Izzie said. Elijah lay perfectly still, his arms stretched to either side, his head on his shoulder, one foot crossed over the other. His chest didn't move and we were petrified, not knowing what to do. "I—I think he stopped breathing," I said. Louie suggested we put a mirror under his nose, to see if he was alive, but none of us moved to get one.

Then Elijah sat up. "That's speaking in tongue," he said, smiling. He really gave me the chills when he sat up, I remember—worse than in a horror movie, when a dead person suddenly comes to life from a coffin. "How you like it?"

"Are you okay—?" I asked.

"Sure," he said, shrugging. "You Jews never see any of that stuff, huh?" He took a piece of chocolate from the dish on the coffee table and popped it into his mouth. "I do better than that in the church—my old man says I'm the best he ever seen for a boy my age. How you like it, huh?"

We all sort of nodded that we liked it, but it was as if we were in a daze. "I tell you what—you get some more guys to come up to one of your houses, pay a dime each, I put on another show for you guys for nothing. Okay?" He ate another piece of chocolate. "Man, I get hungry after speaking in tongue. Mouth dry, too. You got some soda?" he asked me. I went into the kitchen and brought him a bottle of Seven-Up. "Anyway, this was nothing," he went on. "You get ten or fifteen guys, I really go good. This just coming attractions." He handed me back the bottle. "I got to go now, before your folks come home. They won't like me here—that's for sure. I see you guys tomorrow. Twelve-thirty, in front of the Flatbush Theater."

We met him the next afternoon—there were about ten of us, including Kenny Murphy and Corky Williams, who didn't go to Hebrew school—and we chipped in for a ticket for Elijah, plus a nickel a man for getting the rest of us in. Then we stood around the big fire-exit door on Church Avenue, flipping picture cards and playing boxball, trying to act nonchalant. In about ten minutes the door cracked open, the hinges squeaking. "C'mon," Elijah whispered, and we raced inside the theater while he held the door open for us, handing each of us a ticket stub as we flew by. Izzie and I stayed together, jumping into two seats up front, and when the manager came down our aisle with the matron, accusing us of having sneaked in, we showed him the stubs Elijah had picked up from the floor, saying we'd paid the same as anybody else. He grumbled and went away.

In those days the Flatbush Theater was the last place in Brooklyn where they still had vaudeville shows—my folks would go with Louie's parents sometimes on a Saturday night —and we used to have a good time on Saturday afternoons, wise-cracking and throwing popcorn at the people on stage. It was the noisiest theater I've ever been in, and besides the stage show, they used to show three movies. The afternoon we went they had two Westerns and a Bowery Boys picture. We loved the Bowery Boys, and Izzie was pretty good at imitating Leo Gorcey and the way he'd use fancy words in cockeyed ways—I remember what a great feeling it was after the movie, walking down Flatbush Avenue with all the guys,

getting Izzie and Corky to rank each other out, making believe
they were Mugs and Glimpy. The best part, though, was
repeating to each other what a great idea it was to have Elijah
get us in and give us ticket stubs. I think we all felt that he
was a genuine part of our gang now, like Sammy in the Bowery
Boys movies. I guess most of us had always secretly hoped
we could have one Negro in our gang, the way the Bowery Boys did—but until Elijah, we never had. We had lots of
Negro kids in our class at school, but they all lived in a run-
down section about three blocks on the other side of the school
—six or seven blocks away from us—so that even though we
were friendly with them during school hours, we hardly ever
saw them afterwards. They had their own gangs and teams,
and where we grew up you hung around pretty much with the
guys from your own block.

After Elijah had left us that afternoon and we were ready
to break up and go home for supper, Louie reminded us about
Field Day. Having Elijah for a friend was great, he said, but
it wasn't going to help us come in first.

"I'm not so sure about that," Izzie said, narrowing his
eyes the way he had a few days before when I'd seen the idea
begin to stir in his head. We pressed him, but all he would say
was, "I got a plan. You leave it to me."

When Izzie explained his plan to me on Monday, I told
him he was nuts, that Elijah would never go along with it, and
that even if he did, Mr. Gleicher and the rabbi would have fits.
But Izzie said he had it all figured out, and that afternoon he
went into action. For the rest of that week, Elijah went for two
private walks every afternoon—one with Mr. Gleicher and one
with Izzie. The guys bothered Izzie and Elijah a lot, trying to
get them to tell us the plan, but Izzie and Elijah just smiled.
"We got a secret," Elijah said. "Sure gonna surprise you Jewboys—"

Mr. Gleicher noticed that the two of them were palling around a lot, but this only made him praise Izzie to the rest of us, telling us that we should follow his example. Mr. Gleicher was a changed man by then, and we were beginning to believe that he probably was the world's greatest coach. He knew more about running than anyone I'd met, and he kept after us day after day—teaching us how to breathe correctly, to run on our toes, to lean forward and pump our arms the right way. It was as if the things he taught us were secrets that he'd been saving all along for the most strategic moment. By Wednesday afternoon, Louie informed us that we had clipped another four seconds from our relay time—and we were slowly becoming convinced that we might get the Bar Kochba trophy after all.

By this time something else had happened also. We'd run out of money, and Elijah was talking about leaving us and finding new territory. "There's lots of Jewboys in Brooklyn got money to spend," he said. We pleaded with him, pointing out how much we'd already bought from him and telling him that in a week or so we'd have saved up again from our allowances. He told us it wasn't personal, that he liked us real well—we were his good friends—but business was business. "He's right," Izzie said, and he and Elijah went off together for one of their mysterious sessions.

You had to hand it to Izzie. When the stakes were down, he always came through in style. The next afternoon—in his own living room this time—he rounded up a bunch of guys from Hebrew school who hadn't been with us the first time, and he got Elijah to speak in tongue for them. And on Friday Izzie even talked a half dozen girls into coming to watch, getting them to pay fifteen cents apiece, instead of a dime. Elijah went to town for the girls, and by the time he finished and lay stretched out on the floor, they were terrified. A couple of them went hysterical—screaming and crying and shivering —and I was a little worried the neighbors would hear. It took a good three or four full minutes till Elijah sat up this time, and when he did, even he was in a daze.

"Man, that's more like it," he said, shaking his head. "I know I done good when I don't know exactly what happened." He smiled at the girls. "That's speaking in tongue," he said to them. "How you like it?"

We got in an extra practice session at the Parade Grounds the next morning, and in the afternoon we went to the movies, the way we had the Saturday before. Elijah was glad to see us.

"Sure need that money, guys," he said. "The old man's putting the pressure on—I got this brother, a year younger, he been bringing in almost as much as me, trying to push me out." He turned to Izzie. "Our deal still on about tomorrow?"

"Sure," Izzie said.

"Okay," Elijah said. "You guys wait by the door. Let's have your money."

We had a good time again at the movies, but it was hard to relax completely with the track meet one day away —and afterwards, when Louie and Izzie and I got together at my house, we spent most of the time figuring out the points for the different races, and where we would have to place to have a chance for the trophy. It was pretty discouraging. The way Louie had it figured, giving us the benefit of the doubt on all the individual races—which meant having guys like me and Izzie placing in the top three in dashes and broad jumps—we still didn't stand a chance unless we won the relay.

My father came into my room once or twice and I guess he noticed how sad-faced we were. When he teased Louie the way he always did, this time by claiming that Phil Rizzuto was a better all-around shortstop than Pee Wee Reese, Louie just shrugged. My father left our room to speak to my mother, and then he came back and asked Louie and Izzie if they'd like to stay for supper. They said okay—Louie went upstairs and got permission and Izzie telephoned home—but sitting around the table eating we only got more depressed.

After supper, for a special treat, my folks took us to Garfield's cafeteria for dessert, but we weren't too hungry. I had some rice pudding with raisins, I remember. I looked at my parents now and then, and I felt a little bad for them because they were trying so hard to cheer us up. I wished I could get some conversation going, for their sakes, but I couldn't think of anything to talk about.

Then Izzie nudged me under the table and motioned with his eyes to a corner of the room. There was Elijah, going from table to table with a stack of newspapers under his arm. The minute he saw us, he smiled and came straight for our table. I wasn't exactly sure how to act with my parents there, but Elijah shook his head sideways before he got to us—he could see Izzie was going to say his name, I guess—and we played along with him.

"You wanna buy a newspaper, mister?" he said to my father.

"No, thanks," my father said, without looking at Elijah.

"You sure?" Elijah said. "I got the early morning edition already."

My mother sighed and my father looked at Elijah. "I don't read the *Daily News*," he said.

"What paper you read?" Elijah asked. "I get it for you. You just name it."

Maybe if my father had known more about Elijah—and about what had been happening with him and our group of guys—he would have acted differently, but I think he was already pretty annoyed and tired from work all week, and he began to get a little angry, raising his voice to tell Elijah that he had already told him he didn't want a newspaper.

"Maybe you want to get one for your sons here—so they can read the comics—"

"Please go away," my father said, and his tone of voice made me scared and I tried to get Elijah's attention. My father was a quiet man, but if he got annoyed he had a mean temper.

"Ah, c'mon, mister, only fifteen cents," Elijah said. "And I need the money real bad. No kidding. I got to have money—"

"If you don't stop bothering us, I'll call the manager and have you thrown out," my father said. The angrier my father got, the more Elijah persisted. He even put the newspapers down on a chair and took out some pearl necklaces, asking my father if he wanted to buy one for my mother. Izzie, Louie, and I fidgeted in our seats, not knowing what to do. I wanted so much for my father to buy something from Elijah—I remember closing my eyes and trying to concentrate hard and *think* the idea into my father's head—but it didn't help. He wouldn't buy anything, and Elijah wouldn't go away.

"Man," Elijah said finally, picking up his stack of newspapers. "You Jews sure are cheap."

This got my father. He raised his hand as if he were going to hit Elijah. "C'mon, bigshot," Elijah said. "Hit me. Get your sons to beat me up too. Why don't you pick on somebody your own size? Yeah. I like to see you mess with my old man. He lay you out flat—bam!"

"If you don't leave this instant," my father said, "I'll call the police."

Elijah turned and walked away. I guess you couldn't really blame my father—him not knowing about Elijah and Elijah saying the things he did—but I felt terrible anyway. My father and mother talked for a while about the incident, with my mother trying to calm my father down—and Izzie and

Louie and I whispered about Elijah, wondering if he would still keep his deal. My father caught some of our conversation and asked us if we knew Elijah. We said we didn't, but I guess we denied it too hard, because he was very suspicious, and my mother chipped in with some choice comments on young men being known by the kind of friends they kept.

Izzie and Louie thanked my parents for supper and for treating them to dessert, and they left.

"Go on," my father said a minute later. "Go catch up to them—but be home within an hour."

I thanked him and ran out of Garfield's, past the Flatbush Theater, and down Church Avenue, making a left on Bedford —that was the way we usually went. At Martense Street I could see the two of them, walking together up by Linden Boulevard. I was about to call to them to wait, when Elijah came running up beside me.

"Hey, Howie," he said. "Hold on. I got to talk to you—"

It was the first time, I think, that he'd ever called me by my name. "Hi, Elijah," I said. He still had a stack of newspapers under one arm.

"That your old man in the restaurant?" he asked.

"Yeah—"

"He call the police?"

"No," I said. "He didn't mean anything, anyway. He's just got a bad temper."

"You sure he ain't called the police?"

"Sure," I said. We crossed over Linden Boulevard, and Elijah stayed next to me. "I'm real sorry he said what he did to you. He's not usually like that. Honest—"

"You tell him my name?"

"No."

Elijah grabbed my arm and pushed me against a hedge. "Tell the truth, man—you tell him about me?"

"Quit shoving," I said, and pushed his hand away. "I told you the truth—he didn't call the police and we didn't tell him who you were. We made out like you were a stranger—"

Elijah looked both ways. "Your old man following us—?"

"No—"

He brushed my arm with his hand. It was wet. "I'm sorry I shove you," he said. "You want a paper? I give you one for nothing—"

"No, thanks," I said.

"Man, the police get me, I be in trouble. My father, they don't like him much, either." It was dark along Bedford Avenue, and I couldn't see much of his face. Just his eyes. "The police, they real mean." He tugged at my arm. "Listen, Howie, you make sure your old man don't call the police on me, I get you lots of things, you don't got to pay. Okay?" I told him again that my father wasn't going to call the police, but it didn't seem to matter. "I be your best friend, Howie, okay? You give me any orders you want. Just don't want them making blood out of me. The police, they get paid by the Jews, my old man told me. And the Jews, they run everything in this city, lots of kids disappear when you have Moses' holiday—"

"You mean Passover?"

"That's the one," he said, shaking his head up and down. "They get little kids, there's blood, man. I heard stories. — Please, Howie, you tell your old man I didn't mean nothing back there, so long as he don't report me." He stopped. "I even go through with my deal for tomorrow. I don't charge you nothing, either. You tell Shorty and Louie I said so." He straightened up and grabbed my arm. "Only you call the cops on me, there gonna be blood." He giggled. "My old man find out what I do, there be blood anyway." He laughed some more. "I like to see his face, he find out what I gonna do. Oh man, it burn his ass—" He stopped suddenly, and the smile left his face. We walked about a half block toward Rogers Avenue without saying anything. I could see Izzie and Louie standing around the stoop in front of my building. Elijah pulled me over under a tree. "Listen, I got your promise, don't I?"

"Sure, Elijah."

"My brother, I think he on to what we gonna do. He squeal on me, man, I'm dead." He shook his head and whistled. "Izzie, though, he got some good points. I go along with him. See you tomorrow, Howie—"

Then he left. The next morning Louie's father drove Izzie, Stan, Marty, and myself to Wingate Field and we met the other guys by the handball courts. Mr. Gleicher too. It was a beautiful spring day, I remember, and the place was already filled with hundreds of guys, all practicing starts and running around the track. In a little while the stands began to fill and we followed Mr. Gleicher's advice, just jogging around the track, not trying to impress anyone by how fast we were. A few of the guys' parents were there and a lot of people from the neighborhood around Wingate Field, and it felt pretty good, running around on an official track—it was a black one, made of cinders—with over a thousand people watching. Some of the other schools had uniforms, but all we had were these little shields the girls had made for us out of oaktag, with the name of our school on it. We pinned them to the front of our T-shirts.

The whole place was in chaos, it seemed to me, with little kids chasing each other, girls practicing their dances, music playing over the loudspeaker, and teachers and mothers walking across the track to talk to kids—but once the man in charge announced that the track meet would begin soon, things got organized. We looked for Mr. Gleicher on the infield of the track, where all the teachers were, and we found him right away. They played "The Star-Spangled Banner" and then the

"Hatikvah," and Mr. Gleicher gave out square pieces of paper with numbers on them, for us to pin on the back of our shirts. He had a list of the events on a sheet of paper and while speeches were going on and girls from different schools were dancing around as if they thought they were on the plains of Israel, he told us which events came when and who would run in which races. There were all kinds of things you could get your school disqualified for—and the thing he tried to impress on us most was to stay in our spot of the field until our individual race was called. Last year, he reminded us, we had lost points because the judges had found one of our guys sitting in the stands, eating lunch.

Just before the first race, they unveiled a table of trophies and medals and you could hear everybody go "Ooh" when they did. And when they announced that the winner of Field Day the previous year—and the current holder of the Bar Kochba Trophy—was Congregation Shaare Torah, we cheered and shouted as hard as we could, and all the guys from the other Hebrew schools looked our way. Izzie got into some good name-calling with a group of kids from Judea Center, which was in our neighborhood, and when they taunted us about having all our older guys graduate, Izzie yelled back that we had a secret weapon.

Elijah hadn't shown up yet. The announcer called for the guys in the first race, a fifty-yard dash for kids in the first grade of Hebrew school, and Mr. Gleicher got them around him in a circle and reminded them not to look back or stop running when they reached the finish line. The kids listened when he talked, and he was very gentle with them—the way he'd been with Elijah. Mr. Gleicher warned us again to stay in our places, and he went over to the finish line. From where we were you couldn't see much of the race, but when it was over and we saw one little kid from our school jumping up and down, with all the other kids hugging him, we knew what had happened. Mr. Gleicher came back carrying the kid on his shoulders and we gave him a 2–4–6–8 cheer and told each other that this was it, we were going to do it again, nothing could stop us. Izzie even borrowed Louie's ballpoint pen and had him write "Bar Kochba's Raiders" on his T-shirt, and all of us followed his lead.

The track meet progressed pretty much the way Louie had it figured—we did real well in the lower grades and better than we'd expected in the individual races in the upper grades. When the time came for the individual races for seniors, we were in second place, a few points behind the East Midwood Jewish Center. "If we can just pick up a few third places in the senior events," Louie told us, "we can still do it."

Stan and Marty had come in second and third in the race for guys in the next-to-last-year, and Mr. Gleicher had Izzie and me scheduled to race in the senior events. Until we got to the starting line next to the other guys, though, I think we'd forgotten how much bigger than us most of them were. Our race was a hundred-yard dash, and even though we swore to each other that we would give it all we had, I think we knew we didn't stand a chance. "Gleicher should of raced us with guys our own age," Izzie said. "Then we could of at least had a first place for sure—"

The starter told the runners to take their mark and my heart pounded. Izzie got down in position and set his jaw. "Relax," I whispered. "And come up slow—"

"Got you," he said, without looking my way. An instant later the gun went off and the line of us—fifteen to twenty guys—started out. Izzie and I ran neck and neck and for the first twenty or thirty yards, before you really picked up speed, we stayed with the leaders. In fact, at about the twenty-yard mark, I think Izzie was in first place. Being small helped him get a good start. But then, even though I strained with all my might, a few guys passed me and stayed ahead. The same thing happened to Izzie. One guy in front of us, from East Midwood, must have been about six foot one or two, with the longest legs of a guy our age I'd ever seen, and as we passed the halfway point he opened up a lead of almost ten full yards on the rest of us.

Then Elijah showed up, running along the grass on the inside of the track, waving to me and Izzie. "C'mon, Jew-boys," he called. "Catch me, mothers!"

"Yippeee!" I shouted—I was so happy to see him—and as I did I gagged and stumbled, knocking into a guy to my left. The two of us flailed away with our arms for several yards, and then went down in a heap. But Izzie was picking up speed, muttering at Elijah, and churning his little legs as fast as they would go. As I lay on the track and watched him, I could hear in my head the words he was saying, and when he'd gone past the tape and one of the judges had motioned that he'd come in third, I jumped up and ran straight for him and we hugged each other and danced around like maniacs. "I knew I could count on that black bastard—" Izzie said. "I knew it! I knew it!"

We ran back to our group of guys and they surrounded Izzie, punching him around and telling him how great he was. We got a little scared a minute later when the guy I'd knocked down complained to the judges that our whole team should be disqualified, but they ruled that it was nobody's fault, and Izzie's third place stood. Elijah sauntered over to our group then and Mr. Gleicher gave him a big hello, telling him how glad he was to see him. Elijah didn't say anything. He just sat down with the rest of the guys, as if he was one of us.

The broad jump was next, but Izzie and I didn't even come in in the first five in either the standing or the running events and when the announcer said over the P.A. system that the senior relay teams should report to the starter's table for the final event of the day, Louie told us that we were now in third place, eleven points behind East Midwood and eight points behind Temple Petah Tikvah. The relay counted for fifteen points, and when we realized that the guy who had won the hundred-yard dash was from East Midwood, we all felt we were done for.

That was when Izzie put his plan into action.

"I got a stomach ache," Stan Reiss said to Mr. Gleicher. "I think you're gonna have to get somebody else to run for me."

Mr. Gleicher looked around. "You better pick one in a hurry," I said, and Izzie, Marty, and I made as if we were leaving for the track. "My stomach hurts real bad," Stan said.

"Okay," Elijah said, standing up. "I'll run for you—"

Izzie nodded toward our group of guys and we took our cue and cheered and started slapping Elijah on the back. Mr. Gleicher smiled at us and put his arm around Elijah's shoulder.

"That's very nice of you, Elijah," he said. "But I'm afraid you're not allowed—"

Izzie was ready. "Why not?" he asked. "You been telling us yourself how we should treat him like he was one of us." He looked at Elijah and Elijah hung his head.

"It's not that," Mr. Gleicher began. "It's—"

"All that stuff about prejudice and him being an honorary member of our class," Izzie said. "Boy!" he exclaimed.

"You ain't gonna let me run?" Elijah said to Mr. Gleicher.

Mr. Gleicher started to say something, but the P.A. announcer interrupted with a call for the Congregation Shaare Torah Relay Team, and we told Mr. Gleicher that he'd better hurry and decide on a substitute for Stan or we'd lose— and if we didn't come in in the first three in the relay, we would finish fourth or fifth in the total scoring. That hadn't ever happened since Mr. Gleicher had been coach. Izzie nodded to Elijah.

"Look," Elijah said to Mr. Gleicher. "I *want* to be a Jewboy—" He lifted a chain from under his T-shirt and showed it around. It had at least a dozen Jewish stars on it, all different styles. Mezuzahs too. "Izzie been working with me, teaching me," he said. "Honest, Mr. Gleicher. Izzie, he says that if you let me run with the team, that finish me off with the first training for being a Jewboy." He whipped a *yamulka* out of his pocket—a white silk one—put it on his head, and then—just like that—began talking in Hebrew. *"Baruch Atoh Adonai Shalom Shalom—"* Mr. Gleicher looked confused. "Honest, I run real *ma-hare,* show you how much I wanna be a Jewboy. Please, Mr. Gleicher—" He began kissing his Jewish stars, one after the other. "Please let me. *Aleph Bes Gimel Shalom.* Please—" By this time Elijah had such a painful look in his eyes that even I was beginning to believe him. Then he started in about how Mr. Gleicher had to let him be Jewish to save him from his father. "Oh man," he pleaded, "you just got to. I been studying so hard. Listen—*Baruch Atoh Adonai Shalom Shalom—"*

"Last call for the relay team from Shaare Torah—" came the announcement, and Izzie and Louie and I stormed Mr. Gleicher with the arguments we had ready, telling him that he himself had said Elijah was our brother, that color didn't matter, that we should welcome him to our school, that he'd been with us for weeks now and had learned his prayers—

"Forget it," Elijah said, pulling himself away from Mr. Gleicher. "He's the same as all the rest. People always promise you—"

Then Mr. Gleicher was holding Elijah's hand and running through the crowd of kids with him. It all happened so fast after that that to this day I'm not sure exactly what happened. Maybe the judge had a lot of respect for Mr. Gleicher, or maybe he felt sorry for Elijah, or got confused, or—who knows?—maybe Mr. Gleicher even swore on the

Torah that Elijah was a Jew and a member of our class. All I know is the judge pinned a piece of paper with a number onto Elijah's back and showed him where the anchor men were lined up. When the big guy from East Midwood said something about Elijah being Negro, Izzie just said, "What's the matter, you stupid or something—you never heard of the black Jews? Boy, what kind of prejudiced Hebrew school do you go to?" and before we knew it the gun had sounded and Izzie had shot out ahead of the pack, running like a madman, his arms pumping, the baton clenched in his fist.

By some miracle he held on to a slight lead on the first leg of the race, but after he'd passed the baton to Marty we began to lose ground steadily. I was number three relay man, and when I began trotting in the passing zone, and took the baton in full stride from Marty, we were already in third place, about ten yards behind East Midwood. I gave it all I had, trying to make believe Elijah was in front of me, as if nobody else were on the track except us, with him laughing and calling me Jewboy—and I guess it helped, because when I reached Elijah for the last leg I had almost overtaken the number two man. "Watch me go, Jewboys," Elijah said as I ran alongside him and slapped the baton into his hand. "I got Jewgas in my legs!"

The big guy from East Midwood was about fifteen yards ahead by now, but in no time at all Elijah was breezing past him, running free and easy, and laughing in the big guy's face. He only came up to his chest, but he moved his legs across the cinders as if his toes hardly touched the track. The crowd was going wild and in the middle of the field you could see the kids from our school throwing their jackets and sneakers and stuff in the air. Even Mr. Gleicher was yelling and cheering, and when Elijah came to the last twenty yards or so, he did what he used to do with us—he ran backwards! We got worried for a second, because the guy from East Midwood chewed up the ground fast—but then Elijah straightened out the right way, and broke the tape about ten yards ahead of the other guy.

"*Mazel tov!*" Mr. Gleicher shouted, and when Elijah trotted back to us, smiling and proud, the *yamulka* still perched on the side of his head, we shouted it with him. "*Mazel tov*, Elijah! *Mazel tov!*" we screamed—laughing, happy. "Hurray for Elijah the Jewboy!" Izzie yelled, and we all hugged him and pounded him on the back and then Mr. Gleicher hoisted him onto his shoulders and limped around the track with us in a pack around him, giving Elijah *Mazel tov*'s and 2–4–6–8's and every other cheer we could think of.

When Mr. Gleicher let Elijah down from his shoulders onto the grass, the two of them looked happier than any two guys I'd ever seen. "I run pretty good for a Jew, huh?" Elijah said. "We gonna get that big trophy now?" he asked. We told him we were but that they had to announce it first and give out individual medals. "Bet we could get a lot of money for that trophy—" he said, and he strutted around with us as if he owned the place. What he loved most was to see the looks on the faces of the kids from the other Hebrew schools when they'd come over to stare at him and he'd rattle off the words Izzie had taught him. "What's the matter?" Izzie kept asking them. "You stupid or something? You never learned about the black Jews?—What kind of crumby Hebrew school do you go to?"

While they were giving out the medals for the winners of races, Mr. Gleicher was called away by the director of Field Day, and they kept glancing at Elijah. Mr. Gleicher was getting angrier and angrier, and when our rabbi suddenly showed up in his black suit, trying to look important and get into the discussion, Mr. Gleicher became furious. You could tell that he and the rabbi didn't get along well, and as the argument got more and more heated a group of people crowded around them. Then the rabbi pushed his way through the crowd and came in our direction.

"Uh-oh," Elijah said. "Time to split—"

"But they're gonna give out the trophy in a minute," Izzie said.

"I knew my brother'd do it. Help me, guys. Help me." He clutched at my arm. "Do something, Howie. Please. Oh Lord— I got to move, but I can't. Oh Lord—"

Mr. Gleicher had finished arguing with the judge and he caught up to the rabbi and we heard him pleading with him. But the rabbi kept marching toward us. Over the P.A. system we heard the news: Congregation Shaare Torah had been disqualified, and the East Midwood Jewish Center was the winner of the Bar Kochba Trophy.

"No!" I shouted. We groaned and looked at each other helplessly. "No! No!" I yelled again, and some of the guys joined me.

"If you're up there, Lord, now's the time to show your stuff," Elijah said. The guys from East Midwood ran by us, laughing and screaming, and I swallowed hard to keep from crying. It didn't help. Some tears came anyway, and the same thing happened to Izzie and Louie and the others. It didn't even matter that the rabbi was standing in front of us. At that moment we couldn't have cared less what he said or did.

"Help me, guys. I been your friend—" Elijah was saying as he crouched behind us.

And then, just as the rabbi was about to lecture us, this Negro man appeared, planting himself between us and the rabbi. He was a short man, about the same height as the rabbi and wearing a black suit just like him. The only difference was in their hats. The rabbi wore a black one, but the Negro man had on a crazy turban thing with capes and scarves flowing from it. Behind me I could hear Elijah muttering. The Negro man looked our way and I'd never seen eyes like his—the way they blazed at you from his jet-black face made the rabbi's eyes seem harmless. There were jewels in his turban, and rings on his fingers. His neck bulged from his white shirt and there were two long scars that crisscrossed his right cheek. We moved back a step.

"You the Goldberg made my son do this?"

"I am not Goldberg, I am—" the rabbi began, but Mr. Gleicher stepped in front of him. "It was my fault," he said.

"You a rabbi?"

"No, but—"

Then the Negro man shoved Mr. Gleicher aside. "The wrath of the Lord be upon you!" he proclaimed, and let go with an uppercut right to the rabbi's chin. The rabbi fell back and Mr. Gleicher caught him. People were screaming everywhere, crowding around us, calling for the police.

"Now's your chance," Izzie said to Elijah. "Through the crowd—"

"You see the shot he give the rabbi?" Elijah said, and he was laughing again. "That's my old man. I told you, didn't I—?"

Elijah's father came toward us and we shoved Elijah back, but not in time to keep his father from reaching through and grabbing. He got him by the chain and began pulling and you could see it begin to cut into Elijah's neck, making the flesh show like raw steak.

"Now!" I said, and we all shoved back against Elijah's father. Elijah screamed and then the chain snapped and the Jewish stars and the mezuzahs flew into the air. "Won that race," I heard Elijah say. I saw some spots of blood on his T-shirt. "Won that race fair and square."

His father pushed us away, but this time Elijah got his feet moving. He made his way through the crowd and streaked down the track. When he reached the trophy table, he snatched the big gold cup in full stride, then raced for the end of the field, past the handball courts. When he got to the exit, he stopped. He raised the Bar Kochba Trophy over his head, yelling at his father to try to catch him. We all cheered and ran toward the exit, tripping over each other on purpose, getting in his father's way.

"*Shalom,* Elijah!" Louie yelled, and we all did the same. "*Shalom,* Elijah! *Shalom! Shalom!*"

Elijah waved the trophy over his head once more, then kissed it. "*Shalom,* Jewboys!" he yelled. "I see you around—" Then he took off out the exit, swinging the trophy at his side, running fast as lightning, and I think we all knew that that was the last time we would ever see him.

The Pass

ALL MORNING he had been sitting on the porch of his cottage, trying to decide whether or not he should kiss her when she came for him. The minute Dr. Klein had told him that he was giving him a pass to go out with his parents Saturday afternoon, the question had been in his mind. He had meant to ask the doctor, had almost done it, in fact, but then had reconsidered. "What do you want to do, Billy?" That would have been Dr. Klein's reaction. Billy knew he would have thought it was a silly problem—and he knew too that if Dr. Klein had thought it was more than silly, the pass might have been taken away.

Still, he wished now that he had brought it up. He didn't want to do the wrong thing again—the way he had last summer when they'd taken him to his Aunt Harriet's. And only three months ago, on his first pass since the previous summer, he had embarrassed them again. Nothing as bad as at Aunt Harriet's, when he'd been the center of a big scene, because this time he hadn't been allowed to visit anyone. Instead, they'd gone to a movie together, near the hospital. Afterwards,

when they were at a Howard Johnson's having sodas, his
mother had met a friend, and although nothing was said, Billy
knew they had been ashamed of him, of the way he looked. He
had been on heavy medication at that time, and the longer his
mother's friend had stared at him, the harder it had been for
him to keep his eyes open. He had tried, but after a while, he
remembered, they had become too heavy.

"Wanna play ping-pong?"

It was Ira Gordon, a new boy at the hospital. Billy shook
his head sideways.

"Boy, you're all dressed up. Got a pass?"

Billy nodded. He did feel dressed up. Joan had ironed a
shirt for him; Arthur—the boy who slept next to him—had
loaned him a tie, and he had even used shampoo in the shower
that morning. He wanted to look nice this time. Not like the
last time, when his mother had said that she didn't have to ask
him what he'd been eating because his pants could serve as the
menu. She had meant the criticism good-naturedly—as she had
when she'd commented on the length of his hair; still, her re-
marks disturbed him.

"I wish I had a pass," Ira said. "Where are you going?"

"To the beach. My parents belong to a beach club. On
Long Island."

Ira whistled. "Wow—I'd give anything to go swimming. I
love to swim. I really do. I made junior lifesaver at camp two
years ago. Don't you love to swim?" Billy nodded. He wanted
Ira to go away. "Sure you don't wanna play ping-pong?" Billy
was sure. Ira sat down in a chair opposite Billy. He kept rubbing his hands together. Billy tried not to look; he wanted to
stay calm. "There's never anything to do around here," Ira said.
"I can't even leave this lousy cottage. Not unless an aide comes
with me. Everybody's watching the ball game. I don't like ball
games, do you?" Billy said he didn't like ball games either, but

he hardly heard what Ira said after this because he had already spotted his parents down the road, coming from the Administration Building.

His mother reached him first, his father a step or two behind, toting a big shopping bag. "My Billy! Dear—" Before he could do anything, before he had a chance to reply, she had leaned down toward him and her cheek had touched his own. He sniffed her perfume, started to rise, and his lips turned swiftly toward her cheek and pressed in on the skin. His eyes, wide open, looked at her ear, hidden behind wisps of grayish-gold hair, and as his lips stayed on her cheek he realized that her lips weren't on his. Her arm was on his shoulder, though, and as he rose to a full standing position—he was about four inches taller than his mother—he touched his hand to her right shoulder. She broke away and took a step backwards. "How *are* you? It's so good to see you, Billy. It's been so long! Isn't it wonderful? A whole afternoon at the beach, away from here—"

She noticed Ira, standing, staring at them.

"This is Ira Gordon, Mother," Billy said. "He lives in my unit."

Mrs. Fisher shook Ira's hand. "Well, I'm always glad to meet Billy's friends. How are you, Ira?"

"Are you really taking Billy to a beach club?" Ira asked. Mrs. Fisher nodded. "Well, I gotta see somebody," Ira said. He turned and went into the cottage.

"Put it down, Oscar," Mrs. Fisher said, glancing to her left. "There's no need to carry it all the time—and come say hello to your son."

Billy and his father shook hands.

"So, how's my boy? All ready to go to the beach?"

Billy nodded. He turned to his mother. "Your hair looks very beautiful."

"Why, thank you, Billy. Thank you." She turned around

so that he could see the back. "Do you really think so? The man at the beauty parlor who does my hair—he said he thought this little bit of gold in the gray would lend just the right touch. Do you really like it?"

"It's very beautiful."

"Isn't he sweet, Oscar?"

Billy's father shrugged.

"Your father—if I had my head shaved, he wouldn't notice." Mrs. Fisher laughed. "Oh well, come, Billy—let's see what's in the bag. All right? I do hope you like the things I've put together for you."

He thanked her for the underwear, the new pair of Bermuda shorts, the Ban-Lon shirt, the hair tonic, the magazines, but he told her he wasn't allowed to keep the fruit.

"Well, then, we can just take it along to the club."

"Let me sign out—I'll put this stuff in my room."

As soon as he was a few steps away he heard them whispering to each other. Something about his posture being better, but still too "slouchy," his mother said—she wished he wouldn't always be looking at the ground. Billy smiled for the first time that day. That was one good thing about the drugs; they sharpened your sense of hearing. His father said he thought Billy looked perfectly normal, that maybe he'd be out soon.

He didn't hear what his mother said to that, but when they were in the car, on the highway headed toward the North Shore, she kept telling him what a good time they were going to have.

"You do look a little pale, Billy—don't you get much sun?"

"The drugs make me dizzy if I'm in the sun—I'm still on thorazine."

"Don't you remember?" his father said. "Last summer, when he came to Aunt Harriet's with us for the picnic, how he broke out in a rash—"

"I forgot." She put her arm around Billy's shoulder and shook her head sideways. "My poor baby."

"You're no baby, are you, Billy?" Mr. Fisher said.

"Oscar! Watch out—you almost hit that car—you should see the way that man gave you a look."

"I don't think I feel good," Billy said.

"You want to sleep, son?"

Her arm went further around his shoulder and his head rested on her, low, near her bosom. He remembered how she had comforted him at Aunt Harriet's when all his aunts and uncles were standing in that circle around him, watching, waiting, muttering—were some of them crying? He didn't understand why anyone would cry. Maybe it had been what he had said to his father. He couldn't be sure, because he couldn't really remember what it was that he had said; only that as the sun had made him dizzier, just before his stomach had given way, his mother had argued with his father, and Billy had joined her, yelling and screaming when his father wouldn't listen to him. "Poor thing—maybe you'd like to stop for a Coke? That always settles your stomach—remember how I used to keep a bottle of Coke syrup with us whenever—"

"I'm okay now." He sat up. "It was the sun shining on me."

"Of course, dear. You know I was saying to your father, when you were in your room before we left, that to look at you, there's not a thing wrong with you, Billy. You're a little confused, mixed up. Of course. Who isn't these days? And I'll tell you something else—if you ask me, you never would have even gotten mixed up if—" She looked toward her husband and sighed. "Well, there's no sense going into that story, is there? We're here to have a good time . . ."

Billy looked out the window at all the other cars and wondered if he'd ever be able to drive; there was so much to think about when you drove: the other cars, the brakes, the speed limit, people, turns, signs, the gas level, the oil—his father was a good driver. Billy just wished that they could speak to each other about things sometimes. But they rarely did, even on days like this when they hadn't been together for weeks. His mother was still talking, her hand lightly touching him now and then as she used it to punctuate her sentences.

"One thing, though, Billy—and I'm not sure how to approach this. I certainly hope you won't take it in the wrong way—but I see no need to tell people where you are now. Do you—?"

He looked at his hands.

"Now don't be upset—if anybody asks you where you've been, just say you're living with our cousins, Martha and Sam, in Maine for the summer. All right—?"

He nodded.

"Well," she continued, "I just see no need for people to know now—when *you* want them to know, then it's time enough. Even the doctors said there's never any need for people to know until *you* want them to—"

"I won't tell anybody."

"Good—there's nothing to be ashamed of about where you are, either, Billy. I hope you understand that. It's just other people. Let's face it—even you wouldn't *want* to be there if you didn't have to—"

He smiled. "I know," he said. "You—you have to be crazy to want to be there—"

They laughed and his smile broadened and soon he was laughing also. "One thing about my son," his father said. "He never loses his sense of humor."

"You are precious sometimes, Billy," his mother said, between laughs. "Oscar—don't laugh so hard. You shouldn't be so funny, dear—you'll distract your father—"

At the club, he put on a bathing suit so he wouldn't appear to be out of place. All the boys and girls his own age, though, were down at the beach, swimming, sunbathing—and, because of the sun, he couldn't join them. His mother and father offered to play cards with him. At first he said he'd rather not; to please them, though, he let himself be talked into a few games of gin rummy. Then he excused himself, saying he wanted to take a walk.

As he wandered around the club, he noticed that his mother kept glancing up from her beach chair—then from the table where she was playing Mah-Jongg—to keep an eye on him. Finally, to escape her glances, he slipped into the TV lounge and sat down where she wouldn't be able to see him. The lounge was glass-enclosed and air-conditioned, with easy chairs all around. A ball game was in progress on the TV and he watched for a while. In the back of the room, two teenagers —the boy might have been his own age—were sitting on a couch necking and Billy tried not to look their way. He didn't want to embarrass them. The girl's hands were caressing the boy's neck and shoulders, her fingers stroking, stroking while the boy clutched her. Billy noticed that the boy's bare chest was pressed against the girl. Once, coming up for air after a long kiss, the girl caught Billy's eye and he didn't know what to do. He was afraid she would say something to the boy, would involve him in an argument, but she only curled one corner of her mouth, indifferently, condescendingly, and then—as if drugged, Billy thought—her eyelids closed, she exhaled slightly, and her lips, wet, parted, searched for the mouth of the boy. The next time he turned around—two innings had passed, though he couldn't have said which team was ahead— they were gone and he felt relieved.

Outside the lounge, on the shuffleboard courts, a group of children were playing. A little girl in a red bathing suit was examining another little girl, who was stretched out on the ground, mouth open. A little boy—he was the doctor—had a spoon pressed inside the girl's mouth, and the girl in the red bathing suit, who had an empty Dixie cup on her head, kept giving the doctor orders. In her right hand she held a pail from which she took invisible things that she applied to the patient. She pushed the doctor away now and began wrapping what must have been gauze around the patient's head, then picked her up by the elbow, patted her lightly on the rear, and sent her on her way. There were other children sitting in a row and one of them ran forward and sat down. The girl sent her back to the waiting room, conferred with the doctor, and then took one of the patients by the hand—not the one who had come forward—and sat her down on the ground. She stuck a Popsicle stick in the girl's mouth and took her pulse. Billy laughed. The little girl had the biggest blue eyes he'd ever seen.

Two mothers came along after a while, and the children all clapped and shouted—they were going to be taken swimming. The girl in the red bathing suit ran in front of all of them, her blond ponytail flapping up and down, her pail swinging out from her side. Billy was surprised at how graceful she was for her age; and he was particularly taken by her legs, which weren't at all pudgy.

In the middle of a beer commercial he left the lounge. It was hot outside, but a cool breeze blew intermittently and the sun wasn't directly on him. He was hungry and went to where his father was playing pinochle and asked for some money.

At the snack bar he ate two cheeseburgers and sipped a Coke. Only a few old people sat around the clubhouse. Somehow it seemed to him that when he was young there had been no old people at the club. Before his mother had sent him away to camp, when he was thirteen years old, he had spent all his summers at the club. If asked, he couldn't actually have said what he had done during those summers, but he knew he'd had a good time. When you were with friends, you didn't have to be doing anything special. He and his doctor had talked about this, because whenever Dr. Klein asked him what he had been talking about with his friends at the hospital, he could never remember. That, he told Dr. Klein, was what made them friends. With friends you didn't have to talk about something special; you just talked.

There was one thing, though, which he did remember doing. In the men's locker room, right next to the drinking fountain, to the right of the shower, in locker 267—he remembered exactly—there was a hole that they used to take turns looking through to see the women undress. The locker had always been one of the open ones, for guests to use.

Billy wondered if it was still there and he finished his Coke and left the table. He walked into the locker room, down the first aisle of lockers, turned right, then left to the end of the room. He wondered if any of the younger boys would be there now, looking through the hole. He turned the corner and breathed more easily. Nobody was around. No noise in the showers. He looked to either side, then opened the door. To his surprise, nothing happened. He put his hand inside and rubbed it across the back; a piece of cardboard moved. His heart thumped, louder, and he wiped the sweat from his mouth and chin with the back of his hand. Then, looking down the aisle once more, he thrust his head in, pushed the cardboard aside, and pressed his eye to the cool metal.

He exhaled in relief as he spotted no women. He closed his eyes, opened them, and was about to move back and close the door when the girl in the red bathing suit came into view. She was wearing a blue bathing suit now and was being pulled along by her mother. Billy moved closer to the back wall of the locker, pressing his eye flush against the metal. The mother sat the girl down in front of a large locker, almost directly in front of Billy.

"One more chance," he heard the mother say. "I'll give you one more chance." The girl sat and stared at her mother, her jaw set, her eyes fiercely defiant. The mother pointed, and shouted this time. "Now get going—"

Billy switched to his left eye and pressed his cheek against the side of the locker. The edge of the locker cut into his left shoulder, but he wanted to see where the mother was pointing. A few feet to the right, several women were talking, some of them half undressed. He looked away quickly, back at the girl and her mother.

The girl didn't budge. She had her pail in her lap, and Billy saw the Dixie cup in it. The girl looked up, toward the mother, then away, to the right, directly at Billy. But she didn't seem to have noticed him. He licked the sweat that slipped off his upper lip, then drew his bottom lip under his teeth and sucked away the salt that had collected in the crevice between his lower lip and his chin. The mother grabbed the girl and shook her.

"I know your ways, young lady," she said, holding onto the girl's arm. "So help me God, though, if you don't go back and say excuse me to those ladies, you'll sit here all day."

The girl thought, then her eyes opened wider and she smiled: "Then you'll have to sit with me—"

The mother sat down. "Okay, miss smarty-pants, we'll see who can wait longer."

Billy pressed his face to the side again as the girl got up and walked toward the women. She was almost past them and still hadn't said anything. "Get back here, godamnit!"

"There's enough room to go *by*—" the girl protested. "I don't need to say 'scuse me. See—?" She pointed to where the women had stepped back.

The mother took a few steps and grabbed the girl, pulling her back, and sat her down on the bench. The girl pointed to the left. "There's a *back* way—"

"You'll go the way I say, and you'll say excuse me or I'll know the reason why. Do you hear? Your father's so worried about breaking your will, is he? Well, I'll tell you something, young lady. I'll break your will before you break me. Do you hear?"

The girl looked around, trying to find another way out. After a while, though, the fierce look left her eyes and she began to fidget. Billy felt his own jaw set in anger. The girl looked his way again. She squinted and he knew she had noticed him. She didn't give him away, though. Instead, she made a dash for the door, running past the women and mumbling something that must have been "Excuse me, please" as she did.

"Don't tell me, Marge," said the mother, anticipating what one of the women was about to say. "How can I treat her that way? How—"

"Look, Ruth, you bring up your kids the way you want —but if my daughter were half as bright and pretty as—"

"Bright? Sure she's bright. They're the worst kind, I'll tell you that. You know what she's learning now? Do you know what she said to me yesterday when I had to slap her? 'Godamnit, stop!' Can you imagine—?"

"Well, Ruth, let's be honest," one of the other women said. "You yourself curse in front of her. The child just wants to imitate you, to do what you do."

"Do what *I* do? I can have intercourse, can she?"

Hearing no objections to this argument, the mother stalked past her friends. Billy felt his heart pounding. He withdrew his head and slammed the door to the locker. He didn't care if anybody heard him. Something had to be done. His left arm was shaking, quivering the way it used to when he had first become sick. He didn't feel good either. He breathed in deeply. Billy's arm shook more violently and he thought he heard footsteps. He darted into a toilet and locked the door behind him, sitting down on the seat without removing his bathing trunks. Whoever came into the locker room left in a few minutes. His arm had stopped shaking but his stomach was still upset. He left the toilet, went to the fountain, and then he knew what it was he would do. He filled his mouth with cold water but neither swallowed it nor spit it out. It filled his cheeks, pressing them to the sides. He sucked them in, letting the water rest under his tongue, and he walked outside quickly, hoping to head the mother off, but he didn't see her anywhere. He walked all around the clubhouse, then past the snack bar. They must have gone down to the beach, he thought, and so he started walking away from the clubhouse area, onto the sand and down toward the water.

When he neared the shore, he stopped. The blankets were covered with people. What would he do if someone said hello? He couldn't let the water out of his mouth. He'd better wait for her near the clubhouse. She had to come back, if only to change her clothes. He turned and walked back up the beach. To the right of the women's locker room the sun was blocked by a post. He stood next to it, rubbing his skin against its cold metal. He looked at his arms and could see that they were splotchy, red. In his mouth the water was warm now, mixed with saliva.

He didn't know how long he'd been leaning against the post when he spotted her. It might have been ten minutes, or it might have been two hours; the slight dizziness that spun on top of his eyes confused him. The water was almost hot now. He moved his cheeks in and out, pressing air up against the top of his mouth, slushing the water around. She had stopped to talk to some women. He wished the little girl were around to see him when he did it. His arm had stopped quivering, but there was no doubt about the rash now, and if the rash came, he knew what was bound to follow. Two women came out of the locker room and he started, almost swallowing the water. He wondered if they had seen him with his cheeks blown out. One of them looked at him strangely and he lowered his gaze to the ground.

When he looked up, he saw her coming toward him. He slid behind the post so that she wouldn't see him until the last moment. The girl in the blue bathing suit ran after her mother now, the mother said something to her, and then the girl ran off again. Maybe she would turn around in time to watch. The mother came closer and Billy was surprised at how young she was. She was probably no more than thirty years old and she was very pretty. Her hair was auburn and she wore a two-piece bathing suit that revealed a trim figure, wide hips, and two very large breasts. Billy couldn't take his eyes from them. He peeked out from behind the post. When she was about ten yards away, he made a dash toward her, spat the water, hitting her on the right shoulder, and then he continued running, away from the clubhouse, away from her shout, away from what might even have been his own scream. He didn't look back. Not until he reached the water and dove into it and came back out. Some boy called to him, a boy Billy had known in high school, but Billy didn't stop. He ran back toward the clubhouse, just far enough to see the spot where he had done it. The woman wasn't there.

He walked up the beach and sat down near the snack bar. He felt good. Excited, but not anxious. He was shivering from having been in the sun, but he didn't care. He didn't care about anything. The little girl was at the snack bar. His smile broadened.

"Hi," he said.

She stared at him for a second, cocking her head to one side. Up close, her eyes were even more beautiful. Not really blue, as he'd thought, but blue-green, like sea water.

"You were the nurse, weren't you?"

"I was the *sur*geon," she said.

Billy laughed. "Would you like something?"

She hesitated. "Maybe . . ."

Billy dropped down to a deep knee bend position. He felt very old, very fatherly. "Maybe you'd like some milk—surgeons like milk."

She made a face.

"Then, let's see—you wouldn't by any chance be interested in some ice cream?"

"I might."

"Well, how about a Creamsicle—a special one with an orange and green wrapper?"

"Maybe yes . . . and maybe no," she said, but her eyes betrayed her.

"Two Creamsicles," Billy said to the man behind the counter. "A regular one for me and a special one for—" he didn't know what to call her "—for her."

Billy paid and handed the girl the Creamsicle. She took it, ripped the wrapper away, and started licking the orange ice. He bent down again, to her level. "Would you like to—to play something?" he asked. "A game?"

She looked at him. "You're too old," she said; then she turned and ran off, holding the ice cream high in her right hand, as if it were a torch.

Billy stood up. The counter man was staring at him. Billy walked away, toward the card tables. He saw the girl's mother and stopped. He turned a corner of the clubhouse and peered out. The woman was talking to his own mother. His father was being called over and the three of them walked away and talked for a while. His mother gesticulated a lot, his father shrugged, and the woman seemed to be shouting. Once she even pointed a forefinger at his mother. When she left he saw his mother's head sag, then lift, searching for him. He stepped out from behind the building so that she could see him. She waved to him and he walked to her. His father wouldn't look straight at him.

"I've been thinking, dear," his mother said, putting her hand to his cheek, "that maybe this isn't very exciting for you, and here your father and I—selfish parents that we are—sit around and have a good time. Maybe you'd really like to get back to the hospital early—it's Saturday and I'm sure there must be some very special activities planned for you."

He nodded.

"You don't mind?"

He said he didn't mind and then he and his father went into the locker room and changed from their bathing trunks into their regular clothes. His stomach was bothering him; but he vowed that he wouldn't throw up—not in front of them— not, at least, until he was back at the hospital. On the way home his mother talked a lot, and his skin was very itchy. He kept his hands in his lap, pressing the left one down.

"You know," his mother said when they were almost at the hospital, "I'm really glad we came to get you today, Billy. Someday soon you'll be able to go to the beach as much as you want. You'll see. Until then, I want you to know that we're always available—as many passes as your doctors give you, that many times we'll be here to take you places. I even told the social worker, Mrs. Schwartz, on the phone last week—we certainly are glad to give up this little bit, this part of our time for our son. What else do we have to live for? What . . ."

Her voice trailed off. Billy's father shot a look her way,

and Billy felt his stomach convulse, turn, and then he tasted some bile in his mouth. He forced it down. He prayed for one thing now: that his stomach would hold out until he got back in his unit. Nothing else mattered. Everything else, everything that had happened at the beach, seemed unimportant in comparison. His mother was talking again, telling him that she didn't really mean the "giving up" part—she *wanted* to spend time with him. She had loved having him at the club with her, she had enjoyed seeing him look so nice . . . but Billy hardly heard her words. He set his eyes on the horizon and concentrated on keeping his stomach inside him. Her voice came at him from a distance; even when she kissed him goodbye at the gate, he hardly knew she was there, and when he got to the cottage and could relax and let the day's meals splatter the floor, he felt good. He had done it. He had kept it in.

Corky's
Brother

THE FIRST TIME I ever cried about anybody
dying was at Corky Williams' older brother's funeral. I was
fourteen then—it happened after the summer, just before my
first year in high school. I was surprised that it upset me so
much because I didn't even know Corky's brother well. I
wished I did, of course—every guy in our neighborhood did—
but the only way I really knew him was through Corky and
through the newspapers.

Corky's brother—Mel was his name—died from the same
kind of leukemia that got Ernie Davis, and he was probably
the most famous guy in our neighborhood. He had been All-
City in baseball and football at Erasmus and had gotten a
bonus of about $10,000 from the Dodgers when he'd finished
high school. At the time he got sick—he wasn't twenty years old
yet—he was playing double-A ball in their farm system, and
Corky would always come down to the schoolyard with clippings from the Fort Worth newspapers. The night Mel fainted
the first time and was taken to the hospital, he was hitting over
.300, and in the *New York Post* it said that he might be brought

213

up to the Dodgers the next year to fill the left-field spot. The Dodgers hadn't had a steady left-fielder since they'd traded Andy Pafko to the Braves in 1953.

All of us worshipped Mel, especially Corky. Whenever any of us got to do anything with him we'd talk about it for weeks afterwards. Once, I remember, he came down to the schoolyard and we got him into a game of stickball with us. Somehow I managed to strike him out once—he didn't do it to make me feel good either, you could tell that—and when I did, he turned to Corky and said, "Hey, who's that out there— Carl Erskine?" I felt so great, I struck out the next two batters on six straight pitches. The guys kidded me about how red my face got and about the stupid grin I had on, but I didn't care. For the next few months they all called me Carl and no matter how many times they did, each time it made me feel as if Mel were saying it for the first time.

Even though Corky always talked about what a great ballplayer his brother was, he talked even more about the things Mel did with girls. Almost every Saturday and Sunday morning when our baseball team got together at the Parade Grounds, the first thing out of his mouth was—"Boy, you should of seen the piece my brother took out last night!" He said it so many times that after the "Boy" we would all repeat the rest of the sentence with him. He didn't mind. "I mean it," he'd say. "This one was the best yet. You should of seen her!" He'd make a motion with his hand and suck on his lower lip. "*Maron!* What a pair of knockers she had!" Then we'd usually crowd around him and he'd tell us about how he'd been up when Mel had come home and how they'd stayed up and talked till early morning, with Mel filling him in on all the luscious details. "My brother can plug any broad he wants!" Corky would say. That was his favorite word. I don't think any of us ever spent a day or even an hour with Corky when he didn't speak at least once about who Mel was plugging.

Corky and I were good friends at that time, and my parents weren't happy with the idea. They thought he was too wild—and, of course, this only made me feel better about being his friend. He'd do crazy things that nobody else would—and when he wasn't with our group of guys, he'd spend his time with the tough guys from the other side of Nostrand Avenue. They took part in gang wars, and some of them had already been arrested for stealing radios, but Corky never had any part in those things. What he was after were the girls.

The summer Mel was sick, when I'd come home from camp, I used to go with Corky almost every night to the P.S. 181 schoolyard. We'd play stickball for a while, and then, as it began to get dark, the girls would come in and Corky would go to work. The tough guys didn't bother me because I was Corky's friend—so I just used to sit on a bench, fooling with a stickball bat, watching the way Corky would treat the girls. He'd neck with them and chase them around and twist their arms—and no matter what he did or said they seemed to love it. In fact, the more he'd curse a girl or punch her in the arm, the more she'd be willing to make out with him. I knew most of the girls from school—they were the tough ones, the ones who wore tight sweaters and black kerchiefs on their heads and usually had bite marks on their necks and ink tattoos on their arms from whatever guys they were going with.

Sometimes Corky would say to me, "Hey, Howie, you dare me to soul-kiss every one of these girls?" and when I'd say "Yeah," he'd say "Darers go first," and the girls would laugh at me. I didn't mind, though. After spending a couple of weeks with Corky and the girls at night, I got to like them. They may not have been the brightest girls in the world, but at least they didn't talk all the time. "You know why Howie don't make out with any of you broads?" Corky said one night. "Because he got a girlfriend nobody knows about. He gotta be true to her." Then Corky showed them a picture from his wallet and all the guys and girls crowded around. The girl in the picture looked something like Corky—she had light wavy blond hair and a kind of square face with a dimple in her chin. In the picture she was standing next to a well pump with her mouth half open and her eyes half closed. The guys all agreed that she was a piece, and every night after that when I came down the girls would ask me if I'd heard from Sarah Jean. That was her name. Sarah Jean Stilman, and she was Corky's cousin who lived in Pennsylvania. Corky got a big charge out of how I blushed and fidgeted every time her name was mentioned, and I guess I was glad to be thought of as a guy who had a girlfriend.

Sometimes at night, if the guys got bored fooling around with the girls, they'd crowd around one of the concrete checker tables and play poker or blackjack. Corky would keep up a running commentary, announcing the hands as if he were on television. What I liked most, though—and I think this was true for all the guys—were the things he'd say to the girls. "Hey, Gloria," he might say suddenly, calling to one of them. "Do me a favor, huh?" "Sure, Corky," the girl would usually say. Then when she got near the table Corky would say to her, in this very serious tone, "Take a walk to the corner and see if it's raining, okay?"—or something like that, and we'd all laugh.

He was great at ranking out girls—I think this was one of the reasons the tough guys looked up to him so much. There was one exception, of course. About a year and a half before he died, Mel had eloped and gotten married to a girl named Rhoda Miller who worked behind the soda fountain at Ellman's on Flatbush Avenue. When Mel had first started dating her, Corky had been in his glory because Rhoda was generally acknowledged to be the most beautiful girl in our neighborhood. When she waited on tables in Ellman's and we watched her wiggle between the tables and chairs or bend over to scoop out ice cream, Corky would just lean back and smile.

"I told you," he'd say to us, and then he'd give us the details about what Mel was doing to her. A few times he told us that Mel had plugged her right on the rug in Corky's living room. "My brother's really something," he'd say.

When they got married, though, Corky was stunned. He couldn't seem to understand why a guy who could be getting it all over the country would want to settle for getting it from one girl—even if she was the most beautiful girl around. "Why'd he do it?" he kept asking. "Why'd he do it?" After a while, of course, he came to like the idea of having a big sister like Rhoda, and when Mel was away during the baseball season in 1955 he spent almost all his time at her house. She made special foods and pies for him, and according to Corky she could do everything better than any girl in the world.

Corky never did get along well with his parents, and after Mel was taken to the hospital, I remember, they fought more than ever. Any time I'd go over to his house with him, within two minutes they'd be screaming at each other, and when Corky's father would threaten to hit him—usually for the way Corky was treating his mother—Corky would clench his fist and dare him. "I'm ready whenever you are," he'd say. "Just remember one thing. I'm bigger than you are now, you hear that? You better remember that." It was the only time I'd ever heard anybody our age talk to a parent that way. "I hope you both croak," he'd say when we left. Then he'd go to Rhoda's and she would feed him and they'd talk. Or rather, Corky would talk and Rhoda would listen, usually about how lousy his parents were. When Corky visited Mel at the hospital—he didn't do it often because he said it upset Mel to have to entertain visitors—he always went with Rhoda.

The night the news came we were at a party, I remember, and being at a party always made Corky feel uncomfortable. That was the strange thing. He'd be as wild as could be with girls in the schoolyard or at school—but when he had a tie and jacket on at a party you couldn't get him to go near them. If we'd play kissing games, he'd say it was sissy stuff and would sit in a corner reading a sports magazine—and if the girls' parents were gone and we'd play "lights out" or "flashlight" he'd say that the girls didn't know how to do anything, and he'd leave early.

The night it happened we were at Paula Ornstein's house on Linden Boulevard, and her mother came into the living room—after coughing a lot to warn us—and said that Corky's mother had called and told him to come home, there was bad news. The whole neighborhood knew about Mel, of course —I can remember listening to my parents and their friends agreeing with each other that it was "a tragedy, a genuine tragedy"—and when Mrs. Ornstein bit on her lip, some of the girls started sniffling. If the other guys and I hadn't kept busy telling them to shut up, I think a lot of us would have done the same thing. Corky didn't budge.

"Aren't you gonna go home?" Louie asked.

"I'll go when I feel like it," Corky said. We all looked at each other and nobody seemed to know what to do. I jammed my mouth full of potato chips so I wouldn't have to say anything, and after a minute or so Corky broke the silence by doing something he'd never done before at a party. He suggested we play "post office"—and he nominated himself to be first postmaster. Then he whispered to me to be sure to get Ellen Dienstag to deliver the first letter, and he went into the hallway to the bedroom. I couldn't figure what he was up to, because Ellen Dienstag was the biggest snob in the school. She was intelligent and good-looking—we all had to admit that— and she was the only girl in our class whose father was a doctor. She was always taking lessons in ice-skating and elocution and things like that. At a party the week before when we'd taken a break and crowded together in the bathroom to compare notes on who was the smoothest kisser, I'd admitted to the guys that I'd never gotten anything from her—that when I'd go into the hall or bedroom with her for "post office," or if we were on the couch together during "sneak attack," she'd always whisper to me to pretend that we were going to town. "Let's just make believe—all right, Howie?" she'd say, and give my hand a squeeze. Then when it was over she always acted as if I'd really been loving her up. It turned out that she did pretty much the same thing with all the guys. If you were lucky she'd give you a quick peck on the lips so that some lipstick would show. "I know her kind," Corky had said. "She thinks hers is lined with mink—"

A minute after I got her to deliver a special delivery to Corky, we heard her yelp for him to stop. Then they were quiet for a while—but until she came running back into the living room, covering her blouse where Corky'd ripped it open, I think we all figured she was making believe again. Corky followed her into the room and while the tears streamed down her face and the girls crowded around her, he sauntered over to them and started ranking Ellen out. She pushed the girls away from her—her blouse was pinned up by then—and screamed at him that she didn't care if his brother did die, he was still an idiot and a punk.

Corky just laughed. "You know what you are?" he said. "You're nothing but a two-bit C.T.—" Then he went up to her and shoved her on the breasts. "And I'll tell you something else, Lana Turner, you ate it up when I soul-kissed you—you're the one who wanted to keep going. You know why I stopped?" He turned to us. "Cause she's the sloppiest kisser I ever met. I've gotten smoother kisses from a wet sponge." He turned to me. "You wanna bug out with me, Howie? I had enough of this place. Let's get us some real stuff."

When we got outside, though, he said he wanted to visit

Rhoda. "I ought to be with her at a time like this," he said. "Mel always told me to keep an eye on her, to take care of her—" His voice broke then, and I didn't look at him. Then he started talking about Ellen. "I really showed her, huh? I showed her, didn't I, Howie?" he said, and even after I'd agreed with him, he kept repeating it. "I showed her, didn't I? I really showed her, huh?"

When we got to Rhoda's place on East 21st Street, there was nobody home. "Damn it," he said. "She must of gone to my folks' place. What'd she wanna do that for?" So we walked back to Corky's house, which was on Martense Street, off Rogers Avenue. I felt funny going in with Corky, but at the door, when I told him I thought I'd better leave him alone, he insisted that I come in with him. Even from outside the door I could hear Corky's mother crying—I'd never heard a woman cry so loud—she just kept wailing and scream-ing and shouting Mel's name. Corky took a deep breath and opened the door. Inside, it was dark and the apartment smelled as if somebody had been boiling cabbage. Corky's mother was stretched out on the living-room couch with a washcloth over her forehead, and Corky's father was next to her, talking low. Rhoda was sitting in the easy chair, next to the TV, and there were some neighbors walking around the room trying to make themselves helpful.

Corky's mother reached out with her hand. "Is that you, Corky baby?" she said. Corky mumbled something. "Corky, Corky, my love, come to your mother—oh, Corky, why? why—?"

"Easy does it now, Margaret," Corky's father said.

Corky stood there for a second, at the entrance to the living room, and I stood behind him. The neighbors disap-peared into the kitchen, and when Corky's mother started cry-ing again for him to come to her, Corky went to Rhoda instead.

He seemed very tall and sure of himself as he strode across the room to her—but the minute Rhoda raised her arms to him and he lifted her from the chair and let her cry on his shoulder, something inside him seemed to break. He didn't cry, at least not that I could tell—and he talked to Rhoda about how he understood how much they'd loved each other—but something seemed to break in his body, to sag, so that even though he was taller than her and she was leaning against him, he still looked like a little boy. He brushed his pompadour out of his eyes a few times, and when Rhoda had finished crying, he straightened himself up a little bit.

"Your brother's dead, Corky—" his father began.

"Godamnit!" Corky said, turning on his father. "You think you're telling me something I don't know?" Then he walked out of the living room, to his own bedroom. He motioned to me. "Come on in here, Howie," he said.

I went into his room with him and sat down in a chair next to his desk. "Jesus!" he said a few times, and pounded his fist into his palm. Then he paced the room and when he came by me he patted me on the shoulder, as if he were trying to cheer me up, to make me feel good. "You're okay, Howie," he said. After a while he sat down and took some deep breaths. "Jesus," he said. "It's hard to believe, you know what I mean?" I said I did, and I meant it. I could still picture Mel—the way he looked in the newspapers, but more the way he looked when I'd seen him play stickball, the way he'd smile when he whipped the bat around. He was a lefty and swung on a line like Ted Williams, with a really graceful swing. Corky started to unwind then, talking about things he and Mel had done together and about how it seemed impossible that they wouldn't do them again, but the fact that Mel was gone just didn't seem real to him. Not until he went to the closet to show me some stuff. He took out picture albums of Mel he'd collected and some baseball caps from teams Mel had been on, an old baseball glove that he'd given to Corky, a pair of spikes. "See these?" he said, showing me the spikes. The black leather was crusted and cracked from dirt and the shoe-laces had been broken and retied in five or six places. "They didn't belong to Mel," he said. "They were mine. Do you understand? Remember last year when we changed the name of our team to The Zodiacs and started getting more games and things? I got these then. Mel bought 'em for me. When he was back from the Dodgers' training camp in Florida just after spring training—before he got sent to Fort Worth—he bought 'em for me and when he gave them to me he said—he said it was about time I stopped using his hand-me-down's, that I was on my own and he—" And then Corky just started blubbering. The tears came rolling down his face. He stood there holding the shoes next to his face, dirty smudge marks running on his cheeks from the tears, asking if I understood. "He said it was about time I stopped using hand-me-down's . . . do you understand . . . do you?" When he breathed in, he made deep raspy noises and I wished more than anything in the world I could have done something for him. But there was nothing I could do except listen to him repeat what Mel had said. I don't think I've ever felt as helpless as I did then.

Just as he was beginning to get himself under con-trol, the door opened and his mother came in. Corky's father was with her, holding her steady by the elbow, and I could see the neighbors behind them in the living room, looking in at us.

"I'm feeling better now, Corky," his mother said. "I didn't like for you to see me the way I was before—"

"That's okay," Corky said, and he turned his back to her and leaned on the windowsill. He put his spikes on the dresser.

"I heard you from the living room," she said, and took a

few steps toward him. "I know what you must be feeling now —you—you lost your best friend, didn't you?" She had to fight to keep her tears back, I could see. Then she took another step toward Corky and reached out with her hands, to rest them on his shoulders, but the minute her fingertips touched him he whirled on her, screaming like a maniac. *"Leave me alone! Leave me alone—!"* She moved backwards as if somebody had punched her, and Corky's father got to her quickly and held her up. Corky couldn't stop screaming. "Goddamnit, just leave me alone! Leave me alone already!"

"Look at him—" Corky's father said then. Corky's face was beet-red and the bottom of his mouth was spread wide, quivering. "You ain't no good, Corky. I always said it, and I say it again."

"Stop, Frank—" Corky's mother said. "He's upset. Poor baby." Then she was crying again, her chest heaving in and out. "He's lost his best friend—he's—"

"This is my room—so get out! Out!" Corky screamed. "Just get out and leave me alone—!"

"Sure," his father said. "We'll leave you alone—should of done it a few years back, all the good's gonna come of you." He stopped and hitched up his suspenders. "Maybe I never would of said this, not for what's happened—but you're a bum, Corky. Don't know where it come from. Maybe it's my seed— but you're gonna wind up a bum, living all over the country, never settling down. Maybe it's my fault. Like I say, I don't know—"

"Frank, please, I beg of you, stop—" his mother said. She clung to his arm, but Corky's father wouldn't stop now. I just stood there, wishing I could vanish. Corky's father had always seemed a little strange to me and the other guys—to our parents too—but we knew from Corky that before they'd come to Brooklyn his father had run the family farm in Pennsylvania, and I guess we figured that all farmers dressed and talked the way he did. He was the most tight-mouthed man I ever met. In fact, in all the years Corky and I had been friends—he had come into our class in the second grade—this was the first time I think I'd ever heard his father speak more than one sentence at a time.

"You let me speak my piece, and then I'll be done for good, Margaret," he said. "At least your brother, God bless his poor soul, at least he had an excuse with that baseball stuff of his—but you ain't even gonna have that—you ain't—"

Corky leapt at his father as if he were going to kill him and then—it happened so fast I didn't even have a chance to move—Mr. Williams had laid him out with one stroke of his hand. I'd never seen anyone react so quickly. One minute Corky's hands were making for his throat, and the next minute Corky's father had whipped his arm across and hit Corky square on the side of the face with the back of his hand and Corky was on the floor, stunned. His mother bent down, but Corky screamed at her to get away. "I'll kill you some day," he said to his father. "I swear to God I will—"

"I wouldn't doubt it," his father said.

"Frank, why? Why must you?" his mother was saying. "Why now—?"

"The boy says he wants to be left alone, so we'll leave him—" Corky's father pushed his mother out the door and then turned back. Corky was still on the floor, feeling his jaw as if something were broken in it. "One other thing—all my kin's coming up from Pennsylvania for the funeral and I ask you not to shame your mother or your brother's memory the way I know you'd like to. They'll be here by morning. You get this room cleaned up before that, you hear?"

"Like hell I will," Corky said as his father left the room. He got up from the floor and rubbed his jaw.

"You okay?" I asked.

"Sure. He caught me off guard, that's all."

Corky picked up the pair of spikes from his dresser and put them back in the closet with the other stuff from Mel. "If I don't put these away, my old man'll probably throw them out," he explained to me.

"What about your peep shows?" I asked.

"Yeah," said Corky. "You wanna give me a hand—I'll stand on the chair and you hand 'em to me—"

"You got any new ones?"

"Nah," he said. "I'm still working on the Ebbets Field one." He got down on his hands and knees and pulled a big carton out from under his bed. "I'm gonna attach some flashlight batteries here, and some bulbs—" The short end of the carton, like the ends of all the shoeboxes around Corky's room, had a little square cut out of it which was covered with cellophane, and inside, when Corky let light into the top of the box through special slats, you could see a baseball field laid out, with the stands painted on the sides of the carton. "I used green felt from an old pool table—the guy at Ryan's on Church Avenue saved it for me—" I told Corky how great I thought it looked, and he said it would look better when he got the lights fixed on it. At school Corky was famous for his peep shows. They were always putting them on exhibit, and the teachers would say that if he applied the same imagination and skill to his work as he did to his hobby, he "could be somebody." What amazed them, I guess, was the same thing that got us all: how a guy as restless and nervous as Corky was most of the time, could have so much patience when it came to making things on such a small scale for the peep shows. The top of his closet was stacked with them, and I helped him put away the ones that were around the room—winter scenes made with cotton, scenes from foreign countries with trees made from twigs, and scenes with animals that Corky had copied from the exhibits at the Museum of Natural History. I looked into each one before I handed it to him, and it seemed to make him feel better to spend some time talking about them.

"Mel really liked 'em," he said when we were finished. "It was the first thing I ever did, I guess, that he hadn't done—he used to brag to all of his friends about what a great artist I was." He looked up at me. "Boy," he said, shaking his head. "How long you think this is gonna go on, me remembering everything Mel ever said or did?" I shrugged and he patted me on the shoulder again. "You don't gotta say anything, Howie. Come on, let's get out of here before I start getting upset again."

"You ought to get some sleep," his mother said when Corky announced that we were going for a walk. "You'll need it."

"I'll be okay," Corky said.

"Pa's relatives will be here before morning," she said.

"So?"

"I'm just telling you," she said. Corky's father didn't add anything, or even look at Corky. He just sat back in his rocking chair as if he were in another world. He looked very old to me.

"You okay?" Corky asked, kneeling next to Rhoda's chair. She nodded and ran her hand over Corky's blond hair. Then he whispered so the others wouldn't hear: "If you need me to stay here, you just say the word, Rhoda—"

"You go with Howie," she said. "It'll do you good to get some fresh air." Then she leaned over and kissed him on the cheek softly. Her eyes were bloodshot from crying, I remember, but she looked more beautiful sitting in that dark room with her hair messed than I'd ever seen her. When I tried to imagine what she must have been thinking and feeling, I had to swallow hard to keep the tears back. Still, I knew I wanted to say something to her, and I guess I did because in the next instant I was standing next to her chair and she had touched me on the cheek and kissed me too. "Thanks, Howie," she said. "You keep an eye on Corky now—"

"You wanna come with me to see Mel?" Corky asked when we were outside.

"Mel?"

"Come on—" he said. "You don't got to look at me like that—I didn't bust my wig. I mean at the funeral parlor. I wanna see him by myself once—before the others."

"You know which place he's at?"

Corky nodded and turned up Rogers Avenue. I stayed next to him. At the corner of Rogers and Church, in the London Hut, the bus drivers were sitting, drinking coffee. "Sure I know where he is," Corky said. "My old man ain't been talking about anything but the funeral since last spring. He said he had to get my old lady *ready* for it. Bastard—" We walked up Church Avenue, toward Flatbush, past Holy Cross Church. "The way he kept talking, you could tell he was glad Mel was gonna die."

"Come on, Corky," I said. "Your dad may be a louse, but I'm sure he didn't *want* Mel to die—"

"No?" Corky sneered. "You don't know my old man. He's got something twisted in him—ever since he had to leave the farm. Something happened then."

"What?"

Corky shrugged. "I don't remember. I was too young. But something happened with him and my uncle—that was Sarah Jean's father—they ran the place together. There was fighting going on all the time, about money. That Sarah Jean's mother —she's a real bitch. My old man almost killed her once, went after her with an ax—I swear to God! I remember that. Me and Sarah Jean, we were playing in the barn when he took after her—we hid back of the bin of horseshoes. Sarah Jean's old man hadn't come, he would of chopped her head off. You should of seen him swinging that ax over his head—the horses, they were stamping like mad—I still remember that. I expected one of them to rear up and kill 'em both."

"Why'd he do it?" I asked.

Corky shrugged, "I don't know—she was a bitch, that's all. I told you. She was always bugging him." He laughed real loud. He seemed happy again. "He could of chopped her head off in one swipe too! You seen the power he has before, when he slugged me. On the farm he could beat any of the hands at tests of strength—he was always arm-wrestling somebody. The only guy who ever stood up to him was Mel." Corky shook his head emphatically. "Mel never took any shit from that bastard."

We were almost at the funeral parlor, and Corky pointed it out to me. He hitched up his pants, set his jaw, and a minute later we'd walked through the door. The man there looked at us strangely. "What do you boys want?" he asked. The room was lit with a pale amber light. In the next room I could see a coffin, the top open. There were flowers all around it, and the inside was lined with fancy silk.

"Is my brother ready?" Corky asked.

The guy looked at Corky. "Your brother?"

"Mel—Mel Williams."

"Melvin Williams," the man repeated. His hair looked as if it had been drenched in oil. "Yes," he said to himself. "Now I have it. The young man who . . ."

"Cut the jazz," Corky said. "I wanna see my brother. Is he ready?"

The guy started apologizing to Corky in a Holy Joe tone

about not having greeted us in a nicer way. "But we do have some young toughs who sometimes come in here at night and—"

"Come on, come on," Corky said. He was rubbing his palms furiously with his fingertips and for a second I could see him losing his temper and slugging the funeral guy.

"Let me check," the man said. He left us and Corky cursed. "Greasy bastard. He better not touch my brother—" The man returned after a minute and said that the "final preparations" would not be completed until the morning. "You sure?" Corky said.

"Yes," the man said. He started to offer his condolences, but Corky didn't want them. The way his eyes were darting, and the way he kept shifting his feet and playing with his hands I think I must have been scared that Corky was not only going to slug him but was going to drag me down to the basement with him to look for Mel. I had this mad picture in my head of us pulling corpses out of these huge refrigerators, and the thought of the naked bodies, all fleshy and pink, made my stomach turn. I tasted some of the stuff from the party in my mouth, but I forced it back down.

"What time?" Corky asked.

"The family viewing is scheduled for ten o'clock," the man said.

"Will he be ready before that?"

The man thought for a second. "Well, I imagine the preparations will be completed by our staff sometime before that, but, as I said—"

"I'll be here at nine," Corky said. "You better be open. Come on, Howie."

We walked around a lot after that, and at about two or three in the morning we wound up at my house. My father was a restless sleeper and he got up when he heard us come in. I think he was going to give me hell for coming in so late, but when he saw Corky he changed his mind. He told him how sorry he was to hear about Mel, and Corky mumbled back a reply.

"Can he stay here for the night?" I asked.

My father hesitated. "Do your folks know?" he asked.

Corky started to say something but I interrupted him and I surprised myself at how I could raise my voice to my father. "Jesus," I said. "You're not gonna be like that, are you? What's the difference? If you don't want him to stay here, just say so. Yes or no—"

My father looked at Corky, then at me, then back at Corky. "Don't wake your brother and sister," he said. "You want me to get you up in the morning?"

"I got to be at the funeral parlor at nine," Corky said.

My father promised he would wake us at eight and then he said good night and told us not to stay up too late talking. I was proud of him. "He doesn't even need an alarm clock," I explained to Corky later. "It's like he's got one built into his head—he can wake up any time he wants—on the dot."

I loaned Corky a pair of my pajamas and we got undressed. When I'd opened my hi-riser, Corky lay on his back in the bed next to me, smoking. He cursed a few times and he seemed to be thinking about a lot of things. He thanked me for sticking with him and letting him sleep over, but I told him to shut up. Then he turned on his side and smiled at me.

"Bet I know what you're thinking," he said.

"What?"

"Bet you're wondering if your girlfriend's coming up from Pennsylvania. I'll bet you can't wait."

"Ah, come on, Corky—I never even met the girl. I mean—"

He laughed and punched me in the arm. "Wait till you

see her. Last time I saw her was over two years ago—but she looked like she was gonna turn into a real piece. She had some pair of bazookas for a girl her age. Since then I been writing to her and telling her all about you, what a great lover you are—"

"Cut it out," I said. But Corky teased me about how I always blushed when he showed her picture in the school-yard, and he kept asking me if I was going to give her a snow job, and going into endless details about how to get a girl hot. Finally, to stop him, I played along and started bragging that I would plug her if I got the chance. Saying that really got Corky excited and we stayed up for a while after that, imagining to each other all the different ways there were to plug girls. I don't know what time we fell asleep, but I'll never forget what it felt like, just lying there in the dark and talking, and I remember thinking a few times of what it would be like to tell all the guys about it—about how on the night Corky's brother had died he'd stayed over my house with me and we'd talked all night long.

When we got to the funeral parlor the next morning, Corky didn't even wait for the man to show him to the right room. He just started walking through the place with these big determined strides until he found Mel. He looked into the box quickly—I couldn't see his face because I was a few steps be-hind him—and by the time I went up to him he'd turned around. "Okay," he said. "I saw him. Let's go."

We were out of the building almost before we'd been in, and I had only gotten a quick look at Mel. What I'd seen had made me nauseated though: he looked like a wax doll some-body had done up with lipstick and rouge. It made my stomach turn every time I imagined what the men must have had to do to get him to look that way—cleaning him out and things—and I remember that even though I saw that his eyes were

closed I could feel his eyeballs staring through the lids, each
one pointing in a different direction. Corky walked fast when
we left and I had to skip once in a while to keep up with him.
"Bastards," he kept muttering. "Goddamn bastards." He
seemed so mean and angry I was scared that when he got home
he would really kill somebody. I'd never seen him as angry as
he was then, and when he kept repeating the word "bastards"
I couldn't tell who he was referring to.

As soon as he walked through the door of his home,
though, and saw all his relatives sitting around the table eating
breakfast, the anger left. He got the way he did at parties—
self-conscious and unsure of himself. He went around the room
shaking hands with everybody and being kissed by all the
women, and he hardly said anything. He just kept jerking his
head forward the way a very shy guy does when he's introduced to somebody, and mumbling hello's. He shoved his
hands in and out of his pockets and he didn't seem to be able to
look anybody in the eye. He made the rounds of the room,
staring at the floor most of the time, and then came back and
stood by me.

When Corky's mother introduced me, saying I was
Corky's best friend and that I'd stayed with him since the news
had come, I felt uncomfortable, like an intruder. Everybody
said hello, but when they stared at me I felt they were
looking at me as if *I* was the one who'd been responsible
for Mel's death. There must have been twenty to thirty of them
in that small living room—about half of them sitting at the
table drinking coffee, and the rest sitting in chairs, as quiet
as Corky's father. Some of the women dabbed at their eyes
with handkerchiefs once in a while, and Rhoda and a few of the
neighbors walked around in the silence asking if people had
enough coffee.

"They got here about an hour ago," Corky's mother said

to us. "They drove all night to be here—" She started to say something else, but began crying instead. A big woman—one of Corky's aunts—went to her and put her arm around her shoulder. Everybody else ate in silence. That got me, I remember— the idea of twenty or thirty people driving in a caravan of cars through the night on empty highways from these farms I'd never seen. I was certain they hadn't spoken, either. Just stayed awake looking at the road and waiting for the sun to come up.

When Corky's mother had gotten control of herself she asked some of the people about how other relatives and friends were—and then things settled down with everybody talking about who'd married and who'd had children and who'd been hit by disaster or by good fortune. They weren't quiet after that. Even Corky's father talked a lot—asking questions about the farm—and it really impressed me, how much all the men knew about animals and farming and machines. I suppose it was because they came from a world I didn't know anything about, but there was something about them—not just the way they clipped their sentences short or the old-fashioned way they dressed, with double-breasted suits and wide ties, but something else that made me envy them, that made me think that they were wiser than men like *my* uncles, who were all in businesses.

In the middle of all the talk a girl came out of Corky's room and I knew right away it was Sarah Jean. She was dressed in a plain wine-colored shirtwaist dress—and her blond hair was cut short, in bangs straight across her forehead. She was much prettier than her picture—it was almost as if she were the only person in the room who had any light coming from her face—yet she hardly seemed to be there. When she walked around the table and came to us, nobody even turned to look at her. She did it so silently it was as if she had air cushions under her feet. She just seemed to glide across the room, her whole body moving together, not emphasizing any one part, and I couldn't take my eyes off her or stop my heart from pounding. She drifted in between me and Corky and reached up on her toes slightly and kissed him on the cheek. "I'm sorry, Corky," she said. "I liked Mel real well."

She stayed next to us while the conversation went on around the room, and the whole time she held Corky's hand. I kept glancing at her and I couldn't figure out how old she was. Even though her hair was cut short and she didn't have any make-up on, there was something in the way her body relaxed, in the way she was able to stand there without fidgeting, that made her seem much older than the girls her age I went to school with. Her arm touched mine above the elbow—her skin was cool and soft—but she didn't seem to be aware of it, and I didn't move away. I kept glancing at her and getting more and more nervous.

Finally, Corky remembered that I was there. "This is Howie," he said. "I stayed over his house last night."

Sarah Jean nodded to me. "You meet my mother yet?" she asked.

"Your who—?" I replied—or something like that. I was so flustered by the way she looked straight at me that I didn't know what to say. Corky's face seemed to relax when he saw what was happening to me.

"That's her over there," Sarah Jean said, motioning to a tall woman who was collecting dishes from the table.

"Hey," Corky said, leaning his head in front of us and pushing his hair out of his eyes. "Did Howie tell you about how he's been telling everybody you're his girlfriend—?"

"Come on," I objected. "You're the one—"

Then Corky laughed and explained to Sarah Jean about showing her picture. She smiled, and looked at me without blinking. Her eyes were a kind of olive-green color and I couldn't get over how pretty they were, at how they seemed to go with the rest of her face. Her hair was almost white in spots from having been bleached by the sun, yet her skin, even though it was smooth and brown, had a kind of deep red flush to it, mostly in her cheeks and around her eyes. "You're real nice-looking," she said to me, her eyes fixed on mine. She said it as if it were a fact. Corky laughed and kidded me about blushing. "I got thin skin," I said.

"My Ma's looking at us," Sarah Jean said. I looked at Sarah Jean's mother standing across the room, and the look she gave me made me gulp. "Hold my hand, Howie," Sarah Jean said, and she slipped her hand into mine. "I know what she's thinking," she whispered to us, and I looked at her mother. She gave me such a stern look, I recall—as if holy fire were going to erupt from her eyes—that I started to take my hand from Sarah Jean's. With the gentlest pressure on my palm from her fingertips she made me keep it there. "I know what she's thinking," Sarah Jean said again, and her cheeks glowed more than ever. "I don't care, though. You just hold on to my hand, Howie, and don't be scared. She can't do nothing to us."

So I stood there holding Sarah Jean's hand. Her eyes were shining now, and while we stood there and everybody talked, she hummed along in this pretty voice, thin and pale. Then Corky's father said that it was time, that the funeral car was outside.

Downstairs, we got into the back of a Cadillac limousine along with Corky's parents and Rhoda, and on the way to the funeral parlor I looked out the windows, wondering if anybody I knew was going to see me riding with Corky's family.

"I saw him already," Corky whispered, low enough so that only Sarah Jean and I could hear. "It don't look like him at all. Howie and I went to the place this morning. The bastards got him all fixed up like a square—you may not recognize him in this suit and tie and stuff."

"I liked Mel real well," Sarah Jean said.

"It don't look like him at all—" Corky repeated.

Sarah Jean ran her thumb along the back of my hand and goose pimples started up my right arm. Corky's father was sitting between Corky's mother and Rhoda, talking low to both of them, about how it was going to be a great shock to see Mel this way, about how they should prepare themselves.

His words didn't help. When we got there and walked inside, the moment the two women saw Mel it was as if they hadn't understood until that second that he was actually dead. They both started wailing—totally out of control—and one of Corky's uncles went to them quickly to hold them steady. I don't remember what they said or how long they stood there looking at Mel, but I do remember the sounds they both made —not just whimpering and crying and rasping when they tried to stop the tears, but this high-pitched sound, almost like the kind you hear dogs make sometimes. Everybody left them alone with Mel, and when they sat down on chairs away from the coffin, the other relatives began coming forward.

"Once is enough for me," Corky said to Sarah Jean.

She looked at him, then took my hand. "Come on, Howie," she said. "You come with me."

So I went up to the box and got a longer look this time. I still couldn't cry. Everybody around me was, though they all did it softly, but it still didn't seem real to me that Mel was gone. It was as if somebody else was in the box. Sarah Jean cried some and I asked her if she was okay. "I liked him real well," she said. "Here—help me touch his hand." As soon as she said that, I said we should leave to make room for some others to come up and see Mel. "Don't be scared," she said. "Once you touch a dead person, then you feel better—it don't seem so scary after that." And with my hand on top of hers she reached over the side of the coffin and touched Mel where his hands were clasped on his stomach. "Come on," she whispered. "You do it, too, Howie. You'll feel better if you do."

I let my hand slip off hers and I touched Mel's hand but it was so cold and stiff it made me think of the way your own hand feels when it falls asleep—you can touch it, and you know you're touching it, but it seems to belong to somebody else.

A few of the other relatives were standing alongside us now, and from the corner of my eye I saw Sarah Jean's mother approaching us. "He looks right nice, *I* think," she said when she got to us. Sarah Jean looked at her in this absent way and didn't reply. A woman behind us said something about all the flowers that were around the room and how nice they looked.

"Poor Mel," another aunt said—the big one who'd comforted Corky's mother. "We all have to travel the same road, I suppose, but why so soon, why so soon—?"

"Well," Sarah Jean's mother said—she said it stiffly, too, even though there were tears in her eyes. "We know where he is now, though, don't we? We can at least be thankful for that."

Sarah Jean jerked her head sideways and her eyes flared up in anger. Her mother saw the look and repeated what she'd said. "We know where he is now, don't we, Sarah Jean?" Sarah Jean just glared. "I was just repeating to Frank and Margaret about the time when Mel accepted the Lord as his personal savior. It was while he was riding home from town one day when he was a boy on the farm. Reverend Millet had given him a lift—"

Then Sarah Jean did the strangest thing. She started humming. The more her mother went on about the religious stuff, the louder Sarah Jean hummed. It was the same tune she'd been humming when we'd been at Corky's place. It sounded like a hymn and while Sarah Jean hummed it she looked straight at Mel's face, as if she were singing it just for him. The other relatives all grew quiet and Sarah Jean's mother stopped what she was saying. "Don't *you* be singing that," she said between her teeth, low, but Sarah Jean kept singing. It wasn't humming any more, because she'd let her mouth come open so that it was more like singing without words, with a sweet "ah" sound coming from her. Her mother kept glaring at her and whispering for her to stop, saying she had no right, but Sarah Jean didn't seem to hear her. She hummed through the song twice, softly, and when she stopped, one of her aunts came to her and kissed her on the cheek, saying that God must have given her such a voice just to put Mel at peace. Sarah Jean's mother got more upset then— you could see it in the way she clicked her jaw, as if she were grinding on her teeth—and Sarah Jean only smiled and tugged at my hand. I couldn't move. Her mother's stare had me transfixed. Sarah Jean tugged again. "Come on, Howie," she said, and this time I followed her to where Corky was standing in back of all the chairs.

"I got an idea," Corky whispered to us. "How about us three cutting out of here and doing something together?" I shrugged and looked at Sarah Jean. She was smiling, her cheeks glowing. "It's okay," Corky said. "Mel wouldn't wanna make me hang around all day looking at him and saying a bunch of crap to all these jerks coming to say how sorry they are. Bastards. Half the people who're gonna be here never even knew him—they'll just be doing it for my old man and my mother. Anyway, the funeral's not till Monday—we can come back tonight or tomorrow if you want. I'm just too damned restless today—"

"I like Rhoda," Sarah Jean said. "She's real pretty—"

"Come on," Corky said. "Am I gonna go alone, or are you two coming with me—?"

Sarah Jean didn't seem to be listening to Corky. She left us and went to Rhoda. She knelt down next to her and took Rhoda's hand in hers, then said something. Rhoda stopped crying and tried to smile and they talked to each other for a minute. Then Sarah Jean came back. "I told Rhoda," she said. "Let's go."

"Sarah Jean—" we heard from behind as we started out. "Sarah Jean Stilman!" Sarah Jean turned and looked at her mother coming through the rooms after us. "I want to speak with you—" Sarah Jean smiled, and she had this real wild look in her eye. "Come on!" she said, excited. "Don't let her scare you. She ain't God."

Her mother kept calling to us to come back, but the minute we got outside, Corky shouted, "This way!" and we ran down the street together, Sarah Jean between us, the three of us holding hands, zooming in and out of people. When we finally stopped running, way down Flatbush Avenue near the Parkside Theater, we were laughing and out of breath.

"Let's go rowing," Corky said, and we turned up Parkside Avenue into Prospect Park and walked to where you rented the boats. Corky paid. He did the rowing too, and Sarah Jean and I sat in the back of the boat holding hands. It was still early and the lake was almost empty. None of us said anything for a while, but you could tell how happy Corky was now, not only to be away from the funeral parlor but to be getting rid of some energy. When we were away from the islands, in the big open part of the lake, Sarah Jean took her shoes off and let her feet slip over the side. She started humming again, but she kept laughing to herself while she did.

"You been baptized?" she asked me.

"I'm Jewish," I said.

"You don't know then," she said, and laughed again. Then she hummed the tune, and there was something about the melody and the way she did it that made me think it could go on forever. It was beginning to haunt me. "They sing this when you get baptized," she said to me. "It's a hymn." Then she started singing, soft and thin, with this calm look in her eyes: *"Just as I am without one plea . . . But that Thy blood was shed for me . . ."* She didn't seem to breathe between sentences. I took my shoes and socks off and let my feet trail in the water so that the boat balanced better. *"And that Thou bid'st me come to Thee . . . O Lamb of God, I come, I come . . ."* She sang another verse and this time I hummed along with her. What I liked most was the way her voice glided over the words like "am" and "plea" and "Thee"— the ones that carried across more than one note.

"When they baptize you, the preacher, he holds your head under water backwards—that's immersion," she said. "Corky knows." Corky nodded and pulled at the oars. I could see his muscles, and sweat dripping along his neck. "Only thing was," Sarah Jean said, "when they did it to me, this damned preacher, he kept my head under water so long when I come up I bit his hand." Corky caught his oar in the water and splashed us. Sarah Jean clapped her hands, delighted at his surprise. "My mother got so mad she about died." Then she leaned forward and spoke lower, smiling the whole time. "That's why she got so mad before, me singing a hymn for Mel and all—she keeps on at me all the time, how I'm gonna be damned eternally, cause I weren't baptized right. She says the devil must of been inhabiting me, me to do that. —But I don't care. I got even with that preacher. You should of heard him howl, everybody come splashing through the water to us. But I got a real good hold on account of I knew I would only get that chance but once—" She stopped smiling. "He held me under for spite, cause he knew I didn't like him."

"Reverend Millet?" Corky asked. Sarah Jean nodded and Corky smiled. "Mel hated him too," he said, and then—just like that—Corky started singing too, real loud. *"Just as I a-am withou-out one plea—"* He could hardly carry a tune, but it didn't matter. Sarah Jean and I joined in with him and as we glided across the waters we sang the song again and again.

We stayed on the lake for an hour or two, singing and talking and kidding around—Sarah Jean and Corky had fun roaring out a lot of the hymns they both knew—and then we came in and sat at the boathouse and had some French fries and Cokes. Corky wouldn't let me pay for a thing.

"You wanna see where our team plays its games?" he asked Sarah Jean, and she said she did, so we walked through the park to the Parade Grounds. Corky got sentimental then, remembering how he used to be batboy for a team Mel had been the star on, and he couldn't stop talking about him and about what a great ballplayer he would have been. "Yeah," he said. "I'd give anything to be able to make the Majors some-day—the way Mel would of—" He kicked at the dirt. "Ah, shit!" he said.

"You'll be as good as Mel if you want to," Sarah Jean said.

He lifted his head. "You think so?"

"Sure," I offered. "Everybody's always saying how you got the same swing he has—"

"Ah, what's the difference now?" Corky said, staring across the fields.

"You'll be as good as Mel if you want to," Sarah Jean said again, and the way she said it had a calming effect on Corky.

"What time is it, Howie?" he asked. I told him it was after one o'clock and he punched his fist into his palm. "Hey, I know what—let's show Sarah Jean what the Kenmore's like on a Saturday afternoon—" He put his arm over both our shoulders and started talking about how the RKO Kenmore balcony was famous all over Brooklyn. "They got a maternity ward built right in!" he said, and Sarah Jean giggled. Then Corky explained how all the girls went there together on Saturday afternoons and sat in the balcony, and how the matron never asked your ages, so you could smoke and neck and do anything you wanted. We walked up Caton Avenue, then turned right on Ocean. "Howie's never been here on Saturday afternoon,"

Corky said to Sarah Jean when we were at the booth buying tickets, "so you gotta take good care of him—you know what I mean?"

"Howie can take care of himself," Sarah Jean said, and when she said it she tickled the inside of my palm with her fingertip. I shoved my other hand in my side pocket to keep what was happening from showing, and as we passed into the lobby and started up the steps I was really nervous. It was supposed to be mostly the tough guys and girls who would be there in the dark and I didn't know what to expect. Of our group of guys, Corky was the only one who'd ever been there more than once, and he'd always brought back stories about how girls you didn't even know would let you sit next to them and do wild things.

"I almost forgot," Corky said when we got to the landing of the balcony. "Wait for me a minute—I gotta get ammunition!" He ran down the stairs, two at a time, and a minute later he was back with a couple of bars of candy. "Come on," he said, and we went inside. I don't know what I expected, but I was surprised that the seats were only about half taken. There was a lot of smoke and some of the guys had their feet on the backs of the chairs in front of them. There was an old woman in a white uniform standing in one corner, with a flashlight, but she didn't seem to care about anything. "Let me scout the place first," Corky said, and he walked along the back row, looking down the aisles. Every once in a while you'd hear somebody curse, or make a remark back to the movie screen, but most of the time it was pretty quiet. You could hear girls giggling, and sometimes some arguing. "Okay," Corky said. "I see one. Follow me—"

Sarah Jean and I followed Corky down a side aisle until we came to two girls who were sitting together. They looked at Corky, then back at the screen. We sat down, and Corky turned to the girl at his left. "You want some candy?" he asked. The girl gave him a dirty look, but this didn't bother Corky. "Ah, come on," he said. "I ain't trying to be fresh. Honest. This is my cousin Sarah Jean from Pennsylvania and her boyfriend. Come on," he whispered. "We're sitting next to each other anyway and I got more than I can eat, so we might as well share. Here—your friend can have some too."

"It's okay," Sarah Jean said to the girls. "He's my cousin."

For some reason, this seemed to do the trick. The girls took some candy from Corky and the next thing I knew he had his arm along the back of the seat of the one next to him, and her friend was saying she had to go to the bathroom and she got up and left, and then Corky and this girl were at it. I tried to keep my eyes on the movie—Yvonne De Carlo in a Technicolor Western—but I kept glancing at Corky to see how he was doing and then looking around at the other couples. Sarah Jean hardly moved. She just sat up straight and looked at the movie. My hand began to get sweaty in hers and I took it away and put my arm around the back of her seat. Next to me, Corky was starting to use his hands and I had to fight hard not to keep all my attention on him.

I don't know how much time passed before I finally let my arm rest on Sarah Jean's shoulder, but she seemed patient about it, and when I'd finally gotten it there she leaned toward me and let her head rest close to my face. Then she reached up with her right hand and touched my fingers, one at a time. She said something and I shifted in my chair and turned to her. "*I*—I didn't hear you," I said, and when Sarah Jean saw how nervous I was—I squeaked on the first word and had to clear my throat—she laughed and moved closer to me, so that I could feel her breast against my side. The way she laughed didn't make me feel embarrassed at all, and I relaxed a little and let my cheek rest against her forehead. I could tell that she knew I was nervous and that I was working up my courage to make the final move—and what I liked about her, what I still remember most—was that the way she rested against me, so patiently—that's the word that comes to mind—made me feel good inside, confident, grown up. It was as if she were saying, "It's okay, Howie—you just take your time, and when you're ready I'm here."

She was leaning deep into my shoulder by then, and when I looked down at her I saw that her eyes were closed and that she wasn't looking at the movie. I reached over with my left hand to touch her cheek and she gave my finger a quick nibble. We both laughed, and then I leaned down and she leaned up and we met without any fuss or awkwardness.

Time passed pretty quickly after that, even though all we did was neck and fool around, teasing each other—and no matter how much we kissed, it never got boring or sloppy. That was the thing I remember most—no matter how long we'd stay in a clinch, her lips seemed to stay smooth and cool. She was so gentle, the way she touched my face and arms and played with me with her tongue—no girl had ever done that before with me—that I could hardly believe it. And when we'd separate and lean back, she'd snuggle close and smile at me. "I'm real glad I came up to New York," she said to me after a while, and I said I was glad too, though I wished it didn't have to be because of Mel. "You're a good friend to Corky," she said. "He looks up to you—" I was surprised to hear that, because I'd thought it was the opposite, and when I tried to tell her it wasn't true, that I didn't know what she meant, she said that that made her like me even more. "You don't tell him what to do," she said. "I like that." We talked about other things too, and off and on we watched the movie—I think the other picture was a rerun of Randolph Scott in *Gung Ho*—and then, much later, I suddenly felt an elbow in my ribs and I nearly jumped out of my seat.

"Come on, lover," Corky said. "Time to come up for air. It's getting late—"

"Where—where's the girl?" I asked, seeing the seat next to his empty.

"I sent her home," he said. "Come on, it's time to go to the schoolyard for our game of stickball. You'll probably beat me tonight—I'm so stiff from wrestling in these seats—" We stood up and I tucked my shirt in where it had come loose and followed Corky out, holding Sarah Jean's hand. When we were in front of the theater, Corky leaned close to me and winked. "You're okay, Howie," he whispered. "I knew you had it in you—" Then he spoke louder, for both of us. "Someday, what I'm gonna do," he began, "is own a movie theater where they got a section of seats in pairs, without armrests . . ."

On the way to the schoolyard we stopped and had some pizza—Sarah Jean had never had any before and she loved it—and then we walked up Snyder Avenue, to avoid going by the funeral parlor, and when we got to the schoolyard most of the guys were already there, playing stickball or pitching pennies. They came over to us slowly and they were shy about saying things to Corky about Mel. They didn't say much, and when Corky told them to forget about it, that after the initial shock you got used to the idea and that, as everybody knew, it'd always been a question of time—when he'd made them feel better about it by talking like that, they all went back to what they were doing. Still, I had the feeling they understood what Corky was going through better than most guys would have. None of them asked him why he wasn't with his family or at the funeral parlor.

Corky introduced Sarah Jean to all the guys and I was kidded a lot and felt pretty good. We got chosen into a game on opposite sides, and while we played, Sarah Jean sat next to where we had the strike zone chalked on the handball court, and I could tell that the guys thought she was okay.

An inning or two after we got there, Corky and I took over the pitching for our teams and as it got darker my fast ball began mystifying the batters. I struck them out so often that they started calling me Carl again. Corky did pretty well too, but after two innings he suddenly hit one of his wild streaks—he walked about six batters in a row before he switched to the outfield—and I wondered if I should begin pitching bad also, to kind of even things up, but I didn't.

"Why do you think it is?" Corky asked when we were finished playing and were sitting against the handball court, relaxing. "It's the same when I pitch for our team—I'll be going along fine for an inning or two and then bam!—the minute I get a man on base and got to pitch with a stop motion I can't find the plate." He shrugged, and laughed. "Ah, who cares—?" he said.

Sarah Jean touched his hand and she said again what she'd said before: "You'll be as good as Mel some day if you want to—"

Corky bummed a cigarette from one of the guys and smiled. "Yeah," he said. "I guess so. They say that after you develop to your full height and weight your body settles down inside and you get steadier. Maybe my control will improve then. Anyway, I don't have to be a pitcher—you see me blast that ball over the fence off McGowan?—bam!" Corky said, imitating his own swing. "I showed him where I lived, huh, Howie?"

The girls were starting to come down now—it was almost pitch black out—and Corky picked up his jacket and went over to fool with them, telling us not to do anything he wouldn't do. Sarah Jean and I stayed where we were. I asked her if she was getting cold. She said no, but I put my jacket around her shoulders anyway. Some of the girls came over to us to see what Sarah Jean was like, and they were all so polite

I hardly recognized them. They didn't seem to like Corky's horsing around as much as usual—I guess some of them felt strange about doing anything with him on the weekend his brother died. But by nine o'clock I saw him standing by the fence with a girl we'd nicknamed the Splinter because she was so flat-chested, and he was really giving it to her. Then for a long time Sarah Jean and I kissed, leaning on each other and on the handball court and on the concrete and on our elbows all at the same time—we shifted a lot—and I kept my hands around her inside the jacket. Straightening up once, one of them touched against her breast accidentally and I started to say I'm sorry, but she said, "That's okay, Howie," and let me keep it there. Unless you count the sessions we used to have at the corner of Linden Boulevard and Rogers Avenue ganging up on fat Louise, who let you do anything to her, it was the first time I'd ever done that too.

When we finally got up from the ground the schoolyard was empty, and both of us laughed at how sore our rear ends were. I told Corky it was past eleven o'clock, thinking he might want to get back home, but he said that the night was only beginning. He was right. The next thing I knew, we were on the IRT heading for Manhattan. At Chambers Street we changed for the downtown South Ferry local.

Sarah Jean had never been on a ferry boat before and she liked it. The four of us stayed on the outside the whole time, even though the wind ripped through you, and when we got to Staten Island we hiked around until we found a diner that was open. By this time Corky's girl had started getting angry with him, saying he'd promised to get her home earlier. Sarah Jean tried to calm her down, but she whined so much that Corky threatened to leave her stranded. She cursed him and then he began ranking her out about how flat she was, but Sarah Jean got him to stop right away.

On the ferry back to Manhattan Corky and the Splinter made out inside on one of the benches, but Sarah Jean and I stayed outside again. We kept kissing and nuzzling and promising each other that we'd write every day after she went back to Pennsylvania. What I remember most was the way sometimes, after we'd come up from a long kiss, she'd say in a surprised way, as if she were discovering some new fact: "I *like* you, Howie—"

When we'd gotten back to Brooklyn and dropped the Splinter off where she lived—it was almost five o'clock by then —we walked around together, and every once in a while, whenever I got the urge, I'd just stop and we'd kiss in the middle of the street and Corky would laugh at us and tease me. We walked around the neighborhood, showing Sarah Jean where all the guys lived and the places we hung out, and when we got tired we'd sit down on the curbstone and rest. At about seven o'clock we wound up at the corner of Flatbush and Church in front of Garfield's Cafeteria, and Corky announced that it was time for breakfast.

So we went inside and loaded our trays with pancakes and bacon and French toast and Danish and juice and milk and then sat down at a table by the window. We talked a lot about what a great thing it was to stay up all night and then have breakfast together, and I felt pretty good seeing people look over at us, wondering what three kids our age were doing in there at such an hour. After a while—we sat around the table for a long time and I'd finished a second plate of French toast, it tasted so good—we could see people going by all dressed up.

"You gonna go to church?" Corky asked Sarah Jean.

"We'll get back too late," she said, and smiled slowly at him. "Are you?"

"It's only eight-thirty," I said.

"Nah, Sarah Jean's right, Howie," Corky said, catching the look in her eye. "We might as well go to the park again, huh?"

For some reason his suggestion sounded sour to me and I guess I showed it because he got mad, the way he did sometimes. "What's the matter?" he asked. "You got to ask your mommy first?"

"No," I said. "It's just that they'll be wondering what happened to me. I don't stay out like this every night of the week, you know."

"So go home," he said. "The police must be looking for you."

I didn't say anything and Corky didn't either. The thought of repeating what we'd done the day before suddenly made me feel tired. "You call home if you want, Howie," Sarah Jean said, breaking the silence. "Then the three of us can stay together longer."

I looked at Corky. "Sure," he said. "It's okay."

"How about your mother?" I asked Sarah Jean.

She smiled. "She don't worry about me," she said.

"Okay," I said, and left the table. I was afraid my father would yell at me, but when I said that I'd fallen asleep at Corky's house and that nobody had woken me until just now, he said he'd figured the same thing. I guess he was sympathetic because of Mel. He reminded me that my grandparents were coming over and that he expected me home by four or five o'clock. When I got back to the table, I told them that everything was okay but that I had to be back for dinner.

"Yeah," Corky said. "You better—you never know when they're gonna die, old people. Who knows? This might be the last chance to see them together."

I looked up at Corky and I think he knew from my look that I thought his remark was nutty. "My mother killed my father," Sarah Jean said then, suddenly. I turned to her, wondering if I'd heard right. Corky looked at her sideways too. Sarah Jean nodded emphatically. "She took his drink away from him."

Corky laughed.

"It ain't funny," Sarah Jean said, and Corky stopped smiling. "Everybody in the family knew about how he couldn't stay away from the stuff. But he didn't harm nobody with it." She paused. "Him and your father were good friends, Corky—could of stayed that way, my mother didn't—" She stopped and leaned forward. "The thing was, when I was young, at night my mother'd get him downstairs in the kitchen and badger the life out of him." She talked low and we had our heads close together across the table. Her large eyes had narrowed by now in a way I'd never seen them. "I used to sneak right outside and listen. 'Faith without works is death,' she'd say. 'You repeat it after me, Michael Stilman: Faith without works is death. Faith without works is death. Faith without works is death.' She'd keep repeating it and she wouldn't let up on him till she'd made him bawl. Then she'd feel satisfied." She stopped. "I used to think of ways to kill her."

"But—" Corky began.

"It don't matter," Sarah Jean said, as if she knew what Corky was going to say. "I know what I'm saying. If she'd let him be, he would of lived longer. But he didn't have nothing to live for. Your Pa was gone by then and he was the only one my father ever felt real kin to—and they couldn't have no more children after me on account of he had the mumps, so he had no son the way he would of liked. And then she wouldn't even leave him have—" She broke off and started again, stronger. "She'd stand up there over him making him repeat it till he'd grab at her knees. 'Faith without works is death. Faith without works is death.'"

"Hey, lower your voice," Corky said.

Sarah Jean sat back in her chair and her face, which had gone all tight and tense, relaxed. Her eyes opened all the way. "I liked Mel real well," she said to Corky. "He used to let me shoot his BB gun. He said I was a real good shot."

"Maybe for Christmas vacation me and Corky'll hitch down to where you live," I offered impulsively.

Sarah Jean looked down. "You don't got to," she said. Then she looked up and she couldn't keep from smiling. "But it'd be nice." She licked her lips. "You know what else?—I didn't tell nobody yet, but I've been thinking that as soon as I reach sixteen and don't have to be in school no more I'm gonna leave home. I made up my mind."

"Me too," Corky said.

They both turned to me. I opened my mouth as if I was going to say "Me too" also—but I didn't know if I should and I guess I had a crazy frozen expression on my face with my eyebrows up and my mouth wide open, because the two of them started laughing at me.

"Boy," Corky kept saying when we were outside, walking along Flatbush Avenue again, looking in all the windows. "You should of seen your face!"

I laughed when they teased me, but by the time we were at the park and had rented a rowboat again, none of us was laughing too much. We tried singing and making jokes and things, but the longer the day went on, the quieter and more depressed the three of us got. Nothing helped. After we finished rowing, we walked around the park a lot and then took Sarah Jean through the zoo and the botanical gardens. Our money had pretty much run out, so we had to share a couple of hot dogs for lunch. We ate at the Brooklyn Museum and walked around there for a while, with Corky trying to make funny comments about all the naked statues, and then we walked all

the way home. I got to my house at about four o'clock, feeling
pretty low, and guilty somehow for not staying with Corky
overnight again. I told this to Sarah Jean, and she smiled and
said that she'd take good care of him and that they'd both see
me tomorrow.

When I got to the funeral parlor the next morning most
of the guys were already there, sitting in a row near the back of
the room, and I sat down next to them. Corky and his family
were in the front row and Sarah Jean was sitting next to her
mother in the row behind them. There must have been a hundred or so folding chairs set up in the room and around the
sides were baskets of flowers. I'd never seen so many in one
place. The room filled up quickly and before I knew it they
were playing soft organ music and a man was standing at
a little lectern next to the coffin and reading from the Bible.
When he finished and sat down, another man got up and
began talking about Mel. Sarah Jean turned and smiled at me
from in front of the room and I wished I could be with her.
The guys who'd gotten to the parlor early whispered along our
row that Corky had told them all about what we'd done the day
before. "Boy," Izzie whispered—he was sitting two seats away
from me. "She's some piece! They really grow 'em in the country!"

The rest of the service is still pretty much of a blur to
me. There were lots of people from the neighborhood around
the room—some of the guys' mothers, a few of the store owners from Rogers Avenue like Mr. Fontani and Mr. Klein, people who lived in Corky's building—and the man up front spoke
a lot about going to live with the Lord Jesus and about Mel's
great gifts and how they would now be put into the highest
service in exchange for the greatest of gifts. I didn't pay too
much attention to him, but whenever I did I'd think up argu-

ments against what he was saying. Along our row the other guys all seemed as nervous and fidgety as I was—Eddie picked his nose a lot, Louie and Marty talked to each other the whole time, and Izzie kept trying to find out how far I'd gone with Sarah Jean. Whenever the preacher mentioned Mel's age, though, they all got quiet. I don't think that what he said about the Lord working in mysterious ways made much sense to any of them. Aside from Corky, though, Kenny Murphy was the only one of the guys who wasn't Jewish and I thought that maybe if we'd been brought up differently what the man was saying might have sounded right to us.

When he'd finished, everybody started walking up to the casket for the final look at Mel. Some of them did it quickly and some of them stayed a minute or so, and not too many of them could look over at Corky and his family. When the rows in front of us had all emptied out and it was our turn, we all kind of stumbled forward on each other's heels—I was right behind Izzie—and it was then that I cried. It wasn't because it was the last time I was going to see Mel, or because I suddenly realized that Mel simply wasn't going to be in the world any more. What happened was that as the guys all stood around the coffin looking in, most of them with their eyes popping out of their sockets, I suddenly looked at all of them—Louie and Izzie and Kenny and Eddie and Marty, and then quickly back at Corky—and I realized that some day I would be standing in front of a box looking in at one of them, at one of the guys I'd spent a lifetime knowing—and that some day some of them, the ones who were left, would be looking in at me, feeling the same ache. That was what made the tears start. They didn't last long, and I wiped my eyes quickly and followed the other guys out of the room.

One of the men from the funeral parlor asked us to be seated while the family had "the final viewing," and a few minutes later they came filing through. Corky's mother was in bad shape, and he and his father were holding her up. I looked at the other guys and none of us knew what to do. Some of the neighbors had come over to us and asked us questions about ourselves and our families—a few of the guys went and stood with their mothers—but even though I think we all felt grown up to be participating in such an event, when Corky had helped his mother sit down and came toward us, most of us were terrified.

"You guys coming to the cemetery?" he asked. "There's lots of room in some of the cars—just go outside. All my relatives got cars."

We nodded and hurried outside, telling people we were Corky's friends and asking if they had room for us. I got into a car with a man who worked at the bakery with Corky's father, and Izzie and Louie came in with me. The man was as stone-faced as Corky's father, and all the way to the cemetery—it was on Long Island—there was total silence.

It was raining slightly when we got there and we had to huddle inside a tent they'd set up. It was over pretty quickly after that, and while they were saying the final prayers I remembered a funeral I'd been to once of an uncle of mine and of how quiet this one was compared to it. At the other funeral, I remember, my aunt had carried on like a maniac, trying to follow my uncle into the grave—and I remembered also how all the men had gone up, one at a time, and shoveled dirt on top of the box after it had been lowered. They didn't do this for Mel.

As soon as they'd gotten him into the ground, Corky slipped away from his family and came over to me. "Come on," he said. "We got room in the car for you. Sarah Jean too."

All the way into Brooklyn I sat in the back of the car between Corky and Sarah Jean. In front of us Corky's parents and Rhoda stayed pretty quiet—they all looked exhausted, even Corky's father. Corky talked the whole way in, mostly about a guy who had come to the funeral—a fat Irish-looking old man I'd seen him talking with—who Corky said had come to represent the Brooklyn Dodger organization. Corky said that the guy had promised to send him Mel's old uniform, and a lot of glossy pictures that had been taken in spring training. And he'd said that any time Corky wanted to get into a game he should ask for him.

At Corky's house, everybody went inside and had coffee and then all the relatives went right back out and piled into their cars for the trip home. It happened so fast I didn't have a chance to be alone with Sarah Jean. I walked with her to the car, though, and scribbled her address down on the back of a card from my wallet.

"Anyway," Corky said, "at least you two got together."

Sarah Jean kissed Corky goodbye. "I had a real good time last night," she said to him. She turned to me. "Corky and I spent the whole night working on his new peep show," she said. "It's gonna be real good, Corky. Real good."

I didn't know if I should kiss her goodbye or not, but when I noticed the look her mother was giving me from inside the car, I took a step backwards. Sarah Jean smiled and stepped forward, touching me on the back of the neck with one hand and kissing me half on my mouth and half on the side of my face. I kept my eyes open. "When I'm sixteen," she whispered.

Then we were standing there waving goodbye as the line of cars started to move toward Rogers Avenue. "You better get on home," Corky said to me. "Maybe I'll see you tonight at the schoolyard. It depends on how Rhoda feels." He put his arm around my shoulder. "I'll tell you the truth, Howie, if not for her I wouldn't stay myself. But I think she could use me now, you know what I mean? She got no real home to go to, and no parents or anything." He patted me on the back. "You're okay, Howie."

Then he went over to Rhoda and walked inside his building with her, and I turned and walked home by myself.

After that day Corky spent almost all his free time with Rhoda. During the second week after school had started, she went back to work at Ellman's and every day when school was out he would stop by to see her. We didn't have any classes together at Erasmus, but we'd walk to school together and at night if I didn't have too much homework I'd usually find him with the other guys at the corner of Linden Boulevard and Rogers Avenue. Sometimes we'd go over to the schoolyard together and he'd mess around with the girls, but he never seemed to do it with the same spirit any more.

The other thing that changed about him was the way he started studying for school. None of the guys could figure it out. Sometimes he'd even call me up at home just to find out how to do an algebra problem, or to read a composition to me, and sometimes he'd invite me over and I'd eat supper with him and his family and Rhoda—she ate there almost every night—and we'd do our homework together. Rhoda was very proud of the way he was applying himself and this made Corky happy.

For a month or so after Sarah Jean went back we wrote each other almost every day, and I'd show the letters to Corky. I'd tell her about what I was doing in school and about our baseball team and about Corky and Rhoda and about how we were still planning to hitch down to see her, and she would tell me about how much she hated the farm and about her mother and about books she was reading and she'd make up stories that she'd include about a family of mules. Sometimes,

when I was most lonesome, I'd remember the things we'd done
the weekend we'd been together and I'd try to tell her all the
things I was feeling.

It didn't last, of course. There weren't any fights or anything like that—it was just that after a while we seemed to run
out of things to say to each other. By Thanksgiving our letters
were only going back and forth about once a week, and even
though the guys in our neighborhood were still speaking of her
as my girlfriend, by Christmas time we'd stopped writing almost completely. The last letter I remember getting from her
was one that came right after Christmas with a tin box full of
cookies. Corky got one too. He'd sent her a peep show he'd
made—it was a model farm with a barn and silo—and when
she wrote back to him and thanked him for it, she said to send
me her regards. That was all.

Not too long after that—just before our first term in
high school ended—the big news came: Corky's father announced that they were going to move back to the farm in
Pennsylvania. Corky said he should have suspected it, with all
the mail that had been flying back and forth since Mel's death
about bygones being bygones and family being family—and he
didn't seem to like the idea too much. He kept saying that he
wouldn't have as much chance to develop as a ballplayer on the
farm—that he wouldn't get the coaching and the competition
he could get at Erasmus. All of us reminded him of guys like
Walter Johnson and Bob Feller, but it didn't matter. What
seemed to bother him most, though, was leaving Rhoda alone
in the city.

From the time Mel died until Corky's father made the
decision about moving, Rhoda had practically lived with
Corky's family. She ate with them, she went to church with
them, and she slept over their house five or six nights a
week. I remember when I'd tell my parents I'd been study-

ing with Corky and that Rhoda had been helping Corky's
mother around the house, that they'd sigh and shake their
heads, though I didn't see anything wrong with what was happening.

At any rate, the day after Corky broke the news to us,
Rhoda stopped sleeping over his house. Corky spoke against his
parents a lot, about how it wasn't easy for Rhoda to live by
herself every night and how they should have taken her into
consideration, and he even started doing what he'd done when
Mel had been on the Fort Worth team—eating his meals at her
house and spending his evenings with her.

One Friday night, though, after Corky, Eddie, and I had
gone to an Erasmus basketball game together and were
walking along Flatbush Avenue talking about the players and
speculating on which of them would make good college ballplayers, Corky suddenly stopped and went white. Eddie and
I looked where Corky was looking and saw what it was. Coming out of the Loew's Kings Theater, Rhoda had her arm in
the arm of some guy and she was laughing. I don't remember
what the guy looked like, but except for the day Corky and
I raced over to Ellman's to show her Corky's first-term report
card—he'd gotten an 83 average, which was something nobody
could believe—it was the first time since before the funeral
that I'd seen her looking like her old self. She didn't see us.

"Boy," Corky said. "He ain't even dead a year yet."

Eddie and I tried to cheer Corky up after that, but no
matter what we said, he got more and more depressed—then
angry. You couldn't reason with him.

When Corky first got down to the farm that spring—his
family left during Easter vacation—we kept in pretty close
touch, and during the next few years we'd write one another
now and then. By that time he was doing pretty well pitch-

ing in American Legion ball, and I was playing varsity on
the Erasmus basketball team—we'd always save our newspaper clippings and exchange them. The summer of my third
year in high school he came up to New York for a weekend
and we went to a Yankee ball game and spent most of our
time with the guys down at the schoolyard playing three-man
basketball and stickball. Corky's control was still a little bit
off, but being on the farm had made him husky and his fast
ball was as good as any guy's on the Erasmus team. He slept
over my house for the two nights he was in town and he told
me a lot about the things he and Sarah Jean did together.

I suppose I should have suspected something then, but I
didn't, so that on that crazy cold night the following December
when he suddenly showed up after a basketball game against
Madison I was so stunned I didn't know what to say. He
caught me right outside Erasmus, under the arch on the Bedford Avenue side, and when I saw him carrying a suitcase I got
scared. But then this pair of hands was around my eyes from
the back, saying "Guess who?" and when she'd laughed and
given me a hug and a kiss and the two of them started explaining what was going on, I think I was almost as happy as they
were. I didn't feel uncomfortable at all.

I called my folks from Grand Central station and told
them I was staying over a friend's house, and then we were
on the train heading for Maryland and they were explaining to
me how Elkton was the closest place where they weren't under
age and where they didn't have to have consent. They kept
laughing at me because of the way I would shake my head in
disbelief, and Sarah Jean kept saying to me didn't I remember
what she'd said about when she was sixteen, and about how her
mother and Corky's father would have heart attacks when they
found out.

"*If* they find out—" Corky said, and he started telling me

how they were going to get a place somewhere in New York
and how Sarah Jean would work while Corky finished high
school and then he'd either go to college on a baseball scholarship or play in the Minors. Sarah Jean laughed a lot, and she
seemed very beautiful and happy. "You think my mother'll
think this is worse than biting a preacher's hand?" she asked
Corky once, and her eyes were shining when she said it. "I
guess we're just gonna roast in hell, huh, Howie?" she said to
me, cuddling up to Corky and beginning to hum. We kidded
around like that until the train got to the town early in the
morning and then we ate breakfast together in a diner and
reminisced about the other time we'd stayed up all night.

That night I telephoned my parents and told them the
truth—it didn't matter by then—and by the time I got back to
New York the next day—we all kissed goodbye at Grand Central and said we'd be seeing each other—I was half dead.
When I arrived home it all seemed like a dream and my parents thought the whole thing was silly and immature—if I'd
had the strength I would have argued with them, but it didn't
seem to matter. I felt tired and happy.

When I got back to school on Monday and told the story
to the guys, I felt even better. The part they liked best was
about where the clerk had read their application and had
made a sour face and said "I see you're cousins,"—and how
Corky had put him in his place by saying "So were Franklin
and Eleanor—ain't you got patriotism?" I'll never forget the
way he winked at Sarah Jean and me then, and the other thing
I remember most was the story he and Sarah Jean told me
on the train back to New York, about how, the year before,
Rhoda had driven down to the farm with her new husband
and the lousy way Corky's father and mother had treated her.
Sarah Jean was very proud of the way Corky had told everybody off afterwards—and of what he'd said to Rhoda to make

her feel better. The whole thing seemed weird to me, though, especially when Corky was leaning forward across from me in the train, describing all of them sitting around this farmhouse living room together, not saying anything.